THE MISDEEDS OF SADIE QUINN

A GOOD LIFE NOVEL

MERREN TAIT

LOLA PUBLICATIONS

Lola Publications. Raglan, New Zealand.

ISBN: 978-0-473-58968-4

Cover design by Bailey McGinn.

Author photo by Zora Slodicka.

www.merrentait.com

The Good Life series

The Year of the Fox

Bluffing for Beginners

Odd Girl Roar

The Amateur's Guide to the Art of Running Away: A novella

Britlandia series

Real Life and Other Disasters

Romance is Dead

THE BLUE UNIFORM loomed in my wing mirror, obscuring the knowing wink of the red and blue lights of the patrol car. *The joke's on you, Sadie Quinn.*

My tiny car idled on the grass verge of a quiet country highway – a road on which I had a reasonable expectation of encountering a tractor, a utility vehicle or two. Not law enforcement.

"Yes, officer?"

Hoping to buy some time, I hadn't yet wound the window down, so relied on the fact the man could lip read my greeting. Given all I could see of him was his crotch and the lower half of his stab-proof-vested torso, he would have to lip read through the steel of the car's roof.

His right hand made a circular motion.

I reached for the window crank and yanked it into life. The first revolution unplugged the glass from the seal with a *pop,* and the violent movement of the pane against the grimy rubber at the window's base produced an ear-splitting squeal.

It moved little more than a centimetre.

I placed my other hand on top of the first, bent into the movement, and forced the crank around in a series of jerky movements. *Screak, screak, screak.*

Despite the crisp mountain air funnelling into the heat-fog of the car's interior, a band of sweat wrapped itself under my breasts and around my ribcage.

One of the officer's fingers tapped against the cell phone in his hand.

On the fourth revolution, the officer flipped open the phone casing. On the fifth, the pane *thunk*ed home into the window slot and he planted his feet, squarely facing the car door.

"Do you know why I stopped you?"

I pulled my mass of long, brown hair away from my neck to vent some of the heat rolling off my body, and watched the loose, shuddering knob of the gear stick turn one full rotation before deciding on my approach. "I don't, but I'd hazard a guess you wanted a close-up look inside an original Holden Barina. 1988. Classic hatchback."

I thought I heard the officer snort, but given he'd waited for four of my elevated heartbeats to respond, like he was taking the time to gather his patience, I could have been mistaken.

"We've had a call to our Roadwatch line about a car with this number plate weaving across the road. Any partic-ular reason you couldn't keep to the left-hand lane this afternoon?"

I let the breath I'd been holding escape in a *whoosh*. I'd been expecting a "hands where I can see 'em", or at the very least an unintelligible directive shouted through a mega phone on his approach to the car. It might have been disap-pointing if the relief surging through my veins wasn't so complete.

I sucked in a sharp breath as a new fear gripped me.

My possessions, crammed into the boot and above the parcel tray, meant the goat would have been obscured from view on the cop's approach, but it was only a matter of time until he peered into the car. He'd make me set her loose.

I'd had two objectives in mind when I set out on the road from Auckland that afternoon. "Flee" and "with haste".

I didn't want to complicate matters by stealing a baby goat, but when it stepped out onto the road and nearly put a kid-shaped dent in my front fender, it gave me little choice.

Once the smoke from my tyres had cleared and my pulse settled from a drum roll to a rumba, I opened my door and stepped out onto the rough bitumen to ask if it was lost. With a single *blah-ha-ha-ha*, it trotted past me and jumped into the car.

I looked from its disappearing rear to the mountains of the Central Plateau on the horizon, as if I could see into a possible goat-coloured future. Shrugging my shoulders, I climbed back into the driver's seat.

The kid had decided I was hers to keep. Who was I to argue with a goat?

And now the little ball of energy was responsible for my current predicament.

I issued a sigh, knowing I'd protect her at all costs anyway.

The officer's fingers drummed on the roof and I knew I shouldn't have pushed my luck with the "classic hatchback" comment.

From the back seat, the goat nuzzled my hair and mouthed my recycled tin earring with a clack of teeth.

"Shhh," I hissed, even though she'd said nothing.

The officer placed a hand on his hip. "I beg your pardon?"

I pushed the goat away and focused on the blurry edges of the truth of my situation, of what I could pull to the centre.

Grimacing for the benefit of his crotch, and sucking air through my teeth for that of his ears, I said, "No power steering. I've only had her a couple of days and she takes some getting used to. She's an honest car, but drives like a tank." I attempted to give the dash an affectionate pat, but my coordination failed under the presence of his uniformed authority and I ended up slapping it like I was meting out bad-car discipline.

The officer "hmm"ed and stepped in close to the bonnet, his right thigh resting against the peeling paintwork of the driver's side.

He tapped something into his phone. No doubt, the recently expired date of the Warrant of Fitness. "Turn off your engine please."

If the cop was worried about the possibility of me being a flight risk, he hadn't looked closely enough at the duct tape holding on the front bumper or the blockish style of the car's body. The window might have been a clue.

It was then that the goat decided to make her presence known. Her snout found the soft pink shell of my ear and bleated out a shrill goaty laugh. *Blah-ha-ha-ha.*

I jerked my head away from her and my foot slipped off the clutch, throwing the car into a bunny-hop, which would not have been quite so bad in itself were it not for an officer of the New Zealand police force standing in front of the groin-level wing mirror.

The mirror *pumf*ed as it connected with the officer's soft parts.

With a hiss, like that of a deflating balloon, he collapsed on to the bonnet.

His pale eyes locked onto mine and widened. It might have been in recognition, or disbelief at his rotten luck. Possibly both.

There was something familiar about the fairness of his hair, the alarming icy-blue of his irises.

Then they closed and with a *shmeee* of flesh sliding on metal, he disappeared over the end of the bonnet.

CHAPTER TWO

"FUCK," I said to the space above the grill.

Turning to the goat, I pointed my finger at her. "Stay there and don't eat anything I might need to drive the car."

I cracked the door and winced against the prolonged *screak* of the hinges.

In front of the wheel, the officer's prone legs stretched out past the white line of the road's shoulder and onto the highway, toes up. I briefly closed my eyes at the imagined *barrump* as the next car that came along failed to see the obstruction, and bent to grab his ankles.

His Kevlar vest scraped against the rough bitumen as I dragged him sideways to a safe parallel-to-the-road position. His head now lay at an awkward angle, as if he was trying to peer at the rusted underside of my car.

Two things prompted me to brave the bite of the stones and kneel to shift his head onto my lap - the fact he looked extremely uncomfortable, and that I didn't think my immediate future would bode well if he woke to find a six-foot-three, female brick shithouse standing over him (not least one wearing a dress and no underpants).

As I rolled his head towards me and scrutinised the angle of a nose long broken, an ice cube slid down the inside of my ribs and settled in to melt at the pit of my stomach.

I knew exactly who those startling eyes belonged to. The boy who used to live next door to my grandfather.

WHEN I WAS eight and jumping on his trampoline uninvited (having climbed the fence), he came out his back door and stopped, watching me, before he returned inside for a few seconds, re-emerged and told me to look over the top of the roof of my granddad's house. There was an asteroid coming.

I watched and bounced, watched and bounced. No asteroid.

After a minute, a series of giggles broke out from underneath my feet.

I peered through the trampoline's weave.

Three boys lay on the grass staring up at me, or rather, at my knickers, which were on full display beneath my skirt.

A surge of rage at being tricked washed through me like a searing desert wind. My ears roared and my fists tightened.

I jumped down from the tramp, scrambled underneath, and leapt onto the blue-eyed ringleader, who still lay prone beneath. I hit him before he finished his last laugh.

My punches were wild and rapid and mostly ineffective, but one clocked him nicely across the mouth, liberating an already loose tooth from its socket.

He stared at me wide-eyed, then turned his head and spat the tooth onto the grass in a string of red saliva.

I ran back to my grandfather's before the boy's howling drew adults out of the house.

It was another seven years before I broke his nose.

THE OFFICER'S eyes fluttered open, his blonde lashes caging the blue for a second or two before they focused on me. "Sadie? Sadie Quinn?"

As each quick blink took away the fog of unconsciousness, the surprise at finding his head in my lap, and no doubt the throbbing in his groin, brought him to clarity.

He sat up and scrabbled away from me, his boots scraping against the loose grit as he pushed himself backwards.

When he had established a safe-enough distance between us, he raised a one hand as if to ward me off and clamped the other one to his testicles.

I lifted a hand. "Hi, Callum."

Ordinarily, I would have assumed my indignant face, with one brow raised, and dispensed scorn at a man choosing to be affronted or even intimidated by me. It happened often enough that I had my reaction down by rote, but to be fair, Callum and I had only encountered each other three times in our lives, and all of them had resulted in me, intentionally or unintentionally, dishing out a whole lot of hurt.

I kept my eyebrow in line with the other one and attempted to make light of the situation. "If you stopped me to have another look at my underwear, you're going to be mightily disappointed. I'm not wearing any."

My flippancy appeared to ease some of the tension.

The raised hand descended to settle over the top of his other one, and Callum's eyes flicked down my body as if he could x-ray vision his way past the black fabric of my dress.

Before his features could rearrange themselves into a semblance of 'why?' or even, my ego fancied, a look that might have suggested he wouldn't have, in fact, been disappointed, the nasal tone of a 1988 Holden Barina horn erupted into the quiet King Country air. *PAAAAAAAAAAAAAAAAAAAAAAAARP.*

Callum's eyes shot to the windscreen, and I closed mine, counting the long seconds until the goat shifted her head or her arse off the steering wheel.

On nine, the horn cut out, and Callum and I were plunged into a sound vacuum. Any livestock, any birds, who'd made the mistake of venturing within a kilometre of us, had been shocked into silence.

I opened my eyes and contemplated the dandelions weaving their way through the paddock fencing, as if getting a better view of them was why I knelt on the side of the road and not because I'd inadvertently attempted to neuter a policeman.

I didn't have to wait long for Callum's next move.

"Why is there a goat driving your car?" He spoke the words mildly enough, but his underlying tone suggested a belief he'd been sucked into a strange and ill-fated alternative dimension.

I snorted. "The goat is *not* driving my car."

"Looks like it's making a pretty good attempt."

The engine ticked. *Tink tink tink.*

Callum shook his head as if trying to erase the experience from his memory. "Sadie, you have an unrestrained goat in your car."

"Yes."

"Okay," he said, drawing the word out. "And is that why your driving's terrified the locals?"

I replied, "She chose me," as if that explained everything.

With a sigh, Callum pushed himself to his feet, one hand still cupping his groin. "Come on, you can woman-handle the goat into the back of the patrol car. It has a partition. I'll escort you to your grandfather's, which, I presume, is where you're heading, and you can make me a cup of tea and explain how the goat *chose you*."

I watched him waddle his way to his vehicle, his tall, thin frame curved protectively over his middle, and moved towards the car to reason with the goat.

The loose top of the gearshift was gone. As was half my head rest.

I couldn't fault her. She'd done exactly as requested and not eaten anything vital.

She sat, resting on her hind haunches in the front passenger seat, her back legs sticking straight out in front of her and her forelegs placed between them. When she opened her mouth to bleat a greeting a piece of seat padding fell out.

A laugh bubbled behind my ribcage, loosening the strain of the last few weeks. It spilled into the car's interior, mixing with the goat's high-pitched chortle.

"You are utterly ridiculous," I said, reaching for her.

THE SMALL TOWN of Tokawai lay nestled at the bottom of a green basin as if cupped by the hands of a giant. Outcrops of curved limestone dotted the sharply folded hills walling in the shallow valley, and patches of bush spilled over the rocky promontories and advanced down their crevices towards the pasture ringing the town.

Poppy's house was on the outskirts, right at the meeting point between town and country, so that his back yard looked over fields.

I pulled into his driveway as the fuel light winked on my dashboard. His car sat in front of the open garage door as if he'd decided to have an outing and then forgotten why five seconds into it. At least it meant he was home and we could both pretend he had a choice when I announced I was moving in.

Callum emerged from his car a split second after I exited mine and winced as he took a step. Waving away my "sorry", he said, "I'll look in the garage for something to tie the goat up with. Keep an eye on her and make sure she doesn't try to eat her way out of the car."

Ten steps down the driveway, he turned and pointed a finger at me. "Don't think I've forgotten about your expired Warrant of Fitness, Sadie Quinn."

I raised my right cheek in one half of a smile. "Don't think I've forgotten about you fainting, Officer McLintock."

He pivoted on the ball of his left foot and shouted over his shoulder, "I'm comfortable enough in my masculinity to wear that. You need to improve the calibre of your blackmail."

There was no reason to raise the blackmail bar. The WoF didn't matter. The car was a hundred dollar purchase to get me out of town with all my gear. I'd surrender the plates in the next few days and sell it for scrap.

I gave her roof a pat for meeting her end of the bargain and approached the rear of the patrol car.

The goat raised her head from chewing a seatbelt buckle when she saw me and voiced her hello with all her baby might, extending her tongue to bleat as if she had to use all working parts of her mouth to express herself.

I pressed my hand to the window and the goat nosed it, her breath fogging the glass. Then she withdrew her head, confused at the lack of contact.

A movement across the road drew my eye. Mrs White stood in her front garden snipping flowers for a basket at her elbow. Judging from the scowl bruising her hawkish features, she had one eye on me. She had always been quick to let her disapproval known of my and my sister's behaviour, of our play in the front yard or out on the quiet street. It was too loud, too dangerous, too unbecoming.

"Afternoon, Jean."

Her face drew in on itself, her lips puckering like a toilet-deprived anus straining against the pressure of last night's vindaloo. "That's Mrs White to you." She pronounced it 'Hwait', as if she had been raised in Windsor Castle instead of the marshy back blocks of a country half a world away.

The invitation was too good to miss. "OK, Jean."

Before I had time to register her reaction, an "ah, Sadie?" drew my attention back to Poppy's property.

Callum stood beside Poppy's car, staring into the backyard.

It was not the bemusement in his voice that had me running, but the accompanying alarm.

I covered the length of the driveway in a dozen of my long strides and ground to a halt beside him.

In the middle of the backyard, Poppy hung from the washing line.

His skinny, trouser-clad legs poked out from a pair of large Y-fronts, which were attached to the outer line by a set of men's suspenders.

He faced out towards Callum's former back lawn and pumped his legs to get up a swing.

When he'd reached the perfect zenith, he threw his head back and cackled.

CHAPTER THREE

"POPPY!"

His head whipped around, eyebrows raised in a question. "Sadie, my girl!" He glanced at his watch. "About bloody time. Give us a spin."

I looked to Callum as if he might be able to explain how Poppy not only knew I was coming, but that I would be late to make my appearance.

All Callum did was frown and take a large step away from me, presumably to reach a point of safety from my hurt zone.

I frowned back and lumbered towards Poppy as fast as my big frame would allow me. "Stop, Poppy. You'll fall." Halting beside him, I placed a hand on the small of his back and one on his knee and pulled him to a stand still. "All that's between you and putting a femur through your nostril are suspender clips." My voice rang out across the lawn, its pitch increasing with every word. "Are you insane?"

Poppy's eyes glistened. It might have been excitement, or the rheumy-ness of old age. "I sodding well have all my faculties. I'll thank you very much. And it's perfectly safe. I've done it before with pegs." He bounced up and down in his seat. "See? Not going anywhere."

I gripped his hips and held him still. "OhmyGodpleasedon'tdothat." I turned to Callum, who hadn't moved from his spot by Poppy's car. With his gaze fixed on my grandfather, one corner of his mouth twitched upwards, as I said, "You tell him. Pull some 'by the power vested in me' shit and forbid him or something."

Callum waited until he had evacuated all the air in his lungs on a noisy exhale, before taking a step towards us. "That's a priest." Stopping beside the washing line, he casually placed a hand on its metal arm. "Alright, Gerry?"

Poppy looked to me. "Why'd you bring the knobhead?"

I drew breath to remonstrate with him, but Callum beat me to it by pointing out in an even tone that police hadn't worn pith helmets since 1995.

Poppy didn't miss a beat. "Right you are, Callum. Give us a spin?"

As my mouth worked towards the 'O' shape of my forthcoming "No!", Callum pulled back on the metal arm. Then he met my eye and, holding my gaze, propelled it forward.

Poppy shot around clockwise, his legs splayed and his chortle spinning out over the lawn.

I had to step backwards before he collected me on his way past. "What the fuck, Callum?"

Callum ducked to avoid one of Poppy's newly liberated gumboots. "It's Officer to you, Ms Quinn."

I balled my hands and placed them on my wide hips. "What the fuck, *Officer*?"

Another lip twitch. "It's what he wanted." He looked at me then. "Give him what he wants. He's not a child."

"But-" I shifted my gaze from Callum's frown to Poppy's slight frame. The collar of his shirt was loose around his neck and the knobbles of his spine sat in a proud line against the fabric of the Y-fronts. "-He's so breaky."

"I'm sure he knows his limitations." He said it quietly enough, but punctuated his words with a decision to walk off in the direction of the garage. He might as well have shouted them.

My fists slipped from my hips.

The idea that I might patronise Poppy was abhorrent. He'd never assumed he knew what was best for me, unlike almost everybody else who was important in my life. Who was I to assume I knew what was best for him?

Even though Callum was right, it didn't mean I appreciated having a virtual stranger point it out to me.

I raised a hand, locked narrowed eyes on Callum's receding back to communicate my resentment through the power of telepathy, and put all my weight into swinging the line around.

Poppy's head snapped sideways and bounced off the taut length of suspender.

I clapped a hand over my mouth as he emitted a series of loud hacks, like the G-force had sucked his lungs out of his chest cavity.

Before I could slow the line, he had swung around to face me, his mouth wide in laughter. "Switch the sprinkler on, Sadie." Poppy's voice crackled under the strain of volume and seventy years of nicotine addiction.

I palmed the line to maintain its speed and willed my tongue not to betray any condescension. "It's fourteen degrees, Poppy. I'm not turning the sprinkler on."

Callum emerged from the garage with a length of rope

in his hand and strode back up the driveway, ignoring the both of us.

Slapping my hands against my thighs, I turned my face to the patchwork blue and white above me as if it could tell me what had snapped in my grandfather's brain.

As far back as I could remember, he was a grumpy man of few and occasionally offensive words. I had rarely seen him express the notion that something might be fun, and certainly not in any way that would necessitate employing laughter.

My hands closed around the line, jerking Poppy to a stop. The fear my eighty-eight-year-old grandfather was in the throes of a senile episode, lent its weight to the pressure building in my chest to unburden myself. The baggage in my car was only the literal half of a much bigger picture.

I pulled on the line until he faced me, knees to thighs. "Do you mind if we stop...playing for a minute? There are some things I need to tell you."

Poppy reached forward and took my left hand, pulling it onto his lap and placing his other hand over the top. He often did this. He wasn't anything of a hugger, but I knew this gesture carried just as much love. I'd called it a "hand sandwich" for as long as I could remember.

My hand had grown to proportions nobody could ever have predicted over time and Poppy's had thinned. His arthritic knuckles forced the bread into a curve as if the sandwich had been left to curl in the sun.

I longed for that time when he could swallow my hand entirely. It had felt like the safest place in the world.

He grunted. "Figured there might be, with you arriving with the local constabulary."

I wanted to laugh. Point out that was a red herring and

if Callum was still childless in fifteen years, I'd be getting the blame, but the heaviness beneath my breastbone pushed upwards and any laughter stilled in my diaphragm. I shifted my gaze from our hands to his eyes. "You want chronological or order of magnitude?"

Poppy gave my hand a squeeze. "Does Dolly Parton sleep on her back?"

"Magnitude it is." I placed my right hand on top of the pile. A club sandwich meant serious business. "I'm not wearing any underpants, my car's wing mirror took out Callum's fun sack, and I've adopted a kid."

I took a deep breath, as much for dramatic effect as to push back against the pressure in my chest. "Callum's going to tie her to the washing line. Thought I could use the old shed to house her in if it's still standing."

Poppy eyed me. One blink. Two. And played me at my own game. "Good. Been mowing this bloody lawn for seventy years. Could do with a break."

I smiled then. It wasn't much of a one. Circumstances weighed the ends of my mouth down. "You don't mind?"

"Not until she's proven to be trouble of the good kind or bad kind."

"I'm pretty sure she's a good kind of trouble. But to be fair, I have only known her for an hour or two."

"You're not putting her in that bloody shed, though. She can have the old dog kennel." His directive wasn't a surprise. For as long as I could remember, the grandchildren had been forbidden to go anywhere near the old shed. It had been rotting in the depths of the back yard since well before I was born.

It was then that I noticed there was nothing for Poppy to climb on to elevate himself to the height of his makeshift swing. "How did you get up here?"

"Eddie helped me."

"Who's Eddie?"

"My best friend."

I'd never heard of an Eddie before. As far as I knew, most of Poppy's friends had turned up their toes with increasing regularity in the last ten years. But if he had a best friend, it meant he wasn't a lonely last man standing. "Eddie who?"

Poppy narrowed his eyes and shook his head slightly, like I'd said, *What's that stuff that we breathe called again?*

"*Eddie.*"

"Right." My gaze dropped to the over-sized underpants. "I s'pose these are Eddie's?"

Poppy frowned at me. "Eddie would never wear Y-fronts."

Callum emerged from around the corner, a goat under his arm. She bleated when she saw me and kicked her legs as if miming running would bring her to me faster. "I'll be adding a replacement seatbelt to your WoF infringement."

He placed her on the ground and she bolted towards me, stopping an alarming centimetre away from my right thigh. Then she lowered her head and nudged me.

A "heh" bubbled up from the back of Poppy's throat. "A love bump. What did you do to earn that?"

"Not run her over."

Callum shoved his hands in his pockets. "If only all love was so easily won."

The sock on Poppy's gumboot-free foot brushed against the goat's cheek. Without taking her eyes off me, she extended her tongue out of the side of her mouth, pulled the offending item between her teeth and chewed.

"Hey." I tugged on the end of the sock. The goat clamped down harder. "Poppy needs that."

"Leave her." Poppy's toes, now naked in the cool afternoon air, wiggled and flexed. He stretched his leg towards her crown and stroked it, like you might a cat, with his foot. "I have other socks."

I took a step away from him and whispered, "You know any Eddies?" to Callum as he knelt to secure the goat to the pole of the washing line.

"Yep."

"Any Eddies that might suspend an eighty-eight-year-old from a washing line?"

Callum stood upright, stepped away from me, and crossed his arms. "One or two possibilities, but none I'm willing to share if it means you're going to meddle."

He was right, of course. Which only heightened my indignation.

I straightened my spine, pulling myself to my full height, and narrowed my eyes. "If pre-judge were a word, I might be inclined to use it right now. But seeing as it's not and I'm pretty sure you haven't been gifted with mind-reading superpowers and aren't able to determine my action before I do anything, I'm not *inclined*."

Callum, reading my sarcastic sanctimony for the bullshit that it was, narrowed his eyes back. "You owe me a cup of tea and a goat explanation."

"Ah." Poppy clapped his hands together, making the goat flinch. "A cuppa. Bloody excellent idea. Bring the Afghan biscuits out with you, girlie. I made 'em this morning."

I turned and looked behind me as if some other Sadie, who might do tea duty, stood at my left shoulder.

The pressure pushed against my breastbone and rolled upwards towards a verbal release. I swallowed it back down. I couldn't unburden myself while Callum was present. The sooner he drank his tea and was on his way, the better.

I nodded to no one in particular, gave the goat a pat, and headed for the back door.

WHEN I RETURNED with the tea tray, Poppy sat on the bottom step of the back porch with Callum next to him. The goat mouthed the washing line pole and strained against it, as if she could pluck it out of the ground and wield it like a stick.

Placing the tray on the ground in front of us, I sat on the far side of Poppy and handed him his tea. He wrapped his fingers around the cup to warm them, the pointer and middle finger on his right hand still yellowed with nicotine, three years after quitting.

He smacked his lips. "I'd sell my left kidney for a durrie right now. Cup of tea and a smoke on the back step. God-loving bliss."

"Apart from the cancer. Nothing particularly blissful about that," I said, grabbing Callum's cup to pass it to him just as he reached forward to take it. Tea slopped over the side and across his knuckles.

"Jesus Christ!" He attempted to shake the hurt from his fingers. "How do you manage it, Sadie?"

"I don't know," I said miserably. "I'm really sorry. It's not personal."

"Do you have a habit of breaking anybody else?"

"No. Just you. Here." I held out the container of biscuits, hoping the offering might make some amends.

Callum gingerly reached a hand into the tin with one eye on me, as if I might snap the lid closed on his wrist at any moment.

He extracted one without incident and I removed my own cup from the tray, inspecting the biscuits as I did so. The chocolate icing gleamed under a perfect butterfly-wing curl of walnut.

Poppy's Afghan biscuits were Tokawai legend. Large and crunchy from the golden cornflakes hidden inside, truckies would drive a half hour detour to pick one up as a chaser to a Quinn's Bakery steak pie. When Poppy took over the family business at twenty-five, his goods became a local dietary staple.

I sucked back the drool pooling at the sides of my mouth and plugged my lips with my cup in the hope the others might think I'd vacuumed up a mouthful of tea instead of my saliva.

Callum peered at me over the top of Poppy. "You not having one?"

"I try not to eat if I can avoid it."

"Why?"

"Have you seen me? Pretty hard to miss."

Callum stared at me for a beat. "You're kidding."

"Nope." I turned to watch the goat and took a more measured sip of tea. "Seventeen years of only ever having my physical appearance commented on, despite being Dux of my school and holding two Master's degrees." Did beautiful women have a similar issue? I'd trade problems with them in a heartbeat.

A small pool of heat seeped through the fabric of my skirt from where Poppy had placed his hand on my thigh. Nobody said anything. Even the goat had stopped grunting in her effort to remove the washing line.

I wondered if Callum's brain was doing a mental eye roll. How much he wished I wasn't here, so he could shake his head and mutter, "Women," at Poppy. "So," - here he'd choose from a list of interchangeable adjectives - "dramatic/sensitive/neurotic" and make the inevitable comment about our obsessions with body image.

But when he spoke, I looked at him sharply for an altogether different reason. "I want to say 'I'm sorry' on behalf of all the clueless people out there, but that might ruin my rep."

Poppy made a noise like scoria in a blender. My guess was laughter, but then I wasn't very qualified to identify that particular sound from him. "Callum, my son, you can come for a cup of tea on the back lawn whenever you want."

"Thank you, Gerry," Callum said before nodding at me. "So, the goat?"

I sighed. "Things at the moment are very -" I searched for a word that wouldn't betray too much. " - Challenging. The goat is just what I need right now."

The goat sat on her hindquarters and pulled her way across the lawn towards us, like a dog with worms. Her eyelids fluttered in ecstasy.

"I should probably drench her."

The hand on my thigh contracted. "I think a goat is not the highest point in your order of magnitude, my girl. I think that whatever it is, is the reason for this unexpected visit."

"He doesn't know?" Callum looked at me from under his eyebrows.

"Know what?" Poppy asked slowly.

"Judging from the amount of gear packed into Sadie's car, I'd say she's here for more than a visit."

I raised my cup as if toasting him. "Thanks for breaking it gently, Officer Callum."

"I'm not usually a stickler for convention, Sadie, but it's common practice to place the *last name* of the police officer after the rank. And you're welcome. It's the least I can do after today's incident."

I sniffed disdainfully. Then wished I hadn't, given I was halfway through a sip of tea. The steam rushed up my nostrils, encouraging any residual fluid in my sinuses to empty back into the cup.

I wiped my upper lip and eyed my tea with distaste.

Poppy's hand remained on my thigh. "You're here to stay?"

"I need a home, Poppy. I'm hoping you'll be happy to provide me one for a little while."

He retracted his hand, leaving the cold to gather over the small patch of skin. "You know I'm going to say 'yes', but you also know I have to ask 'why's that' and 'is it to do with you not wearing any underpants?'"

My "yes" was out of me before my brain could catch up with my tongue.

I flicked my eyes between the two of them. Then I pointed my finger in the direction of the garage and said to Callum, "Please stand there by the shed, put your fingers in your ears and sing some Whitney Houston or something."

Callum met my gaze for three unblinking seconds. Then he sighed, placed his cup carefully on the tray and pushed himself up from the step. Two metres out from the garage, he turned, locked eyes with me and inserted an index finger in each ear.

I returned his gaze with an equally contrived blank expression and waited.

Callum blinked first.

He shifted his eyes from mine to the heavens as if to ask, 'Why me?'. "I'll give you two choruses and the bridge. That's all."

"Fine."

Callum opened his mouth, and in a falsetto made wobbly by the highness of the pitch, began the chorus of 'I Wanna Dance with Somebody'.

Ordinarily, I would have laughed. Clapped along to encourage him, or mocked him in that careful way that encourages instead of quashes.

But I didn't have time to waste on such luxuries. I turned to a smirking Poppy and did my best verbal impression of ripping off a plaster. "I'm bankrupt."

A blink. "Financially, I hope."

There was no time to wonder at my grandfather's ability to doubt my moral code. As Callum expressed his desire to be warmed by the dancing body of a lover, his voice cracked on a high note and I drew a shuddery breath to prepare for the dam bursting. Then I rattled out a précis of my downfall. "You know how I started an events management company with just-discharged-from-the-army-Jordan? I was in charge of the project management and he was in charge of security? Well, it turns out Jordan has a gambling problem, and he siphoned off the company's profits and sunk it within two months. Too fast for me to notice, and now, after six years of hard graft to reach the point of establishing a business, I have absolutely nothing."

I glanced at Callum. He had his eyes closed and his face screwed up in the effort to hit the high note on the first refrain of the bridge. I had, at best, a half-minute left.

"So, yesterday, I went to his house when I knew he'd be drowning his sorrows at the pub and lifted everything the repossessors hadn't. Took it to a pawn shop and sold it all."

On that last sentence, Tokawai came to a standstill. No pimped-out Toyota Supras with over-sized mufflers rumbled up the main street. No testosterone-engorged and sex-starved bulls roared their frustrations in the adjacent valley.

My blood evacuated all superfluous areas, like my face, and pooled beneath my breast bone in a sharp rush of heat.

Because neither was there any Whitney Houston warbling across the back yard.

CHAPTER FOUR

WITH HIS FINGERS still in his ears, Callum peered down at his feet where a seatbelt buckle, connected to the goat's mouth by a string of saliva, sat nestled amongst his laces.

His eyes moved up to mine. "Guess it's just the WoF I'll be billing you for, then."

My pulse receded from a roar to a thrum. "How much did you hear?" I asked, my voice small.

An expression rippled across Callum's face. It was somewhere between curiosity and distaste. "Something about porn." His eyes flicked again to the unlined area of my nether regions.

In the ensuing moment, the part of my brain that sends instructions to my tongue short-circuited under the groundswell of relief and the desire to correct him, which had been quickly gagged and hog-tied. All it could manage was, "Ah."

It wasn't entirely an impotent response. Better to let him think I'd removed my knickers for money than burgled for it.

Callum shifted his weight from his left foot and shook the buckle free of his right. "Are you sure that's something you want your grandfather to know?"

I pulled my lips to one side as if considering the sensibility of his question.

Beside me, Poppy shook. Then he emitted a series of muted grunts before throwing his head back and spilling his laughter into the cold air.

"Apparently so." Callum bent to pick up the buckle. He wiped it on the grass, his mouth down-turned. When he straightened, he looked me in the eye. "You, Sadie Quinn, are one incredibly lucky granddaughter. Don't for a minute take that or him for granted."

I opened my mouth to retort that I would never - could never - and who was he to think that I might? But Callum turned his gaze to Poppy. "So long, Gerry. You take care. Thanks for the biscuit." And without a backwards glance, he walked up the driveway.

I kept my eyes on the corner of the house Callum had disappeared behind and said, "For what it's worth, Jordan won't report it to the police. I sent him a 'Thank you' text, in case he had any doubts it was me who worked his place over. He knows how much he owes me." I swivelled my head to face Poppy. "I won't bring any trouble to the house."

Up the driveway, the patrol car's door slammed, and the engine fired.

"More than I already have."

Poppy's mouth stretched into a closed-lip smile.

"You're really not appalled at what I've done?"

"Not on your life. It's going to make this next bit a lot easier."

I dropped my chin to my chest and peered at him from underneath my eyebrows. "What next bit?"

He patted me on the knee. "Come inside and I'll show you."

POPPY SAT me down at the kitchen table, pulled something from the bread bin and slapped it on the scratched wood in front of me. Scrawled across the top of a crumpled and crumb-laced piece of paper in shaky cursive script was the word *MISDEEDS*. Beneath it was a list.

Number 1 read *Lace the communion wafers with laxatives.*

"Poppy," I said slowly. "What is this?"

"It's all the naughty things I did when I was young. I want to do them again."

I looked up from the piece of paper. "A bucket list?"

Poppy leant against the back of one of the dining chairs. Even while standing, he was only marginally taller than me sitting. I frequently felt like Gandalf in Bilbo's hobbit hole around him. "It's not an arsing bucket list. I have no intention of dying. Why would I tempt fate by crossing off a list where the unwritten last item is 'die'?" He sniffed and his eyes glistened in the low- slung light over the table. "My list is about living." He tapped the paper with his index finger. "Reliving."

I peered at the list again. "You put *laxatives* in the communion wafers?"

He pulled out the chair he leant on and sat down next to me. "The bakery made all the wafers. Was easy."

A small part of me felt scandalised that I didn't know this part of Poppy's history. That before he was a grouchy adult, he was a havoc-wreaking juvenile delinquent. The far larger part of me was excited by the unfolding of that story. "What happened?"

"I pretended I felt sick to get out of going to the morning service, then lay in wait opposite the church. They didn't make it through the final prayer before the church doors burst open and people stumbled out, their legs clamped together like they'd been hobbled at the knees. It was beautiful."

"How old were you?"

"Seven."

I stared at him for a beat. "Is there, like, some evil genius somewhere in there you've put to bed? Now it's stretching and yawning into wakefulness?"

"I didn't do it on my own. I was *seven*."

"Who helped you?"

Poppy puffed out his cheeks and set his jowls quivering. "Will you help me get through this list or not?"

I eyed it again. My stomach pitched forward on reading number five. "These are pretty spectacular. I doubt they'll be as satisfying the second time."

Poppy slapped a hand on the paper and pulled it to him. "You want to live here? It's my condition."

"I am not helping you put laxatives in the communion wafers! We'd have to break into the bakery for a start and I'm not prepared to tempt any more arrest-gods."

"No, we wouldn't. The church buys in commercially made wafers these days. Those useless buggers at the bakery wouldn't know a wafer from a cracker biscuit. But -" he pointed a finger in the air. "- I make them for special occasions. Like Christmas and Easter."

"Poppy, Christmas is three months away. Easter, seven."

"We do the list out of order, then."

The clock above the stove ticked four times. "Couldn't you just jump out of a plane like a normal eighty-eight-year-old?"

"You want to start your new life at your parents' place?"

I attempted to stare him down, knowing that I'd crack before my first blink. He had the authority of being the elder, and all the leverage.

"Fine," I said resignedly. "But we're not reliving the laxative wafers. They'll work out who's responsible in a heartbeat and you'll spend the rest of your life in jail, which would be a shit finale on any bucket list."

"It's *not* a bloody bucket list. And we'll start at number two. Maybe by the time we've got through the rest of the list, you'll be amendable to doing the wafers."

I "hmm"ed doubtfully. "I have a condition of my own. I'm not sleeping in the room with that creepy statue."

Poppy's eyes flicked to the room in question, like he could see it through the walls. "You'll have to. The front room's turned into a fort."

"You turned the front room into a *fort?*"

"Eddie helped me."

Bloody Eddie. "Well, can't we un-turn it?"

"No. The fort stays. I might bend my knees enough one of these days to play in it."

"I tell you what. We can shift the fort to the back room. I'll even do it without your help. You'll never know it's not in the front room."

"You need to see it to understand." He pushed himself up from the table with a groan. "Come with me."

THERE WAS no way I could replicate what had been created in the front room.

The fort was exquisite. Sheets were draped between the curtain railing and picture hooks to create a multi-level roof line with the promise of a maze of rooms within.

Protruding from the back wall, and towering over the rest of the construction, were several cardboard boxes, cut and painted to look like a turreted defensive wall.

Between the draped sides of the blanket door, cushions and pillows spilled luxuriously across the floor.

"It's awesome," I breathed.

"Wait." Poppy bent and turned on the switch of a power point socket. A rainbow glow of shimmering Christmas lights illuminated the fort from within.

I gasped.

I wanted to crawl into it and pretend I was five years old again, but knew with a familiar pang of disappointment my large frame would prevent me, that I'd struggle to move through the space without wrecking it. I swallowed my resentment down and said, "Your friend made this?"

"I helped a bit."

My fingers twitched to feel the carpet, to slither into the fort on hands and knees.

"Why, Poppy?"

He shrugged. "Because it's fun."

I accepted defeat with the good grace of a grand-daughter who was grateful to be offered a lifeline. "Guess I'm bunking with old smug face."

He bent to turn off the lights and said through a wheeze, "We have a deal?"

"Oh God, Poppy, what if you get hurt, or arrested? I'm going to get the blame for that."

"Girlie, it seems to me like you've arrived here because life has given you a kick in the stomach and you're looking for a boot up the arse in the right direction. What have you got to lose?"

"Nothing. I have absolutely nothing in this world that I can risk. Only you."

"Right, then. You might find that living with one foot dangling over the precipice is exactly what you need to get your mojo back. I know you can do it. If you can burglarise your former business partner, you can help me misdemeanour the buggery out of this town. Shake on it." He hoicked into his palm and held it out.

My stomach turned. "No," I said thickly.

"You want to sleep in the dog kennel with the goat?"

"Fine." I spat on my hand and slapped it wetly against Poppy's. His thin fingers wrapped around the back of my hand, and our palms squelched.

My mouth filled with a bitter mixture of bile and soured tea. I swallowed it back down and turned to race for the bathroom, thrusting my hand under the tap and lathering it with soap.

"You won't be much use to me with such a weak stomach," Poppy called after me. "A few nights with Our Lady watching you sleep should toughen you up."

I ignored him and left to unpack the car and take my things through to the back room.

It was small and dark, with a window obscured by an overgrown camellia bush. Two single beds took up most of the space and faced a low, mirrored dresser and a tall chest of drawers. Atop the dresser was a five-foot statue of The Virgin Mary. The kind you see in alcoves in Catholic Churches.

Poppy had never explained where she came from, or why she had pride of place in one of the bedrooms, no matter how often I asked.

Trying not to make eye contact with the statue while squeezing myself into a pair of control briefs proved more difficult than it should have. She looked down at the occupants of the beds with a benign almost-smile on her face and her hands out, palms upwards, as if imploring.

I'd always felt over the years, when we came to stay, that she was imploring me to be a better person. Smaller, more feminine, happier.

It didn't matter what I did. She always looked disappointed.

AFTER DINNER, I swapped out Poppy's car from the garage with mine, having convinced him if I didn't house it, it would fall apart from exposure. Then Poppy announced that a trip to the pub was mandatory to a) mark our agreed living arrangement, and b) celebrate the first step on his path to reliving the adrenaline-fuelled antics of his childhood.

I protested, stating the responsibilities of a new-found mother, at which point Poppy threatened a goat curry alternative to the standard Sunday night roast if I continued on my current course of objection.

I acquiesced, but only after insisting the first round (and any possible subsequent ones) were on him.

The truth was, the last thing I wanted was to be out in public. I had envisaged a new life in Tokawai doing something wholesome and fulfilling, like weeding Poppy's garden or making goat's milk feta - anything that involved fresh air and talking only to plants, insects or goats. People, I had decided, were not worth the bother.

Poppy was the only exception.

I would accompany him if it made him happy. And besides, who was I to say no to a free drink?

· · ·

WHEN WE ARRIVED, the car park was full.

It wasn't a great start. I had hoped for a quiet drink, a little forced-but-polite conversation with people Poppy knew, and only a few stares and repeated glances.

I gritted my teeth, pulled up my metaphorical big-girl panties and plucked the literal ones out from between my buttocks. Then I strode towards the entrance.

Five steps from our vehicle, I stopped.

On the roof of the pub, and tied to the flagpole, was a bound and gagged naked man. His genitals had been stuffed into a grey sock with the face of Dumbo drawn around it.

Poppy didn't falter. He marched ahead, lifted a chin towards the man and nodded at him. "Mitchell."

As Mitchell nodded back and issued a muffled, "Hi, Gerry," Poppy disappeared through the pub's double doors.

I looked between Mitchell and the pub entrance, then followed my grandfather.

The entire pub lifted their heads to look at me as I walked in. I knew my physique had a tendency to be head turning, but I had never been a room stopper before. A wall of fire swept from the pit of my stomach up towards my scalp, but was extinguished by the patrons' collective "oh" of disappointment. All heads turned back to their beers and their conversation.

I sidled up to Poppy at the bar. "What on earth's going on?" I whispered.

"The Fuzz Cup," he said, raising a finger to attract the bar woman's notice.

"The what?"

"They stage idiotic things to get the attention of the police and place bets on what time they get here to sort it out."

"By police, do you mean Officer McLintock?"

He gave a single nod and said to the approaching woman, "Barmaid, a handle of your finest bitter."

She looked to be about five foot four, fifty kilograms (give or take), and a dress size 8. Just over half a Sadie.

Her grey hair was tied into a bun and a moko kauae decorated her chin. She narrowed her eyes. "I'm nobody's maid, Gerry. Least of all yours. Keep up that kind of talk and you can pull your own bloody beer." The Māori tattoo beneath her bottom lip danced as she spoke.

Poppy grunted. "That's the spirit. Bitter's best served with a slice -"

"- of ire. I know." She rolled her eyes, placed a glass under one of the beer taps, and flipped it towards her. To me, she said, "Fuzz Cup. Brainchild of the tenuous marriage between bourbon and bravado."

Poppy sniffed. "The ol' whiskey lobotomy."

"At the end of the season, the person with the closest number of bets wins the cup."

"It's a season?"

"Traditional pig-luring season gone a little metaphorical. Though we actually quite like Callum, which is why the cup has the somewhat respectful name of Fuzz above any porcine references. It happens this time every year over the course of a month. Excellent for business." She nodded at the crowded tables.

"People try to get arrested for the sake of a tin trophy?" The idiocy of an alcohol-fuelled brain never ceased to amaze me. Then again, the way things currently stood, I'd probably be quite good at beating them at their own game.

"They try not to do anything arrest-worthy, but the limit's always being pushed. Callum has the sense of humour of a saint."

"Don't you mean patience?"

"Nope. But he's got that too." She placed the handle in front of Poppy, who brought it to his lips for three long swallows, then she peered over his shoulder. "Nikora! Put the lighter down."

I turned. At a table behind us, a young man held a guttering cigarette lighter in one hand and a bottle of Blazin' Saddle chilli sauce in the other, his eyes large and on the diminutive bartender.

"Lord help me," she said under her breath, before raising her voice. "You cannot light burps off the fumes of hot sauce."

His eyes flicked between the bottle, the plate of nachos on the table before him, and the glass of what looked to be whiskey at his companion's elbow.

"Don't make me come out there." She took two steps towards the end of the bar and the flame retracted as quickly as gonads in an ice bath.

The bartender shook her head. "Surrounded by meat puppets." Then she turned her dark eyes on me. "Who's your companion this evening, Gerry?"

Poppy placed his glass back on the bar and licked the froth from his top lip. "Granddaughter. Sadie. 'S come to live with me."

She raised her eyebrows. "You're a mightily brave woman. Tēnā koe, Sadie." She held out a hand for me to shake and with a firm grip, pulled me partway over the bar to kiss me on the cheek. "I'm Manawa. Proprietor, sometime bouncer, and bar*tender*," she said, looking at Poppy.

He raised his glass and nodded at her as if there'd been no censure in her words. "Small but mighty, this one." Then his eyes moved to me and he said, "You did remember to put underpants on before leaving the house, didn't you?"

I froze, unsure whether to be mortified or amused at his inability to comprehend appropriate topics of conversation.

Before I could choose the delivery of my response, Manawa said, "I would have thought that was a question for her to be asking *you*, Gerry. I know how hard it can be to get basic things right when you're approaching your third century."

Poppy took another sip of his beer and smacked his lips. "Gets better with each mouthful. You have a go, Sadie. Order a bitter and see how good it tastes when you wind the barmaid up."

I told Poppy I'd take his word for it and ordered a soda water with a slice of lemon in it. Calorie count - six. He raised an eyebrow, but no comment about my decision to teetotal passed his lips. It wasn't his way with me.

When Manawa placed the drink in front of me and got the answer of "indefinitely" after asking how long I'd be in town for, she narrowed one eye. "You looking for a job?"

"Maybe," I answered, picturing gentle days in the sun picking tomatoes in Poppy's garden and wringing out cheese cloth in his kitchen. Being surrounded by people and assisting them on their way to beer-fuelled lunacy was a long way removed from the golden light of that dream.

"Another female presence will help moderate the behaviour of this rabble."

I jumped to the only conclusion I could. "You offering a job because of my gender or my size?"

"Both. Is that OK?"

I wasn't sure. I had spent so much of my life fielding comments about my size, choosing to be offended by them, and watching as people backtracked under the fierceness of my response that I didn't know how to handle her unapologetic frankness.

I turned around to survey the room and for the first time noticed that every single one of the patrons was male.

"This place is a complete sausage sizzle," Manawa continued. "It's like trying to wade through testosterone-flavoured jelly in here."

"It's only ever patronised by men?"

"Nah. They allow their wives and girlfriends to come on quiz night to raise the IQ level."

Poppy snorted.

"It's not quite as bad as that, but it's a lot worse on Fuzz Cup nights. No woman wants to be involved with the idiocy of this lot."

Behind us, the pub doors swung open. Every patron in the bar turned, paused, and let out a cheer.

The publican looked at her watch, shouted, "I make it 7.43 pm," and pivoted to write on a blackboard covered in a large matrix.

I didn't need to swivel on my bar stool to know that Callum, with a resigned expression on his face, waved at the crowd. I saw it in the bar's mirror.

He pointed at two men sitting at the closest table to the door. "Grady, Trenton, go get Mitchell down. And for God's sake, put some clothes on him before you bring him in here."

He turned towards the bar, caught sight of me and jumped as if given a small electric shock.

I waved into the mirror.

He looked around him, decided there was no one else I could be waving at, and with enough pause for two regular breaths or one deep one, stepped in my direction.

I twisted my glass. The perspiration that had pooled at its bottom fanned outwards in tiny runnels.

Callum arrived in my peripheral vision, a safe metre

and a half away from me, and rested a foot on the metal rung running along the base of the bar. "Sadie Quinn."

"Officer Callum. You following me?"

"I was just about to ask you the same thing."

"Are you going to say something cheesy, like 'This town ain't big enough for the both of us'?"

"No. I was going to make some droll comment about the Tokawai trend of burdening children with back to front names and say 'Good evening' to your grandfather."

"Back to front names?"

"Grady, Trenton, and Mitchell. Would you believe Trenton's last name is Johns?"

I leaned away from Callum like he'd said something shocking. He was almost being nice. Or at least attempting to engage me in conversation. "You're a bit more verbose than you were this afternoon."

He turned his back to the bar, leaned his long frame against it, and interlaced his fingers across his stomach. "That would be because the pain in my groin has receded enough to allow other important things, like the socially generous part of my brain, to function." He leaned forward to catch Poppy's eye. "Evening, Gerry. You come down for the sport?"

Poppy harrumphed. "This bunch? Too wet behind the ears to know proper sport if it slapped them in the face. Now, when I was a spy in the war, I used to lob flour grenades at panzer tanks. Made it impossible for the Gerries to breathe in the small space. They'd open the hatch, coughing and spluttering, and we'd pick them off." He fired a finger gun at imaginary German soldiers. "Pock. Pock. Pock."

"Which war are you talking about, Poppy?"

"*The* war. I served under Nancy Wake in occupied

France." He leant towards me and whispered, "For The Resistance."

My stomach dropped to nestle in a pulsating mess between my feet on the bar stool. "Poppy, you were just a little boy during the second world war."

"I was a decorated member of The Resistance. Killed two dozen SS soldiers using nothing but the serrated lid of a tin of spam."

Callum caught my eye in the mirror. His brows bunched and his lips pressed together in an expression that could have betrayed one of three things. Bridled amusement, concern, or pity.

I turned to him and hissed. "This is not happening. Don't look at me like this is happening."

He threw his hands in the air in surrender. "I don't want that possibility any more than you, but who knows what's happening. Don't jump to any conclusions just yet."

Callum may have been right, but that did little to massage out the nugget of fear nestled in my belly.

Before I could decide whether to nurture it or push it aside, someone said, "Evening officer." In the mirror, a middle-aged man approached the bar in a cream suit and matching fedora he was swaggering the cool out of. He placed a foot on the rung next to Callum and tipped his hat. The pale material, seasoned with hair grease, sported a dark ring from where it sat against his head.

"Rick," said Callum.

"You recruiting?" He nodded in my direction. "She'd make a mighty addition to your one-man team." Then his eyes moved to me. "I bet you ate all your greens." He threw his head back and laughed as if he'd issued the last of the great jokes.

Poppy took a sip of beer, Callum pursed his lips at his

interlaced fingers, and I poked at the slice of lemon in my drink with my straw.

Unperturbed, Rick asked, "How'd you get so big, then?"

And there it was. The question I'd been fielding since I was a six-foot, and growing, thirteen-year-old. God, what I'd give to feel normal.

I flicked through my mental Rolodex of answers and settled on, "Positive visualisation. I was five foot two this morning."

Rick's mouth "o"ed, a smile tugging at each corner. Then he slapped a hand on his belly and "ho ho"ed out a laugh. "Positive visualisation. Nice one."

"Bugger off, Rick," said Poppy. "Find another corner to waste oxygen in."

Rick chuckled, wagged a finger at Poppy and pushed himself away from the bar. "Good to see you still living up to your reputation, Gerry. No dust settling on you."

He moved off and sat down at a table near the entrance just as Grady and Trenton appeared. They each pushed open one of the double doors and stood to attention as a now T-shirted and trousered Mitchell passed them and entered the pub.

The floor erupted into cheers and whistles. Mitchell bowed, his ginger pony tail flopping over his shoulder, then casually walked behind the bar as if he owned the place.

"All right, my lamb chop?" he asked Manawa before stooping to give her a kiss.

Manawa's eyes remained closed for a second or two after Mitchell withdrew, a smile on her lips. Then she turned to me. "Sadie, meet my first husband."

I closed my mouth with a snap of teeth.

Mitchell raised a hand. "Hey."

"Hey -" I raised my hand in response, as if we were carrying out some Vulcan ritual. "- Mitchell."

I shifted my gaze to Manawa, who offered a shrug of her shoulders in explanation. It wasn't a dismissal or an apology. The glow emanating from her since Mitchell made his appearance made sure of that. It said very clearly, "Hey. What can I say? We are all happy fools in the game of love."

And at that precise moment, I decided to take the job. It was a combination of affection for the silly but somehow endearing culture of the pub's patrons, my like for a bold woman who didn't, in fact, walk the talk, and the fear nestling in my innards that if Poppy was in a mental decline, I might need to help in paying for support.

And to be perfectly honest, I needed the money.

I thrust my hand over the bar for Manawa to shake. "When do you want me to start?"

IT WAS as Poppy and I were making our way to his car to return home, that a low-slung vehicle bearing the number plate MO1ST squealed out of the car park in a screen of tyre smoke. One of the young men in the back hung out the window and raised his fist in a reverse devil horns sign and poked out his tongue above it, like a KISS fan-boy. "Hey tranny. Show us your fanny."

My "fuck off" was drowned out by a "moooo" issued by the driver.

"I know who your mothers are," Poppy shouted back, but the car had already exited the car park. He turned and gripped one of my hands. "Don't you listen to those mouth breathers, my girl. Nothing between their ears but the fetid air of their own flatulence."

It was easier said than done. Nothing short of ripping

my own ears off could prevent those words from worming their way through my ear canals and into my brain.

As I lay awake, rolling and prodding the nugget of worry about Poppy in my gut and attempting to tune out the incessant keening of the goat from the back lawn, my brain became hitched on a useless point of indecision.

I couldn't work out which was worse - the horrendously misogynistic comments shouted at me in the pub car park, or the fact the number one in place of the "I" in "MOIST" suggested that somewhere else in the country was another mouth breather driving around, brandishing the same mother-shaming number plate.

Near midnight, I got up and took the tin of Afghans from the pantry and brought them back to bed with me.

Mary's eyes glistened in the small amount of moonlight that found its way past the bushes outside. Her gaze was trained on me, the shadows throwing her brows into a frown.

I stuffed an Afghan in my mouth and said, through a spray of crumbs, "Don't you *dare* judge me."

CHAPTER FIVE

I WOKE early and stumbled into the kitchen where I knew Poppy, unable to break a lifetime's habit of rising before dawn for the bakery, would most likely be.

Only he wasn't. As I opened the door, my still half-asleep brain registered the snores coming from the direction of his room.

Standing on the dining table was the goat. She offered a *blah-ha-ha-ha* in greeting and went back to nibbling on the low-slung light shade.

The back door was closed.

When I'd coaxed the goat down from the table, swept up a scattering of tiny droppings and disinfected the floor, Poppy walked into the kitchen, gave the goat a pat on the head and picked up the kettle to fill it.

"You let her in here?" I asked.

He turned to me, eyebrows raised in a question. "What?" His eyes flicked to the goat. "No. Did you?"

I shook my head. "I think she teleported in."

Poppy grunted. "Figures." He placed the jug back on its base and switched it on. "Porridge?"

I answered by pulling out a chair and sitting down at the table. The goat nudged my hand, seeking a scratch. "What do you think of Obi-Wan for a name?"

"Is that Japanese?"

I stifled a laugh. "Where have you been all your life, Poppy?"

A sigh. "Only ever in Tokawai." He removed a bag of oats from one of the cupboards.

"Except when you were in France, fighting for the Resistance," I said with a snort, waiting for Poppy to pass the previous night's story off as a fanciful tale dreamt up under the influence of half a pint of bitter.

"Ah yes. Happy times. Nancy was fearless. Braver than all the men in the regiment."

My breath hitched in my throat and I had to concentrate to coordinate lungs with epiglottis. "Did they have regiments in The Resistance?"

"We did under Nancy. She commanded hundreds."

I placed a hand on my stomach as if its pressure could settle the lump of coal that burned slowly behind my belly button. It pulsed rebelliously, each throb an 'up yours' to my attempt to bring it under control.

I pushed myself up from the table with such force, my chair scraped across the lino and teetered on its back legs. I caught it before it fell and stepped across to the cutlery drawer to find a spoon. Heaping a pile of oats from the bag into my palm, I sat back down again and held them out for Obi-Wan to nuzzle.

She nosed my hand, her breath warm against my palm. I smiled down at her and the lump cooled to an ember.

"Poppy, how do you feel about having a house goat?"

He turned from adding water to a pot. "Looks like we're going to have one no matter how we feel about it."

I loved mornings with Poppy. In the hour after he'd risen for the day, he was all soft and blurry around the edges, like that warm dopiness that smothers you after you first wake clung to him until he showered it off after breakfast.

Turning back to the stove, he gave the porridge a gentle stir. "She needs potty training and I don't want the furniture chewed."

"Of course," I said, prising her jaws from around one of the spindles on the back of a chair.

I offered my hand as a chew toy and her bottom teeth worked their way along each of my fingers. Where her top teeth should have been was hard palate, which I knew from my experience with sheep was a characteristic of ruminants. It didn't mean they couldn't bite down hard.

Obi-Wan rolled my little finger between her bottom molars and her hard dental pad, grinding and squeezing.

With a "fuck," I ripped my fingers from her mouth and shook them out. "I think I'll go into town today and get her some chew toys. Maybe some you put food into, to keep her occupied." At the idea of goat-appropriate snacks, an awful thought flitted across my brain. "Do you think she's weaned? She seems so small."

"She's not that small for a kid. Looks of weaning age to me."

He paused, and I knew he was trying to say that size is relative and judgement skewed by perspective. My perspective of a small thing was more easily skewed than others.

It was true. Obi-Wan looked distinctly less tiny when standing near my diminutive grandfather.

"Judging by the state of my petunias, she's found ample replacement food source."

"Obi-Wan!" I chastised half-heartedly, shifting my

hand out of chewing range by scratching her under the chin. She closed her eyes and her back left leg lifted and twitched. "Aha," I whispered. "Now I know your weak spot. All future resistance is futile." Her eyes rolled under her closed eyelids and she issued a low groan. "She says she's sorry."

Poppy grunted, said, "Needed a prune anyway," and placed a bowl of steaming porridge in front of me. "I've thought of something to replace the communion wafer misdeed."

I stopped scratching and Obi-Wan's eyes flew open. The force with which my "have you?" erupted from my lungs made her flinch.

I had hoped that in his possible state of dementia, he might have forgotten all about the list. "Do we need to replace it? I mean, it won't be authentic. You won't have done it as a child."

"I'll be reliving the thrill of a hit on the church. Same or not. Doesn't matter."

I swallowed a sticky lump of oats. "*A hit on the church.* Does this have anything to do with the fact your delightful neighbour frequents it?"

"Jean?" Poppy asked through a mouthful. "Damnable woman doesn't deserve that level of attention. Not through lack of her trying. She's had her eye on me since her husband died."

I laughed and a glob of porridge shot out of my mouth and hit the salt shaker. I grimaced and wiped it away. "You are joking."

"All but hisses at me if I go anywhere near her. She's so repressed, she doesn't know what to do with her lust."

This time, the porridge shot out of my nose. "You think Mrs White *lusts* after you?"

"Goes out of her way to spit her disapproval at me. What else could it be?"

"General meanness. She's just not a very nice person."

Poppy dipped his head and spooned in another mouthful. "She's ho' for i'."

"Oh ho kay," I laughed. After a pause, I said. "But seriously, do you have something against the church?"

He sniffed, reached for the bowl of brown sugar and soft Poppy was gone. "I want to do this, Sadie. You're going to help me or you can start sleeping in that rust hole of a car."

I gouged a track through the hot oats with my spoon and watched it fill with milk. "Of course I'll help you. We spat on it. I can't go back on it now."

Poppy looked up at me from under the tangle of his eyebrows. "Good. I want to do it tonight."

I dropped my spoon. "Tonight? But I need a chance to acclimatise. Psych myself up to the reality I'm the only thing between you and jail, the hospital, or the morgue."

"You've got all day to get your head in the game. Starting from now." Poppy's eyes shone. He licked the back of his spoon. "I have a fool-proof plan."

I listened, and when he had finished, rolled the plan around in my head while I scraped at the remaining half of my porridge. It had cooled and congealed into little grey lumps. I slid it off the table as quietly as I could and held it out to Obi-Wan who had nestled, like a dog might, at our feet to chew her cud.

Her teeth *clanked* on the spoon and I winced.

Poppy didn't seem to notice.

"How are we going to break in?"

He ferreted around in the back of the bread bin and held up a large metal key. It looked like something that might have been a century old, with a wide, open bow at one end to grip it with.

"Where'd you get that?"

"Lifted it some eighty years ago. Was one of two, but they haven't changed the vestry lock since. I check from time to time, in case I ever need to get in there."

"Why might you need to get in there, Poppy?"

"It's an insurance policy."

"Insurance policy for what? If you're thinking about the afterlife, I'd say that at the rate you're going, it's too late."

"No point worrying about what happens when you die. It's what you do in this life that matters. Which is why we need to go through every step of the plan carefully. You bring a balaclava in one of your suitcases?"

I SAT OUTSIDE on the back steps nursing a cup of coffee and trying not to think about the stunt I was obliged to pull out of filial loyalty and the tenuous bind of a saliva-laced handshake.

A cloud drifted across the sun, sucking the temporary warmth of the early spring air and throwing the garden into a shadowless gloom.

Now was as good a time as any. I pulled my phone out of my pocket and instructed it to ring Dad.

"How's my Amazonian Queen?" he said after the fourth ring.

I let my shoulders slip from where they'd been hugging my ears. It was a good morning. Any other time, any other mood, I'd be his Amazonian Throwback.

Poppy's mother was apparently willowy among her

female relatives at a modest five foot six, and my mother was the shortest of her two sisters by some three inches.

The only thing that could explain my unusual height and breadth was a simple case of baby misidentification. The fact my double crown matched my father's or that my cheekbones had the same curve as my mother's did nothing to prevent the gentle familial teasing about my supposedly questionable parentage.

"Good, thanks, Dad."

"That's the way. Now, you'll have to be quick. I've got six minutes until I meet with Stephanie to disambiguate the touchpoints for the McMillan-Stoltz project. I really want to move the needle on this one, but I'm not sure they've got the bandwidth". Which in English meant *Stephanie and I are going to identify and review all the ways consumers can currently interact with the business. I'd like to introduce initiatives that significantly increase cash flow, but I'm not sure McMillan and Stoltz have the resources to make it happen.*

Dad ran a consultancy firm specialising in business development and devoured every new piece of business jargon like a hatchling guzzling regurgitated viscera from the corporate mother.

He paused, no doubt expecting a coo of business collegiality, a suggestion that perhaps they just target the low-hanging fruit (if I was feeling metaphorical), or actionable items (if I was simply aiming for pretension).

I didn't want him to redirect the conversation and ask me about how my business was going, whether I'd met my quarterly targets yet. It was only a matter of time before he found out the truth of the matter. The blast radius from its spectacular implosion would be spotted from across the galaxy.

The longer I delayed his disappointment in me, the better.

When I said nothing, he continued, "So, to what do I owe the honour of this unexpected call?"

No point beating around the bush when the corporate clock was ticking. But then the corporate clock was always ticking when it came to talking to Dad. "Is there any history of dementia in our family?"

Dad hiccupped out a series of small laughs. "What a question. Not on your mother's side that I know of. Mum died young, so I've no idea there, and with your grandfather being an only child, there's only him to see if his parents' decline is a genetic time bomb."

The lump of fear flared to life. "Genetic *time bomb*?"

"I'd say there's a reasonable possibility we're all destined for an old age characterised by the great renaissance - The Bringing Back of the Bib." Another hiccup. "Quite catchy that."

"Why? What happened to them?"

"I was barely a teenager when it happened, but it was all rather tragic."

"When *what* happened?"

"Dante Kerr even wrote a song about it. 'The Sad Ballad of Doug and Rose'."

"Who's Dante Kerr?"

"Tokawai's famous son?" Dad said, turning the statement into a question, like it should have been firmly within my *knowledge base*. "The country singer?"

Silence.

"Sadie, you surprise me. Anyway, he never recorded it out of respect for the family, but he'd play it whenever he had a home concert."

"Right," I said, the final consonant a snap. "For the love of God, Dad, what happened?"

A hiss issued down the phone as if he had sucked air between his teeth. "Ah, nothing you need to worry about. Yet. Probably best left well enough alone. Why are you asking me this, anyway? You misplaced something? Forgotten where you put your phone?"

"I'm talking to you on it," I said with a sigh.

"Ah. So you are. Phew, aye?"

A series of taps issued down the phone line as Dad wrote something on his computer. After a few seconds, he said, "Your mother saw the New Zealand Film Awards on the tele the other night. Wondered if you were responsible for it."

God love Mum and her aspirations for me.

I stifled a humourless laugh. "No. Not that one."

"She's going to ask when she knows I've talked to you, so tell me, have you got any big events coming up? Anyone famous?"

I thought of tonight's misdeed, said, "Sure." And then, "Nobody famous."

Dad "mm hmm"ed. "Did you really just ring me to ask about dementia, or was that a red herring before you ask for something momentous? Like a kidney. Or money." Three more hiccups.

I didn't laugh with him. I'd been careful not to be one of those adult kids who still holds out their hand, whether for financial or emotional support, knowing that it would be tallied. That there'd be something to owe down the line.

"Yes. I just watched a documentary on it and now I think I'm forgetting more stuff than I should. You know, like when you walk into a room and forget why you went in there? Happened twice this morning." The lie settled sourly in my mouth and I sipped my coffee to wash it away.

"You're a sensitive wee soul, Sadie. Wouldn't know it to look at you. But if you need your Dad to say it, you don't have dementia. There. Everything OK now?"

I flinched as "SADIE," was barked from somewhere inside the house. "You need to fort-train your bloody goat!"

I turned to the open back door as Obi-Wan appeared, dragging a floral sheet from her mouth.

"On no," I groaned and clutched at the sheet as it trailed past me.

Dad's voice rumbled in my ear. "Who was that? Have you got a boy over, Sadie?"

My tongue fired a "no" before my brain had a chance to reach the conclusion that a lie was better than the truth.

"Don't be coy. You're well past the age where you have to pretend you haven't discovered sex yet."

"No, I'm not. I will *never* be past that age."

Poppy marched out of the back door and on to the porch.

I hastily smothered the phone between my breasts.

He snatched the sheet from my hand and snarled, "Ogle San or whatever the damnable kid's name is, is banished from the front room." He pointed a finger at her behind, which shook as she scattered the contents of her bowels beneath the washing line. "Forthwith."

She dropped the sheet and moved off in search of greenery in the flower bed.

"Why on earth did you let her in there?"

"I wanted someone to play with. She said she was up for it."

"Of course she did. She'd be up for playing chicken with solar flares if you asked her."

"Now I have to fix the sodding thing and Eddie's not here to help." He disappeared inside the house, the sheet bundled under an arm.

I pulled the phone away from my chest and returned it to my ear. "Sorry, Dad. Are you still there?"

"Was that...*Poppy?*"

"No," I said, entirely unconvincingly.

"Why on earth are you at your grandfather's?"

Shit. "I just thought I'd, you know, visit. See how he is. I haven't checked in on him in a while."

Dad's change from happy-go-lucky father to disgruntled son was so complete, I heard the gears graunching. "I suppose it's that miserable old man that has you worried about dementia? What's he done or said?"

"Nothing. He's done nothing. I'm just...curious about our family history. I know so little about your side of the family. That's all."

"I might be many things, Sadie, but a fool I am not. Don't you dare take me for one."

"Fine. Fine! I'm a little worried about him, but I'm probably just being paranoid. It's nothing to worry about." I said, "You don't need to ring Uncle Peter," at the same time as he said, "I'm ringing your Uncle Peter."

Encouraging Poppy into a retirement home was not a new topic of conversation, but it was mentioned with increasing conviction over the last couple of years as his two sons realised they would never have the relationship with their father that any child might reasonably expect. The fact Poppy put more effort into his grandchildren than he did his own children didn't help matters.

"It's only a matter of time before that big house gets the better of him. You know what will happen. He'll fall in the garden and break a hip and lie there for a week until someone discovers him. He's his own worst enemy - never slowing down, always doing projects."

"Well, I'm here for the time being. Nobody needs to worry about him or how appropriate his housing situation is."

"What do you mean for the time being? Surely you're only there for a few days."

I placed a thumb against my eyeball and gritted my teeth. "I'm working remotely, Dad."

"Is that something you can do in the events industry? Don't you have to scout venues and project manage teams of caterers and such?"

"Sometimes. It's all under control."

"It's too much for you, Sadie. It's not fair for the elderly to be a burden on the young."

"Dad, I'm perfectly capable of deciding what's fair to me or not. By the time you get to Poppy's age you might change your tune on that one."

"I'll be going into a home. I would much rather cope with the indignity of a stranger wiping my arse than my own daughter."

A female voice issued a question in the background, her words indecipherable.

"I have to go. Stephanie's here. Just...don't make any commitments to your grandfather. We'll touch base soon, okay?"

He hung up before I could give an answer.

POPPY'S HAND shook as he attempted to get the key in the lock. It rattled against the edges of the metal keyhole and the soft *tink tink tink* seemed like bell tolls in the still of the wee hours.

The tremors had little to do with nerves and everything to do with age. Unlike me, whose armpit sweat had already penetrated three layers of clothing and was steadily wicking in an ever-increasing circle, Poppy's focus and confidence was steely.

There was only one potential chink in our carefully thought out strategy.

Obi-Wan's cheeks bulged as she regurgitated her cud. Green grass and gastric juices slid down her chin and dripped onto the cobbled entranceway to the vestry. She emitted a closed-mouthed bleat as if to encourage Poppy.

"Shhh," I said, slapping a hand over her mouth and instantly regretting it. I wiped my fingers furiously over my black jeans. I never wore trousers if I could help it. Long skirts and loose-fitting dresses were the most comfortable and size-masking items in my wardrobe, but they didn't make for great leg-movement range and the chances Poppy and I might need to make a quick getaway were looking likelier by the minute. "Why did we bring her?"

"She's a member of the strike force. A valued one."

"She's a liability."

The key engaged and Poppy swung the door open with a long creak.

We stepped inside and turned our head torches on.

"When I was in The Resistance, goats were our main animal allies. After homing pigeons and camels. Obviously."

"Camels?" The little lump throbbed deep in my belly.

Poppy flapped a hand impatiently. "All the extra water storage in their humps. The goats used to bleat out Morse Code. Very intelligent creatures and easy to train," he said as Obi-Wan licked a glass-fronted cabinet with a bouquet of orange plastic flowers lying on the middle shelf.

A trail of green-tinted saliva slid languidly down the glass.

"I have a feeling they'll be in here somewhere. This place is only used for storage now."

The walls of the small room were lined with the odd oak cabinet and interspersed with newer, taller and cheap storage units.

I opened one and quickly closed it again as costumes and nativity scene figures threatened to spill forth and crush me.

"Ah. Here they are." Poppy held up a box filled with black letters triumphantly. "Time to initiate step two."

I nodded and began to make my way towards the vestry exit when I noticed the distinct lack of goat in the room. "Where's Obi-Wan?"

Poppy pivoted in both directions, looking over his shoulders. "Up to some covert business, no doubt."

I attempted to groan inwardly, but my dismay was too great to be held within the confines of my throat. A noise like a walrus announcing she was in season filled the room.

"Wait here. I'll see if she's done her walking through walls trick." I opened the door to the church and my torch beam glistened on a series of moist, black pellets leading towards the central aisle between the pews.

"Obi-Wan," I hissed, even though there was nobody who could overhear me. "You're jeopardising this mission. Get back here!"

A bleat issued from somewhere near the apse. Her *blah-ha-ha-ha* bounced between the beams of the vaulted ceiling, gathering volume.

"Shhh!" My beam pinned her against the steps leading

up to the chancel at the front of the church, where she helped herself to a large bouquet of lilies. "Stop eating the decoration."

I bent to pick up the incriminating nuggets, which, impressively for such a little goat, led the entire way to the steps.

By the time I'd palmed them all, Obi-Wan had trotted past me towards the church entrance, her hoof steps ringing out on the wooden floors.

"Don't you dare osmosise through that door."

I needn't have worried. Obi-Wan reached the baptismal font, raised herself up on her hind legs and began drinking from it.

"I should have left you at the side of the road." I had the dog's lead I'd bought the previous day wrapped loosely around my neck but, with my hands full of goat droppings, no way to secure it to her.

There was nothing I could do but deposit the nuggets in my jeans' pockets. "They better hold their structure, Obi-Wan," I said as an image of poo juice being strained through the weave of my trousers flitted across my mind.

Securing the lead to her new collar and ignoring the green scurf now floating on the surface of the holy water, I pulled her out through the vestry door and into the crisp night air.

Poppy stood in front of the large sign board facing the street. "Jesus and germs," he read. "You can't see them, but they're both there." He tutted. "These guys aren't helping themselves. Time to up the sign-board ante."

He placed the box on the ground, rummaged amongst its contents and pulled out an 'o'. "Let the fun begin."

CHAPTER SIX

I WOKE LATE.

It was understandable, given the unusual night activities I'd been involved in. But my waking was not the result of having reached the end of a fortifying eight hours of sleep.

Four hard and weighted points pressed down on my chest and abdomen.

"Obi-Wan, how'd you get in here?"

It was a redundant question. Not least because she couldn't answer me, but mostly because I knew her having been shut away in the kitchen for the night, separated from me by two closed doors, had no bearing on her now being in my bedroom.

She shook with a fast twitch, which I knew to mean she was wagging her tail. I suspected it had little to do with her happiness at me now being awake and able to give her the attention she sought, and more to do with her ensuring the evacuation of digested food went neatly.

Sure enough, her shaking was accompanied by a rapid

succession of dull thuds, and the sharp scent of recently digested grass assailed my nostrils.

"Really?" I said to the back of my eyelids. Perhaps if I went back to sleep, I would wake an hour later to find this was all a bad dream.

Obi-Wan lowered her snout until it touched the tip of my nose and let out her displeasure at my lack of initiative to start the day. Her shrill bleat drilled through the walls of my ear canals and into my brain with the efficiency of an ice pick used to open a watermelon.

"All fucking right. I'm getting up." I pushed her off me and sat up, the nuggets rolling into the blanket groove between my thighs.

I groaned and caught the eye of Mary, whose brow had smoothed from the frown she cast on me upon my return from breaking into the church. A branch of the camellia outside the window waved with the breeze, and in the flickering of light, I could have sworn The Virgin's lips moved with the briefest of smiles.

I pulled my eyes away and refocused on Obi-Wan, who had her mouth wrapped around a section of the wrought iron pedal of the old Singer sewing machine serving as the bedside table between the two beds.

The machine would need a clean and an oil, but with its simple mechanics, I had no doubt I could get it functioning adequately.

I carefully swung my legs out of bed without scattering the tiny goat turds onto the floor and gave Obi-Wan's ear a gentle tug. "How do you feel about wearing nappies?"

WHEN POPPY DECLARED he needed to see a man about a dog and grabbed his car keys, I felt it pertinent to point out to him that he had a perfectly good working toilet in the house.

He didn't answer and hurried out the back door without so much as a goodbye.

This, of course, meant I had to walk into town to get the supplies I needed for Operation Goat Turd Control. As Poppy only lived three blocks away from the main street, it wasn't too much of a hardship. Walking, however, meant that instead of passing the church in a three-second drive by, I'd have to endure a minutes-long approach in which my conscience would wrap itself around my brain with all the weight of The Virgin Mary's frown bearing down on me while I attempted to sleep.

And, unluckily for me, it was impossible to avoid seeing the church on the approach to town. A colonial, wooden building surrounded by a large lawn and no other vegetation, it stood proud and lonely at the transition-point between living and spending - a gatekeeper to the commercial life of Tokawai and a reminder to its people that herein lies financial temptation.

Today, however, the church was far from lonely and forlorn.

Cars lined both sides of the wide street and people crowded around its front. A wedding or a christening. Worse - a funeral, and Poppy and I had just made a joke of their grief.

Despite the leaden blanket of cloud above me and the air being more reminiscent of a wintry frost than a spring balmy-ness, I suddenly felt overdressed.

I shrugged my jacket off and tied it around my waist. Then I willed myself to put one foot in front of the other and get myself past as quickly as I could.

Yet, as I neared and the people moved from indistinct

blobs to defined figures, it was clear they were not, in fact, mourning anything.

They shuffled around the sign board, leaning on it, shifting in and out and swapping positions, like a flock of starlings swirling and scattering and regrouping in that hour before the day fades into night.

They were taking photos.

I had intended to cross the road, to distance myself from the responsibility of ruining whatever was being celebrated or mourned, but now that it was clear that it was the sign being celebrated, my curiosity got the better of me.

Four metres out from the sign, I had to push my way through, the bystanders spilling from the church's front lawn and over the footpath.

I tried to step my way around people, but the tiny maze of paths between individuals in a crowd made it hard for someone of my size to get through without minor collisions.

I sidestepped a rotund man just as a young woman (five foot six, sixty-five kilograms, dress size 12. Just over two-thirds of a Sadie) walked into my path. She *oomphed* as we connected and she stumbled sideways.

Reaching forward, I grabbed her arm to keep her upright. "Sorry."

"'S okay," she said, looking up at me, then towards the backs of the people in front of her, and back up at me again. "You're so tall."

"It's the débutante under my dress practising deportment. She thought balancing a pile of books on her head was too much of a cliché."

"And funny," she said, with a wobble of her head and a sarcastic set of her brows. She thrust her phone at me. "I'm going to burrow through. Can you just, like, raise your arms above all their heads and take my photo?"

A bead of sweat tickled the skin between my breasts and rolled down my stomach. I had to get out of there, as far away from the scene of the crime as quickly as I could. "No. I'm actually in a hurry."

As I stepped to move past her, the unmistakable boom of a voice far too big for the small body responsible for it penetrated the hubbub of the crowd. "Sadie! Bulldoze your way through and get in here for this photo. Move aside, people."

As was her power, the crowd parted like the Red Sea to reveal a beatific Manawa. She held her hands out towards me, beckoning.

Mitchell lay across the top of the sign wearing nothing but flesh-coloured shorts, one leg cocked, a hand supporting his head and a lollipop dangling from his mouth in a Burt Reynolds parody.

Below him the sign read *Job hunters: seeking the daily grind? Missionary position available. Apply within.*

"Total classic," she said, stepping forward and pulling me towards the sign. "It's a big improvement on the germ thing." She jerked a thumb in the direction of the church's front entrance. "Someone here's dusting off their joke books."

"Oh, yes. Ha ha." I forced the laughs out of my chest in sharp little bullets.

"Now, you stand there." She positioned me on one side at Mitchell's feet, pulling my arm up and draping it over the corner of the sign. "And I'll stand here." She arranged herself near Mitchell's head. "On three," she instructed the man holding the phone.

I tried to smile. My lips stretched sideways, but failed on the vertical axis.

I had no doubt the photo would show a delighted

Manawa and Mitchell, and a Sadie who looked like she'd casually photo-bombed the shot.

THE RESIGNATION WITH WHICH "SADIE QUINN" was issued from the front of the shop could only mean one thing.

I shouldn't have been surprised. Tokawai was a small town, after all, but the roll of material jumped from my hand as explosively as the "fuck!" that rushed simultaneously from my mouth.

I placed my palm on my chest and apologised to the woman behind the counter. My heart beat against my ribs like a bird trapped in a cage.

Somewhere between my startled curse and my "sorry", my brain collapsed under the pressure of guilt and the fear of discovery.

Left brain hemisphere: *He has no idea. He's just here on his rounds.*

Right: *In a haberdasher's?*

Left: *Don't be judge-y. They might have a high turn-over and a safe full of cash. Or he could crochet tea cosies on his evenings off.*

Right: *He knows. Your goose is cooked.*

Left: *Tongue cluck. You need way cooler metaphors. Say something witty and dismissive at the same time so he'll respect you and leave.*

With a grunt, I forced the two halves of my brain back together and managed, "You have to stop following me, Callum. Coincidence is an excuse that will only get you so far," before bending to retrieve the dropped roll of material.

"You should be so lucky." He stood five steps into the

shop, his thumbs hooked on the armpit holes of his stab-proof vest. "What I want to know is how you always know where I'll be so you can stage an ambush. Do I need my full riot gear today?"

It was a fair question, given the size of the roll of material in my hands. I placed it back in the bin before it slid out of my hands again and crushed a toe. "Didn't pick you as a sewing hobbyist."

"I could say the same thing to you."

"Just because I look like a man, doesn't mean I don't have the skills of a lady."

Left brain hemisphere: *Wait. What? Did you just call out the cop as sexist by being sexist?*

Right: *Shhh. I'm trying to be indignant.*

Callum's hands dropped to his sides. "Why do you do that to yourself? You don't look like a man, Sadie. That's just ridiculous. Height and shoulder width does not a gender make." He walked down the aisle in front of the shop counter and stopped on the other side of the bins of material from me.

"Huh." I extracted another roll of material. "Tell that to the moist boys."

Callum pulled his lips into a thin line. "I'm waiting for the day when they think they're too big for this town and find some other place to pollute. Literally and metaphorically. But right now? Big fish, small pond. It's too easy to fancy themselves as kings." He placed a hand atop a bale of green cotton. "I'm sorry if they've upset you."

I peered into the icy blue of his eyes, wondering at their effect when he turned them on full beam, whether their coolness had the power to cow the moist boys. "Do you believe in karma?"

"I don't believe in revenge. Even if I see enough of it in

my job. But the universe delivering payback? I'd like to think so."

Right brain: *Tell him why you're here. Cute factor ten!*

"I'm making nappies."

Left: *Good one.*

"Wait. What?" Callum's eyes moved to my abdomen and back to my face. "I thought we were talking about the three idiots of the boy-racer apocalypse, but what are you telling me?" He lowered his voice. "A pregnancy is karma for starring in a porn flick?"

"What? No!" I looked over at the woman behind the counter who studiously counted what appeared to be the same buttons as she had when Callum appeared in the shop. "I'm not ..." I dropped my voice. "I'm not pregnant. I'm making them for Obi-Wan."

"Obi-Wan?"

"My goat."

Callum stared at me for a beat. Then he crossed his arms and said, "You called it *Obi-Wan?*"

"*Her*. And yes. I happen to like Star Wars and the name's fitting."

The buttons clacked on the counter-top.

"She's a Jedi Master and mentor?" Callum punctuated his question with a lifted eyebrow.

I saw his eyebrow and raised him a lip purse. "She's my spiritual anchor. I need grounding. Also -" I unravelled and inspected the end of a roll of spaceship-bedecked material. "- She's got powers."

He uncrossed his arms and shifted his hands to his hips. "Your goat has mastery of The Force, but no control over where she chooses to loosen her bowels?"

Left brain: *He has a point. It does sound a wee bit*

idiotic. Perhaps you should have given her a more suitable name for a goat. Like The Masticator.

Right brain: *Or Helen.*

I slid the roll back into the bin and mirrored his movement, placing my knuckles against my waist. "She breaks into the house and nothing I do to stop her works. Apparently, she doesn't want to be an outside goat."

"I see," said Callum. The corners of his mouth twitched. "Speaking of breaking in. Someone had fun with the sign outside the church last night."

I stared at him. All the air in my lungs seemed to have been sucked out and I couldn't find the coordination to re-inflate them.

"Didn't you see it on your way in?"

The desperate need for oxygen overrode the inertia in my diaphragm and I drew in a ragged breath. My hands slipped from my hips. "See what?"

"The job advertised on the church sign. Missionary position?"

"Ohhhhh." I slapped a hand against my thigh as if suddenly remembering. "Yes. I mean, I saw the crowds and thought there must have been a funeral or something." It was true. If only half of the picture.

"Instagram junkies. If there's a sniff of a meme possibility, they're on it like vultures. Mind you, it was pretty funny. You'll have missed it by now. They'll have taken it down."

I nodded. "Uhuh."

Callum looked between me and the woman at the counter. "You're very non-combative today. Few acerbic comments. No cutting sarcasm."

I frowned and apologised.

With a small laugh, he said, "Anyway. I need to continue on my rounds." Taking a step towards the door, he halted and spun back to face me. "Just for the record, Sadie, some men find strong-looking women very attractive. Don't discount that on the say so of a couple of idiots."

Right brain: *When he says some men, does he mean him?*

Left: *Of course not. He's just being nice. You should still thank him, though.*

I couldn't get my tongue unglued from the roof of my mouth before he walked out the door. I jumped as the wood jammed home in the door frame.

The woman behind the counter fed the set of buttons into a cylindrical tube, a little smile on her lips.

***

THAT EVENING WAS the first night of my new job and coincided with Quiz Night.

I knew this not because Manawa thought to warn me ahead of time, like you might expect an employer to do, but because on my approach to the main entrance, it was clear she intended to compete with the church for the town's hallowed Worst Sign Prize.

On a large blackboard screwed to the street-facing wall of the building was written *Saturday Night Quiz Night - a memory test of wholly unimportant information. Who knows? You might have fun.*

I smoothed down the Tokawai Hotel-emblazoned, men's extra-large T-shirt she'd given me (because, unsurprisingly, she didn't have a woman's one big enough), and made my entrance past the collection of muddied gumboots left at the door.

When I opened it and was met by a wall of noise, I understood that Manawa didn't need to make much of an effort to sell tonight's event. With decidedly little encouragement on her part, the place was full.

Unlike my first entry into the pub, nobody bothered to turn to see who had arrived. Clearly, Fuzz Cup nights did not coincide with Pub Quiz nights, which was only sensible. Every grey cell not marinated in beer or bourbon would need to have its sole focus on dredging up tiny nuggets of trivia from dark, cobweb-strewn recesses of brains.

I couldn't see Manawa at the bar over the row of backs of people lining it, but a growled, "This isn't a bloody cocktail bar," told me she was there.

As the patron was informed in no uncertain terms, "Wine spritzer is the fanciest I get," I stepped behind the bar, threw my jacket into a corner and turned to face the sea of jostling punters.

I'd worked hundreds of events in my years of climbing the event management ladder. When things got busy, stepping in was a necessary part of the job. Obviously, Manawa had seen that in me. Otherwise she wouldn't have asked me to start at peak hour without a lesson beforehand.

She flicked her eyebrows up in greeting.

I nodded back, turned to my first patron and asked that age-old bartender question. "What'll it be?"

Ten minutes later, when all but one had settled in to their first drink of the night, Manawa blew a stray strand of hair from her eyes, turned to me and grimaced. "I really need to order in more T-shirts. You look like you've gone camping in a four-person tent."

The one man left waiting at the bar for his drink, fingers beating a drum roll on the bar mat, leaned towards me. "I've got my sleeping bag in the car. I'll crawl in there with you."

Manawa grabbed the handle of beer I'd finished filling

and slammed it down on top of his fingers. "No uninvited lechery in my pub, Tommo. You know the rules."

"Awesome," I breathed, and decided I was a little bit in love with her already.

By the time Tommo removed his fingers from beneath the glass and pulled them into his mouth to suck the hurt from them, Manawa had pulled a pair of scissors on me.

She twirled her finger in the air. "Turn around. This won't hurt a bit."

I took a step back from her. "This T-shirt has just seen you break all the bones in a man's hand. Can't you hear its screams?"

Manawa took another step forward.

I took another one back.

"I hear a whole lot of lip flapping."

"I don't reveal more flesh than is absolutely necessary." I pointed to my face. "I'd wear a face sock with spy holes if I could, but it upsets people."

"Trust me," she said, continuing to advance.

"No."

"One night. If you hate it, you can burn it."

My heel hit the wall and Manawa closed in. The scissors opened and closed in the air between us like a snapping maw. *Shickashicka.* "Please. You couldn't look any worse than you do now in that sheet. I'll keep your dignity intact."

I should have been wise to the fact dignity-keeping is relative.

As Manawa made the last snip and the sour air of beer-breath and socks that had been worked in all day trailed its spongy finger across the top of my breasts, I closed my eyes against the destruction she'd wreaked on the unsuspecting fabric. "What are you going to do with the rest of the T-shirt now you've cut the nipple tassels out?"

"Don't be so dramatic. The ratio of material to skin is still favourable. I think."

It was then that Mitchell stepped out from the back room and any further sarcasm died on my lips.

Mitchell could have been naked, but for the green lycra body suit sculpted to every line, every plane, every bulge of his body.

Small black question marks decorated the fabric. His red hair had been parted and two small buns sat balanced on either side of his skull like a bear's ears. A green Zorro mask covered his eyes.

He spread his arms wide, a black cane dangling from one of them. "What do you think of my new Quiz Master outfit, my honeyed yam?"

A squeak from behind me suggested Manawa had registered the question, but was too overwhelmed to attempt diplomacy.

So I stepped up to the honeyed-yam duties. "I think Jim Carey would be proud."

Manawa let out the breath she had been holding in a whoosh, elbowed me aside, and grabbed Mitchell's hand. "Three minutes to quiz kick off. Plenty of time." And she pulled him into the back room, slamming the door.

I turned towards the crowds on the floor and wondered aloud that I hoped the three minutes were being used constructively. Like finding Mitchell a less ridiculous and more modest outfit.

I poured a house white for a young woman (five foot seven, sixty kilograms, size 10. Two thirds of a Sadie) and we both watched while the surface quivered, settled, and quivered again.

The young woman rolled her eyes. "They're always doing that," she said with a snap of her gum. "Thank goodness she's brought you on. We're usually just left waiting until they finish before we can get our next drink."

"Every night?"

"Most nights."

I whistled. I didn't think even I, at a quarter of a century younger, had the stamina for *most nights*.

I adjusted my T-shirt, tugging it down at the back so that the fabric shifted at the front and covered my cleavage, but the series of knots at the T-shirt's bottom meant my stomach was now exposed above the band of my ankle-length black skirt.

I sighed and pulled it back to its original position.

As the big hand on the clock on the end wall of the pub ticked onto the twelve, the storeroom door flew open. Mitchell stumbled out and staggered his way towards the tennis umpire's chair positioned under the clock.

I poured a coke, then an IPA. No Manawa.

"You okay in there?"

A pause. "Just...putting all my pieces back together," she called back.

I wondered if she meant metaphorically, if Mitchell had moved her heaven and earth and everything in between. Or if she just meant she was having a difficult time locating her underwear.

A series of whistles drew my attention back to the floor of the pub.

Mitchell had arranged himself on the raised chair, so that one leg dangled over the chair's arm in casual abandon, his crotch straining against the tight fabric.

He stretched his mouth into the manic smile of the Riddler. "Good evening ladies and gentleman. Welcome to tonight's delights of trivial curiosities and mind-bending questions. As always, the Quiz Master's word is final and the rules are simple." He waved his cane over the crowd as if magicking them into obedience. "No phones. No heckling. No Jacki Chan-ing."

He spread his arms wide and dropped his voice. "Let us begin."

As he read out the first question, Manawa emerged from the back room, her eyes glassy and her long pony tail askew. She pulled a glass from the fridge, its sides misting from the heat of the room, and poured herself two fingers of whiskey.

Downing it in one, she smacked her lips and cast her eyes over the pub floor. "Right," she said, slapping the glass on the bench. "Business time."

She tugged her hair free of its elastic band and braided it into a French plait. Her fingers worked quickly, the fine bones in her hands shifting under the skin.

Catching me watching, she said, "My mean hair. Hard to ruffle. Won't get in the way."

"For what?"

"Things can get messy on Quiz Night."

I turned and surveyed the room. Everyone studiously wrote on their sheets, or were hunched over their tables, leaning towards their team mates and whispering answers. I couldn't imagine, given the degree of rule compliance, what might ensue.

"Don't tell me they dare to write outside the prescribed line space?" I tutted. "What's the quiz world coming to?"

"Just wait. Something's brewing." Manawa looked out over the pub floor and narrowed her eyes. "They're never this quiet for this long."

I tugged again at my shirt, felt the stale pub air rush in underneath and cling to my belly, and pulled it back to where it was. "Did you have to cut so much off? It's like I've gone in for a wash and trim and you've given me a buzz cut."

"Yes. It looks good. Your cleavage balances the width of your shoulders."

"I feel exposed. And a bit ..." I trailed off, not willing to pass the word over my tongue.

Manawa pointed an empty glass at me. "If you say 'slutty', I will break this glass on the counter and cut your tongue out with it. Women get enough of a hard time from men for being proud of their bodies. They don't need judgement from their own team as well."

I sucked the word back into my brain and settled on, "uncomfortable", which was as much of an understatement as saying the captain of the Titanic had a rough day.

It wasn't just the neckline and the bottom hem that she'd butchered. The sleeves had also lost several inches and my fleshy upper arms, usually hidden in roomy tubes of material, were now on full display.

"Fine. Well, once we get women's T-shirts in your size, that won't be an issue. In the meantime, revel in the beauty of your womanhood."

For one awful second, I thought she'd said "bounty of your womanhood", which while completely accurate, was not something I needed to hear as often as I did.

A hubbub rose as Mitchell marked the papers of the previous round and wrote scores next to team names on a small whiteboard that hung beneath the clock.

Then he climbed back up onto his chair, arranged his limbs, and with sleight of wrist, his genitals, into a comfortable position and raised his voice. "And now. The Manawa Special."

The sibilance of a collective female "yes" penetrated the low drone of male groans.

Mitchell leaned towards the crowd and said in a hushed voice, "The sports round."

"*The* sports round?" a man called out. "Don't we get another one with men's sports?"

The Quiz Master sat back abruptly, throwing the umpire's chair into a wobble. "You will not. Manawa says, and I quote, 'You're lucky to get a bloody sports round at all. So be grateful'."

"Why is the sports round called The Manawa Special?" I murmured to her as Mitchell read out the first question.

"You been to pub quizzes before?"

"Yeah."

"Notice how the sports round - and there's always a sports round - is only ever about male sporting achievements? I make Mitchell only ask questions about women's sporting achievements. In another couple of years, we might have evened things up. Then I'll let him ask questions about men."

"Huh." I pulled the lager lever towards me and watched the bubbles arc and rise in the amber liquid trying to choose which course of conversation to pursue. Congratulate her for her stand or tackle the topic that had been weighing on me for the last day.

The man waiting for the beer I was pouring ran a hand through his hair. It was thin and fine and stood at a diagonal to his scalp, like it couldn't decide which direction to settle in. Just like Poppy's.

"Have you heard of 'The Sad Ballad of Doug and Rose'?"

Manawa shook her head.

The man sucked in a breath with a hiss and tutted on his outwards one.

"What?" I asked him, perhaps a little too fiercely, as I placed the beer in front of him.

He took a sip and said, "Hmm?" as he licked the froth from his top lip.

"Why did you tut?"

Turning to make his way back to his table, he said, "Well, it was all pretty tragic, wasn't it?"

"What was?" I shouted after him, only to receive a chorus of "shhhh" from the floor and a glare from the holes in Mitchell's mask, which might have been intimidating were it not for the fact he looked like his head was being shat out of the arse of a caterpillar.

I'd never been collectively shushed before. I felt like a child who'd been roundly censured, and that child was sorely tempted to shout an apology.

Before I could offend the entire pub, Manawa asked, "Why are you so aggressively interested in a tragi-ballad?"

I emitted a sigh. "It's a song by Dante Kerr. Local country legend, apparently. It's about my great-grandparents, and I want to know what happened to them, but do you think I can find a single recording of it? No covers. No lyrics sheet. No cheeky video taken by someone in the audience. Nothing."

Manawa pursed her lips in thought.

"You cheat!" A woman in a Hello Kitty T-shirt, black-rimmed glasses and pink skinny jeans pushed herself off her stool and stood pointing at a man in short shirt sleeves, a tie, dress shorts and below-the-knee socks. He looked like a salesman who'd just teleported in from the 1980s.

"For reals. He's using his phone." She swivelled to face Mitchell, her hair flicking over her shoulder, revealing a shaved patch above her left ear. "He's looking at Wikipedia."

"Here we go," muttered Manawa.

The salesman affected a round-eyed face of innocence. "I am not. I'm updating my status on Facebook."

Hello Kitty put her hands on her narrow hips. "Hail yes, you were. I could see it under the table."

The salesman pushed himself away from his table, stood and grabbed his team's answer sheet. "I was not. You take that back."

Hello Kitty took a step towards him and pointed at the paper. "Don't you threaten me, gangsta." She turned for the benefit of the crowd. "You all see that? He's threatening me."

The crowd murmured and the salesman dropped the piece of paper and held up his hands, palms outwards. "Alright. Nobody's threatening anyone."

"What on earth's going on?" I asked Manawa.

She closed her eyes and shook her head. "Paper cut fight. Happens every other week."

The two stared each other down like gun slingers in a showdown. Hello Kitty's fingers twitched. Then she made a grab for her team's piece of paper, and as the salesman scrabbled for his own, Mitchell issued a "Manawa!", the plea in his voice throwing it an octave higher.

She'd already pushed herself away from the service bench and was halfway to the end of the bar. By the time she'd rounded it and stepped out on to the pub floor, the two contestants circled each other, bodies crouched, papers raised in strike position.

The salesman smiled at his opponent and jerked forward, feigning a strike, and as the crowd gasped and Hello Kitty staggered backwards out of range, he rumbled out a low laugh like a motorbike engine firing into life.

Somebody called out, "Two metres and closing," and Hello Kitty lunged, striking the man on the forearm with her paper.

He hissed and whipped his arm back with an "ah!"

The crowd "oooh"ed.

And then Manawa was upon them. She grabbed each of the fighters by the ear and pulled them down to her level to a chorus of "ow"s. "I don't accept violence of any kind in my bar." She gave each ear a tug in emphasis. "Stop being fools or I'll ban you both for a month." Then she released them.

Hello Kitty rubbed her ear, the salesman his arm.

Manawa held out a hand to him. "Give me your phone. You can have it back at the end of the quiz."

"But I was on Facebook!"

She pointed at Mitchell. "What did the Quiz Master say?"

The man's eyes shifted to Mitchell, then back to Manawa, and his spine curled between his shoulder blades so that he resembled one of Mitchell's question marks. He slapped the phone on her palm, winced and said, "I need a plaster."

"You don't need a bloody plaster. You need some more brain cells. Woman up and get on with answering questions." She pocketed the phone, clapped her palms together as if dusting off dirt and returned to the service side of the bar. "Speaking of which, your grandfather's not coming tonight, is he?"

"Don't think so."

"Good. He likes to come and show the young people up. Forms a team of one and sits in the corner, taking out top marks on all the categories." She tapped the side of her head. "Mind like a steel trap."

I straightened my back, then rounded my shoulders again when one breast threatened to spill over the top of the T-shirt. "Really?"

"Does it to mock everyone, which is fun for him but shit for anyone else."

"When did he last take part?"

"Couple of weeks ago."

I took a cloth from the service bench and wiped at the bar top in front of me. "So, you wouldn't say he might be in the early stages of dementia?"

"Ha. Not bloody likely."

The lump of worry that had been pulsating in the dark heart of my belly settled into stillness.

Maybe there was absolutely nothing wrong with Poppy. Maybe I was seeing things because I was looking for them, concerned by his age and his appearance of fragility.

I needed to give Poppy the benefit of the doubt and not be so hasty in drawing conclusions.

I smiled, dropped the cloth in the service sink and looked up into the ice-cold eyes of Officer McClintock.

"It's not Fuzz Cup night, Callum," said Manawa. "What brings you here this evening?"

"Sadie Quinn."

Oh shit.

"By the look on his face, Sadie, I'd say he's working himself up to ask you out or arrest you."

Without taking his eyes off me, he said, "You wouldn't happen to know anything about this, would you?"

He opened his hand and nestled in his palm was what might have been, to the untrained eye, a small black berry.

CHAPTER SEVEN

"FOUND under one of the pews in the church. Near the aisle."

I clutched my hands to my chest and stepped backwards as a ribbon of ice wound its way around my lungs and began to cinch itself tight. My ribs creaked with the effort to expand them again, to suck in enough air to make a perfectly reasonable suggestion. "A raisin?" I shook my head. The movement felt stiff, like a wind-up automaton. "Toddlers these days. No respect."

Callum peered out at me from underneath his eyebrows and held out his other hand.

On the screen of his phone was a picture on a Facebook feed of a lollipop-sucking Mitchell draped across the top of the church sign, a laughing Manawa, and a very tall woman looking like she'd just endured a colonic irrigation.

"Seems you did know about it."

I managed to remove one hand and place it with casual abandon on the bar top. "Well, you know, I had a lot on my mind that morning. Like whether cotton or wool has the best absorbency." With great effort, I shifted my other hand to my hip.

"Watcha got there, Callum?" asked Manawa, leaning in for a look at the photo. She nodded as if unsurprised by the content. "Yep, pretty awesome photo, alright. I love everything about it. Apart from Sadie."

Callum pulled the phone around and peered at it. "Yeeees," he said slowly. "That's a look I experience a lot on the force. It says 'I'm very uncomfortable right now, because I'm as guilty as sin'." He shifted his eyes from the phone to Manawa and raised an eyebrow. "I sincerely hope Mitchell is strategically clothed, and *not* exposing himself in a public place."

Before she had a chance to reply, I said, "Look. I just -" I sucked in a breath to buy some time to scrabble about in my brain for a passable excuse. *I wanted to humour my elderly and possibly senile grandfather? If I don't help him 'misdemeanour the arse out of this town' I have to go home to live with my parents, which would crush my soul?*

Callum shook his head. "I mean, who would bring a *goat* as part of their break in plan?"

"That's what I said!" was out of me before I had brought a hand up to slap my mouth closed. I smacked my other hand over my eyes to shield myself from the reality of self-incrimination that would no doubt be written all over Callum's face.

I wasn't sure how long I could stand there for, but if I put in enough effort, maybe I could keep the world closed out until Callum gave up and went home.

Mitchell read another question out. The patrons whispered their answers. Glasses clinked on table tops.

The arm supporting the hand that covered my mouth began to ache.

"I'm still here, Sadie." Callum's voice rumbled against the soft murmuring of the quiz contestants. "I can wait all night, but I don't think your arms are going to make it that long. Would you like to come out now?"

I took a deep breath and slowly lowered each hand.

Callum's mouth was set in a thin line. "So it's your grandfather I need to be talking to." It wasn't a question.

I placed both hands on the bench top in front of me and leaned towards him. I hoped it looked imploring, but suspected it could equally be interpreted as threatening. Or given the amount of breast I now had on exposure, a very unsubtle distraction tactic. "He's not well. In the head. You saw it the other night."

"But instead of stopping him, you helped him."

I stood upright again. "Stop Poppy? I'd have a better chance of rotating the earth on a vertical axis. And besides. We didn't break in. He has a key."

Callum's pale eyebrows knitted. "Why would Gerry have a key?"

I flicked my gaze around the room before I resettled them on Callum, as if I was about to deliver a great secret. "Had it from his childhood, apparently. They haven't upgraded the lock since."

The pale brows rose. Then he pointed his finger at me. "He's - *you've* - still trespassed."

There was nothing else for me to do but accept the cold, hard reality of the situation. "Yes. Though spare the goat. She doesn't know what she's implicated in."

"*Spare the goat.* Sadie, you are -"

"'Pretty bloody gorgeous' I believe are the words you're looking for, Callum," interrupted Manawa. "My design. But it's easy to be inspired by great form."

Not only did her words have the effect of cleaving an

axe to Callum's line of thought, in my indecision to roll my eyeballs or throw my arms across my chest in mortification, I ended up in stasis, which gave Callum the opportunity to check the truthfulness of Manawa's unlikely assertion.

His eyes flicked over me once, and just for good measure, made another pass to make sure my cleavage was still where it should be.

"You're welcome."

I wasn't sure if Manawa had said it to Callum for giving him an opening to scrutinise my assets, or to me for having provided a diversion.

Something told me it was said for both our benefits.

Callum stepped back from the bar and replaced his police hat. "I'll be coming by to visit you and your grandfather in the morning. It's my day off, so you better be bloody home."

CALLUM DID NOT CALL round in the morning, much to Poppy's disappointment.

He'd baked a Black Forest Gateau for the occasion, stating that being caught was part of the game and kudos to "the boy" for working it out.

The prospect of having charges laid against him did nothing to dampen his spirits. He whipped up chocolate ganache with the energy of a seventy-year-old. "I've been many things in my life, Sadie-me-girl, but a con with a rap sheet is not one of them."

When I emphatically stated I didn't want a rap sheet, Poppy slapped a spatula-full of ganache onto the surface of one of the cake layers with a "ha!", then smeared the choco-

late-infused cream in a clock-wise circle. "Could have fooled me."

I left him to decorate the cake and retreated with Obi-Wan to my bedroom to engage The Virgin Mary in a staring contest. It seemed a fitting way to pass the time before having my guilt formally recognised through the strong arm of the law.

No matter how much I squinted to reduce the area of eyeball exposed to the air, I only ever made it to thirty seconds before blinking.

The statue continued to eye me with all the judgemental smugness of a woman blessed with perfection, purity and twenty centuries of adoration.

Obi-Wan, clad in her new polka dotted underwear, quickly tired of my game and engaged her number two tactic to get my attention, now that crapping on me had been removed from the equation.

She nosed my ear and bleated as loud as her baby lungs would allow her.

I swore, locked eyes again with The Virgin and pointed at my eyes with two fingers before reversing them towards her. "Later."

Then I took Obi-Wan outside for a game of No, Don't Eat That.

At a quarter to twelve, the phone rang.

I'd forgone breakfast as a counter-balance to the impending calorie bomb, and Poppy and I had already collapsed under impatience and hunger and eaten a slice of the cake. Exhausted from the weight of a full belly and a morning of cake construction, Poppy had promptly fallen asleep at the table, his head resting on his shoulder.

I had rolled my glazed cherry around my plate, engaged

in a standoff between the rest of the cake and my portion control.

At the phone's *brrring,* I dropped the knife I wielded to cut myself a second slice after conceding inevitable defeat. It clattered onto the edge of the cake stand.

Poppy jerked awake with a grunt and raised his eyes towards me as I pushed myself up from the table. "I'll get it. Go back to sleep."

The telephone, a cheap two-piece connected by a long coiled cable, sat on a low table in the darkened hallway.

"Hello, Gerry Quinn's residence."

"Ah," growled a male voice. "Sadie. Of course."

"Officer Callum. We've been waiting for you. Poppy made you a Black Forest Gateau to celebrate his new life as a felon and says he can't wait to be locked in irons and thrown in the cells."

Callum issued a sigh down the line. "There'll be no throwing in the cells of anybody. Even if the church *did* want to lay a formal complaint."

The ribbon of ice around my ribs released with a *twang.* "They don't?"

"Had a record turn out to mass this morning, apparently. Congregation's been dwindling for years. It seems you've done them a favour."

I rested my head against the wall, closed my eyes and exhaled through pursed lips.

"If I were you, I'd enjoy that cake as a celebration of getting away with it. Oh, and turn that key in to the station in the morning."

The phone line went dead.

When I returned to the kitchen, Obi-Wan stood at the 'rinsing station', assisting Poppy in the baking clean up by licking the plates.

I had long since ceased to remonstrate with Poppy about letting her do this. Obi-Wan, he'd said, could earn her keep while she resided under this roof. Preparing the plates to be washed by removing food debris was part of her contribution.

I sat down at the kitchen table and placed my chin in my hands. "Seems like we're off the hook."

Poppy turned from the sink, his mouth slack with disappointment. "Callum's not going to arrest us?"

I shook my head. "The church is walking the talk and offering absolution. Apparently, they had a record turnout this morning."

He snorted and turned back to the sink. "Wasn't quite what I had in mind, but if they can take a joke, then perhaps they're deserving of a fresh flock."

"Oh, and Callum says we have to take the key to the station tomorrow morning."

"Only fair."

Obi-Wan, having run out of plates to lick, clacked her way over to me and lifted her head for a scratch.

Poppy turned, a cake fork in his raised hand and foam running down his forearm. "You know what this means, Sadie? We've been given a mandate to get on with the second item on the list."

I slapped a hand on the table, making Obi-Wan jump. "You have to be kidding. We only just got away with the first one. The increase in congregation was pure luck. Why on earth would you want to thumb your nose at the law less than twelve hours since Callum made it clear he's watching us?"

A smile. "He said that?"

"He didn't need to. I've been trouble in his life for

almost as long as he can remember, and you're just trouble. You deliberately set out to have that reputation."

The smile deepened into a grin.

"I think we need to give this list of yours a rest."

In a flash, a frown replaced the smile. Poppy slapped the water and suds slopped down the front of the cabinetry. "You're not in any sodding position to back out on me, girlie. We both know this is the best roof for you to have over your head. And besides, we spat on it. You can't break a saliva oath. Twenty years bad luck."

"Huh. Wouldn't make much difference to the way my life's heading."

"Get up here and bloody-well help me do these dishes." He reached for a tea towel and threw it at me.

My world turned checker-board green and orange.

I pulled the tea towel from my head, pushed myself up from the table and stepped in line next to him. "I just -"

"You just nothing."

"If you're really determined to do this, Poppy, why don't you get your friend, *Eddie*, to help you with it and leave me out of it."

"Eddie's already helping. It's you who needs to pull their blasted weight."

I dried a plate, placed it on the bench and prepared to call his bluff. "Guess I'll be sleeping in the car, then."

Poppy raised a finger so quickly, soap suds strafed my shirt like machine gun fire. "Don't you make me make you. I'll bloody-well do it, Sadie. I've had sixty more years than you to practice my mule impression. I'll out-stubborn the arse off you."

My phone vibrated in my back pocket. I pulled it out and looked at the display. Dad.

"Poppy, I've got a call. I'm going to take it outside. I'll dry the dishes and fight with you after."

His grunt burbled in the back of his throat so that it emerged more growl than gruff acknowledgement.

I answered the phone as I pulled open the back door. "Hi."

"Sadie. It's your father."

"I know dad. That's the genius of modern phones. They tell you who's calling."

A "hello, darling" issued from somewhere in the background.

"Hi, Mum."

"Alan, ask her if she organised that TedX event. The one with that Swedish girl. Greta somebody."

The speaker distorted with a rush of air, no doubt a sigh. "Your mother wants to know –"

"No," I said, rolling my eyes. "I didn't do the TedX."

"Goodo," Dad said, not bothering to relay the message. "You still at your grandfather's?"

"Yes." I walked down the back steps and stepped out on to the lawn.

"Excellent. I've done some blue sky thinking with your Uncle Peter about what's best for everyone and we've agreed there's no point boiling the ocean about what to do with your grandfather." *Uncle Peter and I have been trying to think creatively about what's best for us in regards to Poppy's future and we can't be bothered wasting time on alternatives that aren't in our interest.* "So, you're going to be the change agent, Sadie. I'm sending you some marketing collateral." *We want you to do the dirty work. The retirement village brochures are in the mail.*

Ducking under the washing line, I said, "Poppy doesn't

need to go into a home, Dad, and for the love of sanity, can you please talk to me without the corporate patois?"

A sigh. "They're all in the district. Not flash, but functional, which is probably all the old bugger can afford, even with the sale of the house."

I walked on to a wooden plank placed between beds of vegetable seedlings. "You're not listening to me, Dad. I'm here. Poppy is perfectly happy, and he doesn't need to go anywhere."

"He's eighty-eight years old, Sadie. What happens when you decide to go back to the city? You can't keep running a business from the armpit of the King Country. Who's going to check he's still healthy and happy then? I am not burdening you with him, as broad as your shoulders are." Dad's references to my size were made often enough, that I knew he was not just speaking metaphorically.

I stepped onto another plank and stopped. The wood rocked beneath my feet on the uneven earth. "It's not a burden. I like living here with him. And I'm perfectly able to keep things ticking along from a distance. I'll be here for the foreseeable future."

"Sadie," he said in a voice low with warning. "This is actually not your decision."

"It's not yours either! Poppy would be miserable in a home and you know very well he'd make everyone else miserable with him. If and when he's unable to look after himself, then we consider a different living situation for him. Back off, Dad."

I hung up and marched into the house, interrupting a tea towel tug of war between Poppy and Obi-Wan. "Fuck it, Poppy. I'm in. I'm in for the whole fucking list. Let's do this."

THE HORSE HAD BEEN REARING atop the Bertram building for generations.

Originally designed as a marketing gimmick for Tokawai's general store, it had seen businesses in the building below come and go, the meaning of its commercial symbolism long since gone.

But it was a Tokawai icon, and part of the collective subconscious, either in its original wooden form, or as the garish fibreglass and neon-lit replica that had replaced it in the 80s.

No one noticed it any more. It had become as normal and mundane as the blue sky above them, which, presumably, was the reason for its current state.

The colours were faded to a whitewash, a milky hint of what they might have once been. Only one of its raised hooves was illuminated in glowing blue. The mane flickered, not by design, but through ageing circuitry. Only one yellow strand of the tail's hair remained lit. The effect was somewhat alarming - a tape worm making an enthusiastic bid for freedom from the horse's rear end.

As an occasional visitor, the horse had never become background noise for me. It had captured my imagination as a child and I wanted to set it free from its eternity on the building. Loosen the bonds holding its back feet to the roof and watch it leap onto the verandah below and down on to the road to gallop out of town.

It seemed I wasn't the only one who'd had childish dreams of the Bertram's horse.

"How the hell do we get up there?" I said, peering up at it from the dark of the main street.

Poppy grunted. "Scale the building. I've got a couple of grappling hooks in the bag."

The bag, slung over my shoulder, was heavy enough for

two such devices. I hadn't looked inside when Poppy passed it to me to carry. "Please tell me you're joking. Neither one of us has the skills to scale a building using a rope."

"There's a metal ladder around the back. Eddie showed me."

Eddie. Should have guessed.

"Then what's in the bag?"

"Bolt cutters. The ladder's padlocked."

"Right." I scanned each side of the street. "You thought about any CCTV issues?"

"Nope," said Poppy, setting out across the road. "Unless they're watching it twenty-four seven, I'm not wasting any bloody thinking space on spy cameras."

Obi-Wan and I followed, her hoof-steps ringing out in the pre-dawn air.

Poppy stepped into a dark service lane that led to the back of the building. "Now, when I was in the posse, we had no need of spy cameras. People did the spying for us."

My stomach roiled as if a storm brewed and the fear I had dismissed the previous evening surged back to lap at the inside of my ribs. "Which posse was this?"

"The one the sheriff employed. She was a commanding woman. Gave me a pair of Colt six shooters. One for each hip. I only ever had to use them in a showdown once. Mostly it was stake outs and flushing the bad guys out of the saloon like rats from the ribs of a dog."

"A dead dog I hope?" I barked a solitary laugh after I said it. A ridiculous noise for the question. It echoed between the walls of the buildings on either side of us.

"Shot dead in the street. Rabid."

Despite my unease, I couldn't help wanting to dig more, to scratch the mosquito bite, knowing the itching would get worse. "The sheriff was a woman? Was this before or after you were in The Resistance?"

We stepped out of the service lane and into the sharp glare of a security light. Poppy looked up at me, his features gathered in puzzlement. "Why does there need to be a before or after?"

"Most things have a before or after," I said, before realising that it had no bearing on these events because they didn't happen. Chronology had no importance or existence in Poppy's 'remembering'. I placed a hand on my stomach in a redundant attempt to settle it. "I see the ladder."

Eddie was indeed right. The metal ladder ran up the side of the building to the roof. At its base was a round protruding frame with bars blocking access. The bars were hinged to swing open, but secured in place with a padlock. Flakes of rust crusted the ladder.

"Is this the same ladder that was here when you were a kid?"

"Dunno. Can't imagine so." He gripped a side rail and gave it a shake. "Seems solid enough."

"For you maybe. Not for a person the size of a small house."

"Well, just as well neither one of us is. Pull your tongue back inside your head if you can't say anything sensible."

I followed the line of cancerous metal up to the top of the building and the world shifted sideways.

The bag slid from my shoulder and hit the ground with a *thud*.

Putting a hand on the metal base of the ladder to steady myself, I ignored Poppy's "okay?" and crouched down to retrieve the bolt cutters. "You sure these will work?"

I couldn't see Poppy's face with his back turned against

the light, but I could imagine his frown. "Two words. Knife and butter. Now stop gabbing and get on with it."

"Yes, Sir," I said, knowing full well that *sphincter and straining* was likely a more apt description.

With a fair amount of grunting, and helped by Poppy's motivational, "Put your bloody back into it," I managed to squeeze the blades through the metal.

It was a bit of an anti-climax. The padlock wobbled, but didn't explode or fall to the ground with a clatter that threatened to give us away.

Poppy removed it, released the gate, and the ladder was free to climb.

"You go first. Then I'll catch you if you fall."

"I'm not going to arsing fall." He flicked on his head torch. "The arthritis turns my hands into vice grips. You'd have to pry them open for me to let go."

It was almost a super power worth wishing for, if it also didn't mean a whole lot of pain for the rest of the time the disease wasn't useful. I knew with absolute certainty my palms would start sweating on the first rung, so that even if I was required to catch Poppy, I'd have no chance of holding on.

I helped him up onto the ladder, slung the bag across my shoulders, and as I put my hand on the first rung, something small and hard butted my thigh.

"What are we going to do with Obi-Wan? She can't climb a ladder."

"She's a goat. She'll work it out. Those things scale cliffs."

I ran an eye up the side of the building, noting its smooth brick, the tiny grooves afforded by the mortar. Then wished I hadn't. Closing my eyes against the spinning, I gave her a pat on the head. "Don't run away. We won't be long." I reached for a rung and pulled myself upwards.

Poppy was as good as his word. Or so I assumed. I had sealed my eyelids as soon as I'd levered myself off the ground, but his shouted, "Get a bloody move on, girl. The next millennium's already on its way," suggested he'd reached the top when I'd only managed five rungs.

The problem wasn't just the vertigo. Yes, the spinning and the tilting weren't pleasant, but it also wasn't real. Falling the distance of two storeys and ending up a quadriplegic for the rest of your life, was.

When my breath came in uneven sips of air and my legs started shaking, I tried to think of a happy place and realised I didn't have one. Poppy spinning out over the lawn? The ridiculousness of Callum singing Whitney Houston, face screwed up to hit the high note?

When at last my upwards grasp found nothing but air, the hot and grassy breath of a ruminant met me. "Obi-Wan?"

She answered with a quiet closed-mouth bleat.

I scrambled up on the roof, eyes still closed, and lay spread-eagled and panting. "Jesus Christ, that was horrible."

"You're up now. Whingeing about what just happened is as useful as catching a fart with a colander."

I tipped my head back and looked up at him from my prone position, but all I could see was a pair of legs disappearing up into a blinding light.

Blinking the glare from my eyeballs, I rolled over and raised myself to hands and knees. "Where do you want me to take the photo from?"

"Down on the street where the first photo was taken."

There was a couple of things about his statement I took issue with. The least being that I hadn't actually seen the original photo, so didn't know where the photographer had stood. I peered out at him through my curtain of hair and counted to five.

It didn't help. I gritted my teeth and forced my words out between them. "If you wanted the photo taken from the street, why didn't you tell me *before* I climbed the ladder of fucking death. You're obviously more than capable of doing it on your own."

"I thought you might want to give the horse a slap on its rump first. And maybe enjoy the view."

"Of what? There's nothing to see. It's still night, Poppy."

"Suit yourself. Take the bag with you when you go. Leave the hat and the can openers."

I unzipped the bag and pulled out a cowboy hat and a cracked pair of spurred, leather boots.

"Where'd you get these?" I set them down on the ground with a jangle.

"Eddie."

I should have known.

After swapping out his sneakers for the boots and positioning the hat on his head, he turned away from me, taking his spotlight with him.

With my full vision returned, I could see I was wrong about it still being night. A pale band of new day had begun to appear on the eastern horizon. We didn't have much time before the town woke and began its day.

Right now, the illuminated parts of the horse were visible from the street, but little else. The gathering dawn would give enough light for Poppy to be visible in the photo, but hopefully not visible enough to be noticed by passers-by.

I stood at the top of the ladder and counted to three. I

counted to three again, and began my sweaty-palmed, closed-eye descent.

As I hurried back towards the main street, two cars, their lights bright against the dim street lights, drove past the end of the service lane. Soon there would be more. There was no time to find the best vantage point for the photo. As long as the horse was visible, Poppy would have to be happy with what he got.

I crossed the street, pretended to look at the goods displayed within an illuminated shop window when another car drove past, then turned to look up at the horse.

It continued to rear in its eternal solitariness. No Poppy. "Where the fuck is he?" Each word was a little puff of white in the cool dawn air.

Another set of headlights appeared down the street. It wouldn't take long before my loitering was noticed.

It was then that the wailing began. A high-pitched rise and fall that belonged unmistakably to a certain kind of beast.

A squad car.

A wave of frigid water washed over me. We had been noticed and this time, Callum would be less likely to go easy on us.

I peered up the street into the brightening gloom, a foot hovering over the curb, ready to make a dash across the street. With a scrape of cement, I pulled it back. By the time I made it back up onto the roof, Callum would already be here.

"Poppy," I hissed.

Nothing. No reply. No movement.

"Poppy! Get down. You need to climb back down."

The horse's mane flickered. Its second raised and unlit

hoof was now visible in the growing light. Still no Poppy. Perhaps, hearing the siren, he was already on the ladder.

The patrol car had reached the commercial area of the main street, its siren ricocheting between the buildings' façades. There was no time left for Poppy to be indecisive. Either he was down off the roof and readying himself for a 'walking the goat' lie, or we were screwed.

I pulled myself back into the safety of the shop entrance as a low-slung car with a spoiler roared past. Its number plate, reflecting a rolling flash of red and blue, read MO1ST.

Two seconds later the patrol car tore past.

I unclenched my fists, my palms hot where my nails had bitten.

A "now!" barked from above.

Stepping out from underneath the shop verandah, I raised my phone, took the photo, shoved it in my back pocket, and hurried back across the street and into the service lane.

Obi-Wan bleated at me as I turned the corner into the car park. It reverberated in the empty space.

"Shhh." I flapped my arms as if warding away the echo of her greeting. Then I stood still, listening for approaching footsteps.

When ten seconds had passed without any shouts of alarm or returning police sirens, I hissed up at her, "Put your energy into getting back down here."

A series of chimes like coins clinking into an outstretched hand cascaded down from the rooftop, and Poppy's head appeared over the side of the building. "Hi ho, Sadie. The bangtail's been tamed. Time to ride out of these badlands."

"For Christ's sake. Lower your voice. People are up and about now."

Poppy saluted me with his finger gun and reached for the top of the ladder.

He grasped one side of it and shuffled around to get his body into position to lower his foot onto the first rung. A cochlea-exploding screech rent the still morning air.

Poppy froze. Then his eyes shifted to meet mine.

And because my insides had crumpled in on themselves, my "Poppy. Let go!" came out as a whisper.

He splayed his fingers, releasing the ladder.

With a whine, the top of the ladder swung out from the wall, stopping two feet from the edge of the roof so that it formed a shallow triangle with the brick façade.

I held my breath, willing it to teeter back and settle against the side of the building.

Then, with the slow grace of a wronged lady fainting into her petticoats, it descended towards the earth and hit the concrete of the parking lot with an almighty *CLANG*.

I looked from it to Poppy, who peered down between hands clamped to the roof edging.

"Shit."

CHAPTER EIGHT

BY THE TIME the fire brigade arrived, a small crowd had gathered in the parking lot.

I'd taken the opportunity in the down-time between my phone call and the truck's arrival to stash the bag with the bolt cutters in the car and try to find the padlock in the twisted metal of the ladder. It wasn't there, presumably flung off at the point of collision.

Obi-Wan, who, unsurprisingly, had found her own way down, nosed my hand as the spectators parted to reveal a very tall blonde man in police uniform.

From the way his hands clasped his narrow hips so that the knuckles matched the colour of his hair, it may have been fair to say he wasn't particularly impressed.

I pretended not to have seen him and looked up towards Poppy, now safe in the bucket of a cherry picker, and smiling and waving at the crowd below like a messiah descending from the heavens.

This grandfather, the one who exercised all the smile muscles in his face several times a day, and not only in the blurriness of just-waking, and who acknowledged other people in ways that might be considered polite, was not one I would have recognised prior to my recent arrival in Tokawai.

He was happy.

A suspicion fluttered at the edges of my mind, its touch the faintest of tickles, like someone had traced a feather over the bumps and hollows of my brain.

I knew Poppy had been a grumpy, distant man for most of his life. A disposition that was natural, so Dad said. But maybe he wasn't an uncaring, callous bastard.

Maybe he'd just been shaped by unhappiness.

If I was right, God. What a way to have lived. A lump formed in my throat and wedged itself beneath my larynx.

I swallowed it back down, sucked in a deep breath, and turned to face Callum. Whatever the reason for the change, and for how long it lasted, I was going to protect it at all costs.

I mirrored his stance, placed my hands on my hips and opened my mouth to make an aggressive case for our defence, when Callum held up a finger.

My inward breath stuck in my throat.

He retracted his finger, and like a puppet on a string, I closed my mouth.

Damn him and his blue-eyed authority.

"But -"

Callum gave a slight shake of his head. "No."

"He's-"

He held up a palm. "Stop."

"Will you just -"

"Listen? No, Sadie. I don't think there's anything you can say that would give you a legitimate reason for being up on that roof."

"Fine." I mimed zipping my mouth closed and pulled

my phone out of my back pocket. I thumbed open the photo I took of Poppy and showed it to Callum.

Bathed in the golden light of the sun's first rays, Poppy rode the Bertram's horse with one arm flung wide, a cowboy hat in its grip, and a broad grin on his face.

He might have been making a grand gesture before riding off into the sunset, were it not for the goat standing on the horse's head.

"This is meant to exonerate you, how?"

"Look at him. He's deliriously happy. How many times have you seen Poppy like that?"

"Ah. Just a few days ago?"

An image of Poppy's head thrown back, his mouth wide with glee as he swung from the washing line projected itself on the inside of my skull. "Apart from that."

"I presume he was pretty happy when he made a celebratory Black Forest Gateau?"

I raised a finger. "But not before that, right?" I didn't wait for his answer. I knew my facts were solid. "He's always been a notoriously miserable bastard, but something's happened recently that's made him want to chase happiness. Who am I to deny him that? He's my *grandfather*. And a very old one. He probably doesn't have too much time left to try and change his way of being."

"So-" Callum thrust his hands in his trouser pockets. "-What you're telling me is that you've enabled your elderly grandfather to trespass *twice* in the pursuit of happiness."

"Yes."

"Oh, well in that case, I'll stop my line of enquiry right here."

I eyed him for three heartbeats.

"You're being facetious," I crossed my arms. "How unlike you."

"Of course I'm being facetious. If the building owners want to lay a formal complaint, I won't stop them. At the very least, the fire brigade will fine you a few hundred dollars for the call out."

"What about the health and safety violation? There was nothing to suggest he couldn't climb the ladder. It could have been kids who scaled that death trap." I shifted my hands to my hips. "It was totally irresponsible of the building owner not to secure it."

Obi-Wan clattered forward and presented her head to Callum for a pat, which he declined. Then, with a bulge of her cheeks, she regurgitated the padlock onto his shoes.

My insides clamped together.

Callum peered down at his feet, then up at me, eyebrow raised.

I did the only thing I could. Shrug.

It was deliberately ambiguous. It might have indicated guilt. Or it might have suggested I'd never seen such a device before.

Callum bent and pincered it between thumb and fore-finger, his other fingers sticking straight out as if scared to get too close.

With the index finger on his other hand, he poked at the silver shackle. It swung open revealing its sheared off end still locked in the body of the padlock.

"Huh," I said. "See? Total neglect. Even the padlock was dysfunctional."

"Sadie. I don't suppose, should I search the contents of your grandfather's car, that I would find a pair of bolt cutters?"

I rolled my lips together as if smoothing out freshly-applied lip balm. "Nope." My voice rose in pitch like I was issuing a question, rather than a denial.

Callum shook his head. "You're a terrible liar. Take me to the car."

Fuck.

"Don't you need a warrant?"

"No, I do not need a warrant, because you are going to willingly comply with my request."

I peered over the heads of the bystanders to try and find Poppy. He was being helped from the platform of the cherry picker, which was now nestled back on its base.

"Poppy!" I turned from Callum and hurried towards the fire fighter assisting my grandfather.

Callum growled a singsonged "Sadie" like a father might to a naughty child.

Wrapping my arms around Poppy, I enveloped his small frame and said for the benefit of the crowd, "That must have been terrifying." Then I hissed into his ear, "Play along. Callum's hot on our case."

Poppy nodded, eyed his waiting audience and "yee haw"ed. Affecting a southern American accent, he declared, "That was quite some rodeo. Been squaring off with that bronco for eighty years. Hasn't got the better of me yet."

I closed my eyes and groaned inwardly. Between Obi-Wan, Poppy and my ability to blurt incriminating sentences, we were the world's worst con team.

Poppy turned to Callum. "Do you know how strong she is? Cut through that padlock like it was a meringue. I didn't think it could be done, but with a bit of pep talk, she nailed it in about five seconds."

I pressed the heel of my hands to my eyeballs and willed time to suck me back to when I set up my company with Jordan. At which point, I would knee him in the crotch and start it up without him.

AS WOULD BE OUR LUCK, the building's owners, too frightened of being prosecuted for failing to provide a safe route of evacuation from the building's rooftop, and having a near miss, refrained from making a formal complaint about us trespassing.

Callum delivered the news a day later via the telephone with his customary resignation and suggested that perhaps Poppy could continue his pursuit of happiness in less law-bending ways.

I promised to have a word with him, then winked at Poppy when I hung up. "Which word would you like to share?"

"Word?"

"I promised to have a word with you. Are you partial to any words in particular?"

"Insubordination."

"Right insubordination it is. You take the first three syllables. I'll take the rest."

After Poppy and I had chanted "insubordination" into a frenzied crescendo, and he then took the car and disappeared without a word of goodbye, Obi-Wan informed me she needed a walk. Ever since the introduction of the dog lead, she'd thrown herself into the role of canine pet as completely as Daniel Day-Lewis method acting his way into shoe cobbling.

I led her to our usual spot - a soccer field and playground surrounded by thick stands of tall, triangular kahikatea - and let her off the lead. She sproinged her way across the first half of the field in little four-hoofed leaps, located a stick and sproinged back to me.

I picked it up and threw it, knowing there would be

pointing from the playground, and barking from dogs using the park, but Obi-Wan and I had become adept at ignoring the noise and attention.

What I hadn't expected was to turn around and see Officer McClintock, takeaway coffee in hand, watching us with a bemused smile on his face.

I jumped with a "Jesus" and rearranged my surprise into the semblance of a scowl. "How do you manage to materialise exactly where I am? Have you planted a locater beacon on me somewhere?" I patted myself down as if searching for it.

"Microchip. You'll never find it." He sipped his coffee.

A chirrup at my knee announced Obi-Wan's return from the previous throw. I picked up the stick and hurled it towards the trees. "If this is a stake out, you should probably hide behind or in something. A car is fairly standard."

"You think your misdemeanours warrant a sting operation?"

I followed Obi-Wan's progress, the tiny clods of dirt thrown up by her hooves. "Well." I pursed my lips. "Considering Poppy and I continue to evade capture -"

"*Evade capture.* I take it from your verbal swaggering, you didn't have your promised word with Gerry."

"Oh no, I did. 'Insubordination' has never been so thoroughly had."

Callum eyed me for a beat, then threw his head back and volleyed laughter into the grey sky above. Still smiling, he levelled his eyes with mine. "You are something else, Sadie Quinn."

It sounded like a compliment, but with my track record of either breaking him or testing his professional patience, I couldn't be sure. "Why *are* you here?"

"Station's on the other side of those trees. I walk through

here to get a barista-made coffee when I need a bit of down-time. Re-fortify myself. This -" he pointed at Obi-Wan. "- Is great medicine."

She skidded to a halt between us, spat the stick onto the grass and looked up expectantly. Given the position of her eyes on either side of her narrow skull, it was hard to tell who she'd bestowed the throwing honours on.

Callum looked at me.

I shrugged, then nodded in Obi-Wan's direction to give my permission.

He picked up the stick and threw it with the practised arm of a cricketer. It travelled a third further than my attempts.

Obi-Wan charged after it, her ears flapping against her skull and my heart constricted. She was so goofy, such a little thing with an impossibly big personality.

"Couldn't she just use The Force to return the stick?"

"Where's the fun in that? The thrill's in the chase, as you would know, Officer."

"Oh yes, I know," Callum said, his voice a low rumble. "Although sometimes it's hard to know if the chase is worth the risk."

I looked at him sharply. The dropped volume suggested a sub-text, that perhaps he wasn't only talking about high-speed pursuits, but Callum's eyes were fixed on the goat's trajectory.

A gust of cold wind funnelled through the stand of trees on either side of the park, whipping my hair across my face and pinning my long skirt against my legs. I might have been naked from the waist down such was the force of my sense of exposure. Mortification flamed across my cheeks.

I plucked at the fabric, pulling it away from the solid

girth of my thighs. It tented where my fingertips pinched it, but continued to cling everywhere else.

The gust dropped. I released my skirt, and looked up to meet Callum's eyes. They were unreadable.

He drew a breath as if to say something, then closed his mouth and turned his head away to watch an incoming Obi-Wan. He bent to pat her head, and tugged the stick from her mouth. Then he feinted and threw it in the opposite direction to which she'd started running.

"You know, you could have just kept walking."

He swivelled towards me, a question in his raised brows.

"I'd have thought you'd want to give me a wide berth."

Callum's cheeks bunched into a smile. "Things are never dull when you're in the vicinity, Sadie Quinn." He nodded towards Obi-Wan. "Case in point."

"I thought I'd have induced irritable bowel syndrome by now. Or at least a stomach ulcer."

"Don't flatter yourself." He placed a hand in his pocket and sipped at his coffee. "I wouldn't need to recalibrate with a coffee walk if all the undesirables were at your level of criminal."

"I haven't put a spike in your blood pressure levels?" I tried to sound as incredulous as our game of out-sarcasm-the-other required me to.

"You haven't raised so much as a stress pimple."

"I don't believe you. All your huffing down the telephone suggests otherwise."

"I have to maintain a professional front."

I smiled and shook my head. "You are so full of shit."

Callum's cheeks bunched again and the skin around his eyes crinkled.

Out on the field, Obi-Wan paused mid-run for a refortifying nibble of the turf.

"What does 'something else' mean?"

"Hmmm?" Callum said through a mouthful of coffee.

"Earlier you said I was 'something else'. I just want to see if what I think you mean matches up with what you think you mean."

He pushed his bottom lip out and nodded. "I find you...interesting."

"Ah. That eternal euphemism," I said as if I knew exactly which word he was avoiding, when the truth was I had no idea. Unhinged? Entertaining? Beguiling? Or perhaps he was alluding to my supposed sex-tape past.

"It's no euphemism." The edges of his lips curled upwards. "I can't work you out. Someone smart enough to get a double Master's, finding herself in a situation so desperate as to be reduced to boxes in a rusted out car and begging a bed off her grandfather." He turned his head and met my eye, the smile gone. "How does someone like you get involved in an industry that exploits women?"

Right. So it *was* sex-tape interesting.

"You only heard a tiny snippet of our conversation. You shouldn't be quick to judge or assume or whatever it is you're doing based on what you thought you heard, because it might not be representative of the truth."

"OK." Callum swivelled back to face the field. "What's the truth, then?"

I released a long breath. "I had a momentary lapse in judgement." More like a momentary descent into madness. "That's all you need to know."

"Cryptic. Contradictory. Evasive. I stand by my 'interesting'."

"I'll take it." It was a generous alternative to the other possibilities.

WHEN I ARRIVED at the pub that evening for my shift and stepped out of Poppy's car, my heart tried to beat its way out of my chest.

Someone had crashed into the back wall. They'd hit the building at such speed that it had swallowed the front half of the car.

Cinder blocks lay strewn around the ground and on its roof. A gaping hole ringed the car's body, revealing the pub's dark interior like the broken-toothed maw of a battle-defeated dragon.

No emergency services were on the scene to free trapped occupants or crushed pub patrons, no fluorescent tape cordoned off the area. Nobody stumbled out of the building, wondering if the sky had just fallen in.

I squinted my eyes against the glare of the car park's external lights and heel-toed my way towards the wreckage of the car as if approaching a dangerous and sleeping animal.

As I neared it, the gaping holes in the wall lost their depth and reflected the halogen-yellow light. Black paint.

The car, instead of being a crumpled mess, looked like it had been neatly sliced from driver to passenger door with an angle grinder, and fit snug against the wall.

It was Fuzz Cup night.

I pushed open the door to the pub, smiled in acknowledgement of their well-executed efforts and let the collective well of disappointment wash over me.

"You know any Eddies?" I asked Manawa by way of greeting.

"No," she answered, placing a pint on the bar and taking a twenty dollar note from the waiting patron. "I know an

Ed." She raised her head in the direction of the tables beneath the big screen TV, which was playing women's cricket. "Hey Ed!"

Nobody looked up.

"ED!"

A middle-aged man with neatly combed hair turned in his seat to face the bar and raised a hand and a smile when he saw us looking at him.

Circling his neck above his black shirt was a dog collar.

"That him?"

"Unlikely."

Ed dropped his hand and turned back to the group at his table.

"Why are you interested in Eddies?"

I pulled two Coronas from the fridge behind me and popped the caps off. "Poppy has a best friend called Eddie and they seem to hang out quite a bit, though I've never seen him. They're just as mischievous as each other. I want to know who he is." I inserted a slice of lemon in the neck of each bottle and passed them across the bar. "He's sneaky. Sets Poppy up with a game and vanishes before anyone can tell him he's irresponsible or thank him for having a play date with my grandfather. Cause that's what they do. They play. Like they're five-year-olds."

"It beats sleeping in an armchair all day, waiting to die."

A crash at the double doors to the smokers' garden drew our attention.

Mitchell was flattened against the glass, his cheek and palms yellow from the pressure and his breath fogging the pane.

He wore blue stubbies, the short shorts piped with white edging, a tight T-shirt and sweatbands around his head and wrists.

And roller-skates.

"What's he doing?"

"He thinks delivering food by skates will be faster, but he hasn't accounted for his lack of skill. I've had to take chowder off the menu."

"You could just make him take the skates off."

"Why would I do that?" Manawa turned her face to him.

Mitchell had by now peeled himself off the door and rolled inside.

"Look at him." Her nostrils flared slightly, her mouth gave the smallest of curves and her chest expanded.

I could bottle that look of want and sell it for a small fortune to the lonely.

I tried to see what she saw, but the best my brain could do was objective. Mitchell was a wiry middle-aged man with red hair, dressed as an 80s tennis player on roller-skates, and doing a fairly good impression of a squid attempting to Moonwalk.

"He does have good entertainment value," I conceded.

"Oh, you have no idea."

I thought back to my last shift when I had to catch a bottle of gin that had edged its way off the shelf above the fridge. The *entertainment* Manawa had received in the back room was so vigorous, the glasses had clanked with increasing frequency. "I have a fairly good idea."

Mitchell rounded the end of the bar, using the counter to pull himself along. "Sadie, you're looking delightful, as always."

Mitchell might be a clown, but you couldn't fault him for charm.

I smiled despite myself.

"And you, my little soup de jour, are ravishing."

A shiver rippled through Manawa and she closed her eyes. "Speak to me in French again."

"With pleasure, my chicken cordon bleu."

Manawa exhaled on a long and shaky "hoh".

Then her eyes snapped open. She grabbed Mitchell by his sweat-banded wrist, towed him into the store room, and slammed the door shut.

I reached under the bar and turned the volume up on the music.

When I looked up, a woman (five foot six, fifty-five kilograms, size 8. Three-fifths of a Sadie) rested against the bar like she'd just materialised there.

I jumped.

She had a shaved section on one side of her head, thick-framed glasses, and wore a My Little Pony T-shirt.

The woman from the paper cut fight.

She looked at her smart watch. "One minute and forty-seven scconds is the time to beat, which is pretty impressive for a double banger. If you know what I mean."

I looked between her and the closed storeroom door. "Are you *timing* how long it takes for Mitchell and Manawa to...check the stock?"

She tipped her head to one side and looked at me earnestly. "I'm hoping to start a new betting league. I mean, it's ripe for the exploitation. It's funny and it's not restricted to a season. But these losers -" she jerked a thumb over her shoulder. "- Have standards, would you believe? They'll do stupid shit like staple their skulls to the front of their cars as hood ornaments if it meant it got Callum's attention, but they won't go as far as timing a couple reaching the point of mutual pleasure."

I wrinkled my nose. "So, you're timing it anyway?"

"I'm not going to let these asshats look down their noses

at me. Somebody might see the comedic light at any moment."

"I'd say they're well and truly blinded by the fear of upsetting Manawa. You've canvassed her opinion on this?"

"Uh uh." She shook her head. Then she propped it in her hand and peered up at me. "You're really tall."

I didn't bother responding. I didn't think I needed to, considering I was already cognisant of this fact.

"You should own it. Pull your shoulders back. Not try to make yourself look smaller. If I was your height, I'd want people to know I was looking down on their shit."

"Yeah." I picked up a glass and gave it a polish with a tea towel. "I'm not really into intimidating people."

"Shame. You should at least look proud of who you are. You look like you're trying to disappear into yourself. Like, you wish you could melt yourself down a bit."

"Probably because I do."

"Well, you cain't, sister. So own it."

Easy enough for a person of average size and weight to say. "What's with the cute T-shirts?"

"They're ironic. Obviously."

"Obviously."

"Because I'm not cute."

She had a small nose, and large eyes with thick lashes behind her chunky frames. She was pretty cute.

"I'm totally meta."

I had no idea what that meant. Was it a sexual orientation I wasn't aware of? The generation after the Gen Z-ers?

"Meta?" she said as if I'd been living under a rock since the turn of the twenty-first century. "Like, you know." She waved a hand in the air.

I didn't. And told her so.

Her "existential self-awareness and stuff?" didn't offer

any clarity. Which I also told her.

She managed both a tongue cluck and a sigh in the same breath. "Anyways, I'm Flick." She thrust out a hand for me to shake and lost me immediately in a complicated sequence of hand grasping. "My name's not Felicity or anything. I just like how it sounds. Bit street. Bit badass. Be a good ho name. You know, like, one with an indie business model? If that's where my career aspirations lay."

I wasn't sure which question to ask first, such was the number being jettisoned around my brain. My tongue chose, "They have business models?"

"For reals. If you don't want no pimp, you're independent. Like an indie music artist."

I nodded sagely. "Yes. I see the similarity."

"I want to be an assassin. Like Nigella Lawson. But brown."

Biting my lips together, I wiped at a wet patch on the counter and let her words trickle over my brain, syrup-like. "I don't think Nigella Lawson gets enough time away from the kitchen studio to take people out."

She raised a finger and wagged it. "Don't let the curves and flirtatious smiles fool you. That beeyotch is deadly. She's got the perfect cover. Sexy domestic confidante. Non-threatening. Gains your trust, gives you a hard on - not necessarily in that order - and BAM!" She punched a fist into a palm. "Kittens."

"Curtains."

"Whatevs. She is one deadly femme fatale. I am *so* right about her."

I thought about pointing out that she wasn't so right with her grammar. That a femme fatale didn't need the extra adjective, but the storeroom door whined open, Mitchell rolled out and Flick turned towards the pub floor, her hands raised in the air, index fingers pointed, and shouted, "And we have a new record. One minute and forty-two seconds. Give it up, homies." She clapped vigorously and "whoop, whoop"ed.

Nobody raised so much as a sneer.

Flick turned back to the bar and slapped both palms on it. "Philistine lardheads. Can I have a vodka and Red Bull? I got some heavy shit I need to pull later."

"Stuff'll rot your insides," I said, reaching into the fridge for the energy drink and immediately feeling like one of those judge-y adults I resented as a teenager. I attempted to rebuild the bridge I'd just taken a flame thrower to. "You don't happen to know any Eddies, do you?"

"Nope."

I eyed her ironic T-shirt, the shaved patch of hair, the neat sequence of sleeper earrings lining the edge of her left ear, and decided that as unlikely as it was, I had nothing to lose. I mixed the drink and said, "Ever heard 'The Sad Ballad of Doug and Rose?'"

"Yuss! See? You're totally all over it. That song is like a full meta anthem. I *knew* you understood me." She took a slurp, turned and made her way towards the tables. "Laters."

"Wait! What does it say?" I said as the storeroom door banged shut behind me.

I turned to find Manawa leaning against it, eyes closed above a smile, and the tag of her inside-out T-shirt protruding under her chin. "Is Callum here yet?"

A collective gasp drew my attention to the double doors of the back entrance. They twitched. Then they swung open and a young man in jeans and a plaid shirt, bearing an uncanny resemblance to Officer McClintock, stepped into the room with a wave.

The patrons erupted into cheers, Manawa shouted, "I

make it seven-o-nine," and I waited while my brain reconciled this man in civvies to the one I knew in uniform.

He looked good. He appeared longer without the bulk of the stab-proof vest. Lean and lanky, the sinewiness of his frame evident in the close-fitting clothes.

He walked towards the bar, the muscles of his thighs shifting against the fabric of his jeans.

An icy coldness flowed over the fingers of the hand holding the glass I was filling.

"Shit." I released the lever and shook the beer off my hand.

"Eyes on the job, Sadie," Mitchell said into my ear as he rolled past with a plate full of fries. "Perving's for after hours."

"I wasn't *perving*," I whispered at his disappearing back. I eyed Manawa. "It's probably against the rules, anyway."

"Unwanted innuendo, lewdness, and touching, yes. Looking's OK, as long as there's no leer associated with it."

I flicked my eyes back to Callum, then averted them. As long as I didn't look at him, I couldn't perve, let alone run the risk of stumbling into leering territory.

I dropped ice cubes into a glass, ran a double shot of whiskey across them and punched the charge into the EFTPOS machine. The transaction went through and I inputted the amount into the till.

A large hand with fine, golden hair appeared on the bar in front of me.

"Sadie."

His hand was wide, the fingers long and fine. "Callum."

"Lager please."

"Sure." I pulled a glass from the fridge and tipped the lager lever towards me to fill it.

"Your   grandfather   recovered   from   yesterday's excitement?"

"Yep." I glanced again at the hand resting on the bar. It was a nice hand. Oh God. Was I *hand* perving?

"Is there something wrong with your eyes?"

"No."

"They don't seem to be able to move upwards."

"I'm concentrating on my work. I don't look - you don't get the beer you want."

"Good. Because it seems as if you're avoiding looking at me."

A small flame lit itself somewhere behind my belly button, the heat fanning itself up towards my face.

"If I had the ability to point my eyeballs in different directions, I assure you, I would employ it right now, but I've put all my super-human powers into growing."

"Uh huh." He waited a couple of seconds before saying, "Are you guilty of something else I don't know about yet? It won't matter. I'll only have to wait two minutes until you manage to incriminate yourself."

I raised my eyes then and met his gaze with studied cool.

"Are you undercover?" I leaned towards him and whispered, "I don't think it's going to work. They already know you're a cop."

Callum blinked heavily, as if attempting to not reduce himself to eye rolling. "I'm off the clock. I do have time off, you know."

"I did wonder. That was an early car chase yesterday morning. I was beginning to think you never slept." I placed his beer in front of him.

"The behaviour of *some* citizens of this town makes it very difficult for the only cop to rest." He handed over a ten dollar note.

"I can imagine. Cameos at idiocy tournaments and chasing wandering cows off the road must be a real challenge to your policing skills."

Callum's lips briefly quirked up, and then he issued a sigh. "Flocks of sheep. It's always bloody flocks of sheep, and no, they don't teach you to round up livestock at police college."

I pursed my lips and nodded. "I'd have thought we'd be the highlight of your week, what with all the detectorising you've had to do."

"Detectorising isn't a word and so far, the highlight of my week has been a prostate exam, which was preferable to the reckless antics of you and your grandfather."

Wrinkling my nose, I said, "Admit it. We bring sunshine to your mundane professional existence."

Callum's mouth twitched, but he offered neither an admission nor a denial. Instead, he attempted to ensnare me in the glacial blue of his irises. He held my gaze for four seconds before I felt the vertigo hit, and I had to brace myself against the service bench.

I dropped my eyes and busied myself with working the till. "So, um, what happens when you *are* off the clock and Floss, the runaway ewe, is straddling the centre line of Highway 30?"

"They bring in somebody from Turangi on my days off and all calls are triaged through them when I'm sleeping or finished for the day."

I passed his change, palming the coins into his waiting hand. My fingers brushed against his warm skin and as the flame *fwoomp*ed into full roar, Callum's eyes flicked down the front of my new, better fitting and perfectly intact Tokawai pub T-shirt. "I see you're a little more..."

"Self-respecting?"

"I was going to say 'conforming'." He nodded at Manawa, whose T-shirt was now orientated correctly and right side out.

"Have you seen Mitchell this evening?" I asked.

He took a sip and used his bottom lip to suck the beer off the top one. "I have. Mitchell's a team of his own. He doesn't count."

Manawa said, "You're looking pretty sharp tonight, Officer. Isn't he looking sharp, Sadie?" She nudged me with her elbow. "How tall are you, Callum?"

"Six-five."

"Good height for a six-two woman, right Sadie?"

I narrowed my eyes at her and edged away. "I wouldn't know. I'm six-three."

She shuffled over, closing the gap, and pressed her knee against the side of my calf. Then she leaned on the service bench, chin in hand, and stared at Callum. "You know, if you pouted more, you'd look a bit like Daniel Craig."

"And if your nose wasn't quite so broken," added a passing Mitchell, three plates of burgers and wedges in hand.

"Yeah," said Manawa as if it was a great tragedy. "I can't remember you without it. How'd it happen?"

Callum's pale eyes flicked to me, then out to the pub floor as if he had the power to deflect attention through the use of his eyeballs alone.

Manawa gasped. "Did *you* break it, Sadie?"

Callum turned then to face me squarely, both hands on the bar. I wasn't sure if his posture was designed to dare me into telling the story, or intimidate me into keeping shtum.

It didn't matter. I had nothing to lose by disclosing the truth. Callum already had his eye on me as Tokawai's most notorious offender. What difference would it make if I also embarrassed him?

"It was a...joint effort," I said in an attempt to be diplomatic.

Callum smiled ruefully and leaned against the bar in resignation.

Manawa propped her head in her hands and gazed up at me. "Tell me."

Wiping my hands on a cloth, I looked to Callum, but his eyes were on the tables full of punters. "Well," I began, "when I was fifteen, I caught Callum perving at my sister."

"Callum!"

Callum shrugged. "I was fourteen. Completely at the mercy of my hormones."

"It was dark and I was out in the back yard playing with Poppy's new set of glow in the dark golf balls."

Manawa raised her eyebrows. "Who plays golf at night?"

"I dunno, but they were cool. Anyway, I hear this cracking coming from the side of the house, so I go to investigate. There, bathed in the light from the room my sister's sleeping in, is Callum, eyes glued on the window and attempting to climb the fence to get a better view of whatever's going on inside."

"Wait," Manawa said. "Please tell me your sister was eighteen, or something, and not eight."

"Jesus, Manawa. I was a normal, curious fourteen-year-old, not a sexual predator."

She held up her hands. "Alright. Just getting the facts."

"So, I creep up to see what he's looking at and my sister is in her underwear, posing in front of the mirror, squeezing her boobs together and trying to make her cleavage look bigger and stuff. Callum doesn't notice me, of course."

Callum's features were carefully arranged into a blank

expression. He took a sip of his lager and continued to watch the punters on the floor.

"He gets one foot on top of the fence and I place the head of the golf club I'm holding against his chest and say in a deep voice, 'What do you think you're doing, son?'. He shits his pants, loses his balance and topples over the fence."

"And break my fall with my nose."

As Manawa laughed and Callum smiled ruefully, a short, middle-aged man in a dress shirt and dark blue jeans placed an empty wine glass on the bar. "Callum, Manawa."

"Justin," they chorused.

He turned his dark eyes up at me. "Wow, you're a big girl. I'd want you on my side when the anarchy starts."

Callum shifted position and I felt his eyes on me, waiting to see how I'd react.

My indignation momentarily flared but was staunched under the pressure of his gaze and the weight of years of people passing comment.

It was Manawa who rose to the challenge. "You're fucking kidding, Justin. What part of your brain thinks it's OK to comment on a woman's size, let alone patronise her by calling her a *big girl*." She pointed out towards the pub floor. "Go and sit down. You can come back and order when your brain's re-engaged."

"What?" said Justin, like he was the victim of a great injustice, but he walked back towards his chair, regardless. "I was being nice. She can be on my team."

Manawa turned away from him, crossed her arms and glared at Callum.

"Yes?"

"You could have stepped in at any point."

"Sadie can handle herself. Anyway, she knows how I feel about the situation."

I suddenly felt drained, exhausted by the relentlessness of people passing comment, of their belief they have the right to. I sank down on to the service bench and rested my head in the V of my hands. "Can we talk about anything else? Tax imputation systems or the ringworm on the inside of Poppy's elbow?"

"I vote tax imputations systems," said Manawa.

I looked up at Callum. "Have you put any more thought into who this Eddie is?"

"No. I told you not to meddle."

"Yes, and I do everything a man commands of me."

A snort. "See?" he said to Manawa. "She doesn't need me to be chivalrous." He drained his beer and placed it on the bar mat. "Thanks for the drink, Sadie. Try not to court any trouble in the next ten hours. I'd prefer not to have to wake to the news I have to arrest you."

The speed and pitch to which I rattled out, "You're leaving already?" might have been construed as an expression of disappointment if anyone was paying close enough attention.

"Early start tomorrow. Had to put my head in for the sake of the competition."

"You're a good sport, Callum," said Manawa. "Pō marie."

I raised a hand in farewell, said, "Goodnight", and watched him disappear back through the double doors.

"Well done," said Manawa. "Not one iota of leering."

I pivoted towards her. "I wasn't perving!"

"I agree. *That* look was almost wistful."

I reached past her and grabbed a round serving tray. "I'm going to clear glasses. Project your need to live vicariously onto someone else." Then I turned and walked towards the end of the bar.

"I'm not the one who needs to live vicariously. I have all the love I want."

"*If* I was looking for love, it would not be of the two-minute-clinch-in-a-cleaning-cupboard variety."

"It's a storeroom. I would never reduce myself to a cleaning cupboard. And, yes you would. If Callum suggested a screamer against the boxes of vodka pre-mixes, you'd be in there in a heartbeat."

I gave her my *you are talking out your toilet hole* face and continued on my glass-gathering errand, attempting to ignore the little flutter behind my belly button at the thought of any kind of screamer with Officer McLintock.

WHEN I ASKED Poppy where he disappeared to on the afternoons he wordlessly drove off on, he answered, "Ag Day tomorrow." It was unsubtle evasion of the highest order. He then placed a bowl of porridge in front of me, and Obi-Wan placed her head in my lap.

She didn't need to ask. I always gave her half my breakfast. I pretended it was because of her newly learnt puppy eyes trick and not because porridge with whole milk had a calorie count of 268.

"Do you want to go?" An Agricultural Day meant candy floss and watching men out-testosterone each other by racing tractors and throwing tree trunks as far as they could. I *loved* Ag Days. "We could enter Obi-Wan in the goat competition. If they have one." I stroked her soft ear and she murmured a bleat.

"We have to go. No way of seeing our handiwork otherwise."

"What handiwork?"

"Item number three." Poppy retrieved the list from the bread bin and placed it in front of me. He scraped his chair out from the table and eased himself into it while I attempted to decipher his cursive handwriting. "You painted a sheep to look like a clown?"

"Big red nose and everything. The clown feet were a bit of a bugger. Sheep wouldn't lift its feet high enough. Kept tripping over them."

I eyed him for a beat. "You made *clown feet* for a *sheep?*"

"Nothing you can't do with a bit of cardboard and twine. Now." He placed a spoonful of porridge in his mouth, swirled it from cheek to cheek and swallowed. "Jock McAllister will have his prize ram there. The ram always starts the day's proceedings and he'll have delivered it today to the big wool shed on site to protect its wool from any overnight rain. It's a merino. The fleece on this thing is about a foot deep. Bloody ridiculous-looking."

"You think a ram's going to stand still while we attach clown feet to it?"

"No." He slurped down another mouthful. "We're not going to turn it into a clown."

And in that moment, I knew exactly what Poppy was asking of me. "I can't."

"Yes, you can. All the gear you need will already be there."

"It's been years."

Poppy held up the index and middle finger of his right hand. "Two words."

"They better not be 'knife' and 'butter'. That didn't work out very well last time."

"'Riding' and 'bike'. What time do you finish work tonight?"

CHAPTER NINE

THE CROWD FUNNELLED into the woolshed for the eight o'clock start of Tokawai's annual Agricultural Day. The shed wouldn't be able to hold more than a hundred and fifty people, so those who were sticklers for tradition and formality arrived early to jostle for position when the wooden doors rolled back at five to eight.

Between us, Poppy and I had little trouble finding our way inside. He was small and sharp. He stuck his elbows out like he was doing the chicken dance and used them as paddles to get purchase between the bodies.

It also afforded him good viewing room. Nobody wanted to come within poking distance.

I, of course, had the benefit of height and size, had Poppy not been plenty efficient at moving people for the both of us.

It was just as well. All but my frown muscles had seized after last night's athletics. I wasn't sure I could turn my neck, let alone coordinate limbs to bulldoze my way through the crowd.

Poppy settled in two-people deep from the front, so as not to seem too anticipatory for what was to come.

Jock McAllister's merino ram, Barry, had won prizes for at least the last five years. The fleece was exceptionally fine, they said. Seventeen microns in diameter. The ram's temperament was on the calm end of the volatility spectrum. Perfect for showing.

And for the last five years, according to Poppy, it had been the official mascot of Agricultural Day. It would be brought up onto a raised platform and handed a pair of scissors to cut the ribbon.

I had a fair idea Poppy might have been pulling my leg about the last part.

After all the official stuff, a Scottish piper would lead the ram around the first section of the show grounds - one of five paddocks of the Parata farm.

As Poppy elbowed a clearing large enough for four people and turned his face up to the raised platform, it became obvious things were far from okay backstage.

Raised voices wended their way through the slats of the sheep-holding area. The rhythmic groan of a set of discordant notes, like someone was jumping on the bagpipes, drowned out the first set of shouted words.

The pipes emitted a single, shrill and prolonged note. "Get the bloody thing off me!"

"I can't! He's. Not. Cooperating," replied someone, as if through a set of tightly gritted teeth.

"Winiata," Poppy said and rubbed his palms together as one of the Parata brothers climbed across the slats and walked onto the make-shift stage. He gave the microphone a tap. "Ah." He cleared his throat. "Tēnā koutou. Nau mai, haere mai. I think, ah -" He looked back over his shoulder. "-

We'll just get under way. Things will be a bit different this morning. Barry isn't, um, feeling the best, so won't be making an appearance i tenei ata."

A collective groan rolled around the shed.

I looked at Poppy. This wasn't part of the plan. If there was no sheep, there was no thrill. Which meant no happy Poppy.

I needn't have worried. He turned his face up and winked at me.

Winiata grimaced as a crash and shriek, whether of human or bagpipe origin, rang out behind him. "But we'll start as we normally would, with a karakia. Kia inoi tatou. Let us pray."

As he lowered his head, the clatter of running hooves echoed through the sound system.

The ram, determined not to miss its moment in the limelight, emerged from the holding pen, a red-faced Jock McAllister in tow. He leant back against the lead attached to the ram's neck and dug his heels in as it pulled itself up the ramp to the raised platform.

The animal was far too powerful.

Jock's feet caught on the bottom of the ramp and he stumbled forward, the slack in the lead giving the ram a chance to surge forward and pull the rope from his grasp.

It clip-clopped to the centre of the platform and arranged its body in competition stance, legs planted, head high.

The crowd gasped.

Jock McAllister's prize-winning ram no longer resembled one. The front of its neck had been shorn, but the top of its head sported a splay of floppy wool and the back of its neck had been trimmed into a neat rectangle. Perfect rings of wool circled its legs and at intersections along its abdomen.

"It looks like a poodle with a mullet," someone in the crowd called out and a wave of laughter surged towards the stage.

Jock shook a fist at the crowd. "One of you buggers did this. I'll bloody hunt you down, you mongrel."

Poppy threw back his head and cackled into the rafters.

The throng rushed forward, phones in hands, camera apps open.

I grabbed Poppy's arm to pull him from the crush, turned, and recognised the broken nose a split second before I walked into it.

I DABBED at the blood beneath Callum's nose with a wet serviette, trying not to wince at the pain in my muscles as I lifted my arm. "You have to stop following me."

"You have to stop hurting me."

We sat on a picnic table beside a caravan selling hot chips and battered sausages on a stick, Callum astride the bench, me side-saddle.

"I wouldn't have to if you didn't have your nose in my hair, snorting my rose water shampoo."

"You smell like a Turkish Delight. I couldn't help it. Your hair's like the White Queen of Narnia tempting me to the dark side." His eyes twinkled. "And I wanted to see what mischief you and your granddad were up to."

I ignored the tightening in my chest. I couldn't tell if it was because I was only a blurted confession away from arrest, or because Callum and his lovely hands were mere centimetres away, millimetres with each dab. So far, I'd wiped without incurring the electric buzz of any touching. "You're off the clock. The only reason you'd be scoping us out would be for your own perverted pleasure."

His lips stretched into a small semblance of a smile. "I needed to see what I'd have to run away from if I was to avoid working on my day off. Seems I'm safe, though."

"Good," I said, a swell of relief cresting under my lungs. Then the shearer within me added, "Why's that?"

"Shearing a monster ram? I don't think Gerry's up to it."

"And what, me being a woman wouldn't have the skill?"

"I don't know any female shearers. Do you?"

My dabbing hand dropped into my lap with a *bumff*. "I paid my university fees doing the summer shear, I'll thank you very fucking much. I was so fast, I'd be *invited* onto shearing gangs. No sexism amongst that lot, surprisingly. Unlike a supposedly enlightened policeman I could name."

Callum winked at me and I understood what he'd done. I groaned and turned my knees and face away from him.

"Nice detail. I particularly like the way you feathered his fringe. Who'd have thought a mullet on a sheep could look so becoming?"

I watched a small child being led on a pony in the neighbouring fenced-off area. "Thank you." The pony wickered and shook its head, and the child burst into tears. "What are you going to do about it?"

"Well, as it's for Poppy's happiness, *and* it's my day off, I thought I might do nothing."

I let the breath I'd been holding out in a *whoosh* and swivelled to face him again.

"Also, I found it very amusing. I wouldn't want to curb your comedic flair by arresting you."

"That's a fairly long list of reasons. Are you sure that's everything?"

"Jock's a bit of a dick."

My lips turned up of their own accord. "Pretty unprofessional of you to be choosy about whose cause you take up."

"You want me to change my mind?"

"No, Officer McClintock, I do not."

Callum eyed me for a beat. Then he shook his head and rumbled out a laugh. "God, I can't believe what you did to that poor beast. You really are quite remarkable, Sadie Quinn. If a little unconventional."

I wasn't sure if he was referring to my ability to wrestle my way through a flock of sheep armed with clippers, or my supposed foray into the porn industry. Hopefully, he wasn't talking about my size.

A fresh trickle of blood edged itself out of his right nostril.

"Jesus. Doesn't it hurt?" I gripped his chin and plugged the nostril with a piece of serviette. His skin was smooth and emitted the faintest hint of cinnamon from his shaving cream.

My fingertips crackled with energy and I whipped my hand away to reach for a new serviette from the pile beside me.

"You destroyed all the nerves in my nose when you broke it the first time. I can't feel a thing. I'm lucky I can still smell with it."

"*You* destroyed it when you allowed your penis to overrule your brain."

"My penis overruled my brain for about six consecutive years. It was a long-standing dictatorship. I had no choice but to obey its whims."

I involuntarily shifted my eyes from Callum's blood-smeared upper lip to meet his blue gaze and fire flashed through me.

I tracked its path up my chest and neck and into my face, and cursed its traitorousness. Callum, and anyone else within hearing and seeing range, would know I'd been thinking about his penis.

My eyeballs, oblivious to my mortification, didn't help matters by glancing at his crotch. I tried to act like his groin was in the path of my trajectory of observation, and swung my gaze across the grass at our feet and out on to the group of people lining up at the food caravan.

"I'm no longer a slave to my penis, if that's what's on your mind."

I snapped my eyes back to him. "Can we please stop talking about your penis?"

"Sure. Though I'd like to point out that you mentioned my penis first."

"Here." I placed the wad of damp serviettes into his left hand and the wad of dry into his right. "Clean up your own blood."

Callum placed the serviettes back on the table, weighing the dry ones down with the wet so that moisture wicked through the first layers. "Can I ask you a personal question?"

And here it was. The question he couldn't let go. Why did I decide to chase fame and fortune with my vagina?

"That depends."

"On what?"

"What the question is."

"Okay. How are you going to determine if it's a question you want to answer without hearing it first?"

"I know what you're going to ask. And I'd prefer if you didn't."

"How could you possibly know what I'm going to ask?"

I raised an eyebrow to let him know I had read his game and knew his next move. "It follows on logically from the penis conversation."

"I'm not going to proposition you, if that's what you think."

It *wasn't* what I thought. And the small "oh" that escaped my lips made it pretty clear to Callum that while that hadn't crossed my mind as something to be concerned about, I might have been amenable to the suggestion regardless.

"Do you have a question you'd *like* me to ask?"

I didn't want to say, "I do now," and give away my entire hand. But another sprung to mind as quickly as the question that Callum said he wouldn't ask fell away.

"Yes."

"Alright then. How about we count to three and you ask the question you want me to ask, and I'll ask the question I want to ask at the same time. Then you can decide if you want to answer my question, and I can decide if I want to ask yours. Deal?"

"Sounds dangerous, but okay. Do we say it on three, or count to three then say it? Which would really be saying it on the count of four."

Callum's mouth twitched sideways. "Count to three, then say it. Ready?"

"Yes?" I said, sure this was a terrible idea.

"One. Two. Three."

"Why didn't we play together more as children?" I said as Callum said, "Why do you always wear black?"

That was the question most pressing for him? If he found me remarkable, I constantly found him surprising. The answer was simple. "It's slimming."

"Ah, yes." Callum swung his foot over the bench seat and leaned against the table top, his fingers clasped over his stomach. "Your size is a real issue for you, isn't it?"

I cast my eyes over the throngs of people shifting between stalls. "I've been teased my whole life by my family about what a genetic anomaly I am. You know, the old 'Did we take the wrong baby home from the hospital?' joke. It never gets tired. Apparently." Then I whipped my head around to face him. "Not Poppy. Never Poppy."

"You two are close." It wasn't a question. "He's not the easiest of men. I imagine it isolates him a bit, so it's nice he has you."

"I'm lucky to have him, too. I don't have to try and navigate my way around any disappointment. He's very accepting of me, and I know how rare that is. I don't think he's particularly accepting of anyone else. He's probably at the kindergarten cake stall hassling the parents on the lack of pride in their presentation, and their inability to ice a cupcake without dripping it down the side of the paper casing. I'm surprised people don't tell him to 'fuck off' more. He deserves it."

A rumble of laughter. "Yes he does."

The pony, on a break from bearing children, poked its head through the fence and began to graze. The grass squeaked in protest as it was torn away from its base.

"Can I ask you another question?"

The pony's eyes were black-lined, like they were ringed with kohl, its lashes impossibly long.

"You know, Callum, when people ask that question it usually means they're going to ask something that's going to make the person answering extremely uncomfortable, so I'm not sure I want to say 'yes'."

"I promise I won't make you feel uncomfortable."

I raised a hand, palm upwards, as if to say with reluctance, "Go ahead, then."

"Why didn't we play together more as children?"

Laughing out a "ha", I turned to face him again. "I don't know. I hardly ever saw you. It's like you spent your whole time hiding from me after I punched you in the face."

Callum chuckled and his hands bobbed up and down on his belly. "You hardly ever saw me because I was hardly ever there. You visited Gerry during school holidays and I tended to visit my dad during school holidays."

"Oh," I said. Then, "I'm sorry. I didn't know it was just you and your mum there."

A shoulder shrug. "I was pretty young when my parents split and didn't know any different, really. And then we moved to Turangi after the summer *my penis* broke my nose."

I threw my hands in the air. "You lasted two minutes without talking about your penis." I said, "It's almost as if you don't want me to forget about it," and immediately wished I hadn't, such was the upwards rush of blood. I turned my head back to the pony and regretted not leaving my hair down so that it might curtain off the burn in my cheek.

"I didn't want to disappoint you. I think you secretly don't mind talking about it."

I whipped back around and said, "Don't presume to know what's in my mind," knowing he was winding me up.

He pointed to his nose and said mildly, "Do you think I can unplug this now?"

I sat back against the table top with a *flump*. "No idea. I've never broken my nose."

"Only mine."

"I'm now thinking about breaking other parts of you."

"It's only a matter of time, given your record." Callum pulled out the wad of bloodied serviette and looked down his nose as if he could see past it to detect any blood. His nostril remained dry. "I'm sorry you don't feel normal, that some people don't allow you to."

I said nothing.

"You know, how you feel about yourself isn't objective. I'm looking at you now and objectively I see a tall, strong, curvy woman with thick hair and cheekbones other women would kill for, which is a pretty good list I would say."

He swung his leg over the bench seat and straddled it again. Shifting a hand along the wood, he extended his index finger and ran it along my knuckles, leaving a trail of sparks beneath my skin. Then he wrapped his finger around my little one and gave it a gentle shake.

"*Sub*jectively, I see a woman with flesh in all the right places. With lovely hair and incredible cheekbones."

Flesh in all the right places.

I glanced up from our hands to his face. The glacier blue of his irises held me captive. I couldn't have looked away from him if I'd tried.

Surely he wasn't earnest. Yet, the fire that ignited with a *fwoomp* behind my belly button was fuelled by a large pyre of hope. The rising hot air stirred my tongue and before I was fully cognisant of the thought, it had flapped. "I'd break you."

A smile. "I'm pretty sure you wouldn't."

What did that mean? Was that an invitation to do my

best? I didn't know which way to go in this world of suggestion, of half meanings. What was the next move?

Callum's eyes dropped to my lips.

Oh.

Was he about to kiss me here? In a place where most of Tokawai had gathered, and where most of Tokawai would then talk about it?

My gaze shifted of its own accord.

There was a tiny piece of dried blood lining the smallest of grooves in his top lip.

"Gangstas!"

Callum and I whipped our heads towards the showgrounds, whatever spell had woven its way around us, broken.

Flick stood a couple of metres away, legs astride, knees bent, and shooting a pair of imaginary six guns into the air. "I *knew* I'd find the law enforcement over here. I was standing in line to pet the Angora rabbits and I got that feeling. You know, when either someone really bad, or a soul brother or sister is within homing range?"

Callum was going to kiss me.

I narrowed my eyes and tried to look like I was thinking about her question.

"I'd just slipped my fingers across the silky fur of the grey one with the black ears and my pubes stood on end. I've got this weird-ass sixth sense in my hair follicles, like I can divine good or evil with my curly fries. And I knew a professional womb-mate was nearby. My brother," she said, slapping her hand against Callum's palm and gripping it.

Callum stared up at her, his eyes large and unblinking as if he'd been pulled into the same strange alternative dimension he'd visited when I'd tried to remove his testicles with my wing mirror.

I tugged my brain back into the present, and said, "Callum, this is Flick. She wants to be an assassin. Like Nigella Lawson."

Callum's mouth made an 'Oh' shape, but it appeared his voice box had been shocked into silence. Eventually he said, "Right. I don't actually kill anybody. I'm really hoping to keep it that way."

"You won't have to. That'll be my job. I'll do the hits on the big-time crims. The ones the law struggles to touch, like mob bosses and real estate agents. You can stick to the petty stuff." Flick straddled the bench beside me so that I had to shift perpendicular to them to be able to see them both. "So, Sadie. What do you think of my new T-shirt?"

It had a stardust-throwing Rainbow Brite on it, her head disproportionately large where it stretched across Flick's breasts.

"Very meta."

"For reals, right? I bought it online at a store that sources straight from Japan. I'm saving up for a Care Bear one." Flick looked past me, winced and said, "Bruv. What happened to your nose?" like she hadn't already been talking to Callum and looking at his face for the last couple of minutes.

"Sadie happened."

She put a closed fist up to her mouth and hooted. "No shit. Turn sideways so I can see which part of Sadie fits into the dent."

Callum obliged. "Should be a forehead-shaped curve right about here." He pointed to a flattened area above the tip of his nose.

"Look at that. You guys are like two interlocking pieces of a jigsaw puzzle." She made Vs with her fingers and demonstrated just how effective our interlocking parts were at interlocking.

A tiny bird stretched and ruffled its feathers low in my belly, just above my groin.

"Oh my God." Flick gripped my wrist and I jumped. "I can't believe this fell out of my brain until just now. Dante Kerr's playing in the wool shed at noon."

I sat up straight. "Dante Kerr?"

"He hasn't played a home gig in over a decade and just got back from Nashville, apparently. It's going to be E-PIC."

"You're into country, Flick?" Callum asked. If there was any incredulity behind his question, he hid it well.

"I'm into Dante. Gotta support home-grown. Nothing like a bit of blind patriotism to nurture the creative arts. I'm also into burn outs, macramé and riding the Bertram horse."

"Huh," I said, giving Callum a smug sideways glance. "You too?"

"Yeah, though some muggle broke the ladder, so that pursuit's on hold."

"That's a well-rounded list of artistic patronage," Callum said. One side of his mouth was cinched up like he couldn't decide to be amused or point out that it might not be in her best interest to disclose such hobbies to the local cop.

"Obviously, I draw the line at the Fuzz Cup and hot boxing. I'll save that shit for the Captain Stupids."

Callum nodded solemnly.

A hot rush of nerves and anticipation and fear washed over me. I had a chance to find out what happened to Poppy's parents. To know once and for all if I had anything to be truly worried about. I placed a hand on each of their thighs and squeezed. "We have to see Dante Kerr."

"Hail, yes, we're going to see him. As the great man said himself, 'Wild mustangs couldn't drag me away'."

"I don't think Dante Kerr came up with that concept," said Callum.

"Do you think he'll play 'The Sad Ballad of Doug and Rose'?" I asked.

"He'd better, or I'll be hog-tying him and asking for my money back."

"Noon, huh?" Callum looked at his watch. "We've got a bit of time to kill. What do you want to do first?"

"Speed milking," said Flick as I said, "Cowpat sculpting."

I NEVER STOOD a chance in the great milk-off between Callum, Flick, and me. I might be able to shear my way through a flock of sheep blind-folded, but the fact I'd never milked a cow, either by hand or more modern methods, or that my muscles felt like they had been fused to my bones, put me at a distinct disadvantage.

Callum and Flick had either turned their hand to it before or had beginner's luck. Their jets of milk hit the sides of their metal buckets (the stall was nothing but authentic) with a series of gentle *patang*s. I couldn't coax any more than a trickle from each teat.

However, I knew with a reasonable amount of certainty that I would be able to hold my own in the cowpat sculpting tent.

Flick had never experienced the satisfaction of squeezing a cold grass-fed turd through her fingers, but she approached the task with her standard level of enthusiasm. She entered the gazebo, eyed the barrel of green manure and shouted, "I know what I'm making!"

"Ah," the man managing the competition said. "We're actually a genitalia-free zone."

Flick dropped the hand she'd been shooting the competition off the drying shelves with. "Oh".

"Apart from," continued the man, gesturing at Flick's chest and groin areas. "What you come in with. Obviously."

Callum and I wandered over to the shelves. Most of the sculptures were children's, sweet in their blockish rendering of cars and dogs and ice-creams. One was the impression of a face. Some brave soul had lain their head in their designated cowpat and pushed into the cold gloop.

"I hope they wrapped their face in cling film first," I said.

Callum bent over and peered at it closely. "Are their eyes open?"

"You'll be wanting these." The man passed out pairs of surgical gloves. "You've got five minutes to create your masterpieces. Please set the timer on your phones and start on my 'Go'."

Flick made a mounted head of a unicorn, which looked like a camel with a phallus growing out of one of its nostrils. It was an ironic statement, apparently.

Callum tried to make a teapot, but with one minute to go and the handle and spout wilting like they needed a good watering, he rolled his pat into a rectangle and put a small ball underneath to form a lump. He called it 'Where are my bed socks?'

I made a goat. It had a passable likeness to Obi-Wan, all the way down to her puppy-dog eyes trick. I tried not to gloat as we placed our entries onto the drying shelf, but given I'd been roundly humiliated at speed milking, I didn't feel particularly inclined to hold my bragging rights in check.

I placed my goat between their sculptures. "In the art world we call that a shit-gilded frame. Sandwiching a masterpiece between two embarrassments to emphasise its superiority."

"Yeah?" said Callum. "Let's see how you go at sledding."

Sledding involved sitting on an upside-down car bonnet and being pulled across long grass by a utility vehicle.

Desperate to go first, Flick decided she was going to surf it. She stood on the bonnet in a crouch, arms out like a surfer from the 1960s and yelled at the driver to, "Book it!"

"I think I like her," said Callum as she whizzed past, giving us a double-handed shaka salute.

"I don't think she'd give us a choice in the matter. She'll enthuse her way into our hearts, like an energetic puppy."

"Wanna go tandem?"

I eyed the sled sceptically. "You think it will tow the both of us?"

"I sincerely hope that isn't a reference to my weight." He nudged me with his shoulder and I staggered forward. When the sled finished its second pass and slowed to let Flick off, Callum said, "Come on. I'll sit behind."

The thought of Callum riding pillion behind me did strange things to my skin. It was suddenly hyper-sensitive. My dress felt too tight, too warm for the sunny spring day, the fabric scratchy.

I climbed on to the bonnet, sat with my legs out in front of me, groaning as my muscles strained to support the movement, and tucked my dress under my legs.

The bonnet rocked as Callum climbed on. He placed his long legs on either side of me, careful not to make contact.

As soon as the vehicle accelerated, I slid down the metal and into the U of Callum's crotch. My back hit the hard planes of his torso and the breath from Callum's laugh warmed my ear.

I shivered and a chirrupy laugh bubbled unbidden from my throat.

The cage of his body made me feel small and I had a sudden and fierce wish for the ride to never end.

The vehicle changed direction, sending me sideways, and I clamped my fingers around Callum's thighs just above the knees. The muscles were rigid from bracing against the movement of the bonnet.

"Alright?"

"You're not going to fall off the back?"

"No, I have handles. How's the view from up the front? I can't see anything except for your hair. Your pony tail's wild with excitement."

It wasn't the only part of me. "Sorry. I should have put it in a bun."

"I don't mind. I like your hair. It's making me hungry, though. Do you think Turkish Delight would make a decent meal?"

Callum may not have been intending any innuendo, but such was the sorry history of my love life, that last sentence was the most erotic thing any man had ever said into my ear.

My nipples pressed against the fabric of my bra with a dull ache. "Depends on how large your appetite is."

"Sadie Quinn, are you flirting with me?"

"I think so. To be honest, I'm so out of practice, I could just be discussing dessert preferences. Which option would you prefer?"

Callum was silent for a moment. "There's only one option we can do anything about now." Before I could wonder if he was about to attempt to pull off some make-out acrobatics on the underside of a speeding car bonnet, he said, "Hot dog or spit-roasted lamb for lunch?"

. . .

THE WOOL SHED was already full by the time we arrived. We edged our way into a space at the back, which while fine for Callum and me, didn't much suit the diminutive Flick. Announcing she was heading for the mosh pit, she slipped between the bodies of those standing before us and disappeared.

"What kind of country does Dante play if there's a mosh pit?" I asked, knowing Flick had been, as usual, just shifting hot air around with her tongue when she said it.

"I wouldn't put it past Flick to create the first one in the history of the genre. You a betting woman?"

"Only on Saturdays."

"Well you're in luck then. I'd bet the people at the front are all middle-aged women with coiffed blonde hair and manicures. And they'd be right into a mosh with Dante."

"You think this dude has rabid fans?"

"He's a bit of a sex symbol in the country arena. Or at least he was. He's got to be pushing seventy now. But I think once a musical sex symbol, always a musical sex symbol. Think of Tom Jones."

"I try very hard not to."

As Callum laughed, making his Adam's apple bob and sending a tingle across my skin, a cheer brought my attention back to the stage.

The band appeared, taking up their positions and toying with their instruments. Once they had settled, a thin guy with the face of someone who'd exclusively sourced their oxygen through the butt of a cigarette sauntered onto the stage.

The accompanying whoops and whistles were deafening.

Dante Kerr, dressed in a shiny black western shirt, boots

and very tight jeans, tipped his hat to the crowd, sending them into another frenzy.

"Tokawai! It's been a long, long time." His voice had the affectation of a drawl and the snarl of vocal cords soaked in degreaser. "But you know what they say. You can take the boy out of Tokawai." He wagged finger and mouthed 'but' and the ovation from the audience swelled once more. "I thought it would be appropriate to start with something -" He dropped his head, looked out at the crowd from under his eyebrows, and growled, "Local."

A chorus of shrieks issued from the front.

Callum leaned into my ear. "Hear the calibre of that scream? Definitely blonde and manicured."

My pulse stuttered. It was as much the heat from Callum's breath as the certainty that "local" meant he'd sing 'The Sad Ballad of Doug and Rose' and I'd find out once and for all the truth about Poppy's, and my, mental pedigree.

An acoustic guitar strummed a sequence of minor chords. And then, after an arpeggio of plucked strings, Dante Kerr began to sing.

"Doug met Rose on a Tuesday,

Pretty little darlin' in a checker-print dress.

He held out his hand, said 'Will you be mine?'

By Friday, she said 'Yes'.

Let's build a life, my lovely,

A home, a chevvy, and little 'uns too.

Meet me in the church all dressed in white,

My dreams belong to you."

The chords shifted to a more upbeat sequence, signalling the chorus.

"You're wedded to my heart, my Rose, my Rose,

My search for love is done.

Nothing we can't do, my Doug, my Doug,
Our strength is us as one."
"It's a bit cheesy," I shouted in Callum's ear.
"Isn't that a ballad pre-requisite?"
"No idea. I'm fairly uninitiated," I said, wondering at
Flick's degree of song-worship. What did she hear among
the sentimental platitudes that I was missing?
"All their dreams in a shop,
Little children wept at their Neenish Tarts,
Steak pies brought men to trembling knees,
Their hopes soared in their hearts."
I grinned at Callum. "It's funny. Is it meant to be
funny?"
He chuckled and shook his head. "I don't think so."
A young man in front of me turned, shushing us and
hissed, "Have some respect."
I grimaced up at Callum, who winked back, and I faced
the stage again, smile reinstated.
After another couple of verses about the realisation of
their dreams and the calibre of their apple turnovers, Dante
sang about "a shadow creeping in". Amusement slipped
from my face and foreboding set in. If there had, in fact,
been any joking, it was well and truly over.
"Years went past, their joy ebbed.
Crumbling hearts sucked the sweet from their tarts,
Pastry now cracked and brittle as their minds,
Their dreams had fallen apart."
On stage, Dante closed his eyes against the words of a
different version of the chorus.
"Forty years has past, my Rose, my Rose,
Our dreams have worn us down.
My heart is hollow, my Doug, my Doug,
My strength in you is gone."

And then, the third act drew to its climax and the full picture revealed itself in all its terrible detail.

"On the cake racks lay our Rose,
Her womanhood covered in blue butter cream.
She begged all who entered to join in the feast
With the devil that supped on her spleen.
In a pie crust, Doug placed his head,
And garnished his hair with turnip and corn.
As he shuffled towards the oven's wide maw,
Asked God to be reborn."

I slapped my fingers across my mouth. "Oh God."

Callum leant towards me, frowning. "This is about your great-grandparents?"

I couldn't answer. It was so awful, it had to be real. Kerr couldn't have dreamt up such misfortune with a universe-worth of creative licence.

Poppy was well and truly fucked.

As Dante began a repeat of the first chorus, a figure pulled itself up onto the stage. It wouldn't have been a great surprise for Flick to launch herself into the mosh pit, but was that even something you could do during a ballad?

The person stood up. They were small, and skinny, and very old. And looked like thunder.

Poppy.

Dante smiled at him as he sung, beckoning him to come and join him.

Poppy did not smile back. He turned to the mic stand positioned in front of the keyboardist and pulled the microphone from its cradle. Was he going to *sing*?

Holding the cord, he dropped the mic, stopping it an inch away from hitting the stage. Then he began to swing it above his head like he might twirl a lasso for the calf rope competition. The circles got bigger and bigger as if he fancied himself as Roger Daltrey, twirling the mic above his adoring crowd.

Then with a little shuffle forward, he thrust his arm out and clocked the microphone against Dante's temple. It connected under the brim of his hat with a *THOCK*.

Dante gave Poppy a bemused smile.

And toppled off the stage and into the mosh pit.

CHAPTER TEN

THE INTERVIEW ROOM WAS COLD. Poppy tried to warm it up with a smirk that smouldered across his weathered features, but it didn't help me.

I wrapped my arms around myself and watched the fabric of my dress dance as my left leg jigged of its own accord.

Womanhood covered in blue butter cream.

I closed my eyes against the lyrics and another line wormed its way across my brain.

Garnished his hair with turnip and corn.

Poppy's father had tried to bake his head in a pie. God, it was so unbelievably awful.

Leaning forward, I cradled my head in my arms. Perhaps if I hid myself away for long enough, this would all disappear.

Footsteps rang out on the vinyl floor and entered the room, followed by two *thunks* on the table top.

"Here's your tea, Sadie," Callum said softly.

"Uarm," I said against the flesh of my arm. It was

intended to be a "thanks", but that one mashed syllable seemed to have piggy-backed a subtext of *Please take me back to the point of my conception and ask me what I think about the whole idea.*

Poppy sucked at his tea with a *shwuuuurp.* A lone cricket chirruped mournfully outside the window. Callum shuffled papers on the desk top.

"I'm really sorry, Gerry, but it's likely I'm going to have to charge you over this one. I expect Dante Kerr to lay a formal complaint. You knocked him out."

His "yes I did" sounded far too self-satisfied to be helpful for the shit storm he had whipped up. "Little shyster."

"He's still at the hospital getting checked out."

"He took my family's breakdown and tried to turn it into local legend."

Callum's chair scraped across the floor and his words were issued closer to my head. "You're likely going to have to front up to a court hearing."

I turned my face towards Poppy, one eye peeking above the crook of my elbow.

He leant forward and jabbed a finger into the veneer of the table top. "He never." Jab. "Bloody." Jab. "Asked." He sat back in his chair and crossed his arms. "That stuff's private."

"I understand you were angry, Gerry. But to hit a man over the head with a microphone? Couldn't you have just called a meeting and asked him to stop performing it?"

"What's the arsing fun in that?"

"Word of advice. Don't present that attitude to the judge. It won't do you any favours."

I pushed myself off the table and sat up in my chair. "What'll he be sentenced to? It's not something he'll get jail time for, is it?

"For assault with a weapon? Not likely. But it's up to the

judge. He might get diversion or a hundred or so hours community service. *If* he looks like he's taken responsibility for his actions."

I stood up and paced across the room. "He's going to fuck it up," I said to no one in particular. I turned and paced back. "He's going to say something stupid." Turn. "Like 'I've got no regrets'."

"I don't."

"'The peacocking sod deserved it'." Turn.

"Couldn't have said it better myself."

Slapping my palms on the table, I leaned over him. "I need you to not make this whole thing worse."

"What whole thing?" said Poppy and Callum in unison as my phone rang.

I pulled it out of my jacket pocket and swore. Dad.

My blood pressure soared from stratospheric to bobbing about with the space junk in outer orbit.

I stepped out of the room and walked towards the station's front door. Swiping the phone to accept the call, I placed it to my ear.

"Sadie? You there?"

"Yes, I'm here," I said, on an outward sigh.

"Please tell me your grandfather hasn't been arrested."

Jesus. Had the man tapped into the station's CCTV?

I screwed up my face, wondering how I could say 'yes' without it sounding like 'yes'. The best I could come up with was, "Kind of."

"The Lord help us, that man's a liability. Did he really try to kill Dante Kerr?"

The only thing that was reliable about Tokawai's grapevine was its speed and its ability to warp the truth for the sake of good story telling. "No."

As I pushed open the front door to the station, Dad said, "Don't protect him, Sadie. He doesn't deserve your pity."

"I don't *pity* him, Dad." Didn't I? Wasn't I already anticipating a decline into a confused second toddlerhood? "And even if I did, he certainly deserves my loyalty." And love.

A snort. "Goodness knows how he earned that."

The plain speak, the distinct lack of a single piece of business jargon was as good as a battle cry.

I straightened my spine, mentally pulling up the draw bridge and readying the boiling pitch.

"Do you know what I have in my hands right now?"

"No. How could I?"

"A clipping from the Tokawai Monthly Telegraph with a picture of your grandfather in a cherry picker. You wouldn't happen to know anything about that, would you?"

My lungs suctioned onto my ribcage. I jumped down the front steps to free them so they could inflate. "You've got somebody *spying* on us?"

"I've asked a person, who shall remain anonymous, to keep an eye on your grandfather and let me know if there's anything I need to be aware of. Like him being *arrested*."

I kicked at a loose stone in the parking lot, sending it skittering into a bush. "You've organised an *informant*? Jesus, Dad. How desperate are you to shove Poppy into a place where you can forget about him? Have you forgotten I'm here? There's no reason to ask *anybody* to spy on him."

"Sadie, I am concerned about your grandfather's welfare and I don't trust you to give me the full picture. Would you have told me about the arrest if...my informant hadn't?"

"No. Why should I? You're not interested in Poppy's welfare at all, at least not in any way that serves him."

"He's out of control."

"He's fine. He just showed a small lack of judgement."

"Small? His *small* lack of judgement has required a fire brigade rescue from the Bertrum's roof and a trip to the police cells."

"He's not in the cells."

"Do you know what he said about the rescue? He said, and I quote, 'Second best ride of my life. After Claudette Beaufort in 1941. Those Parisian women knew how to treat a man'."

Oh God. Poppy gave an *interview?*

"I mean. Apart from the lewdness of it, it's absolutely bonkers. He's lost his mind and this kind of behaviour, scaling buildings for goodness sake, is not acceptable."

"To who? You and Uncle Peter?"

"To *the law* for a start. I'm sending someone. You can expect them in the next couple of weeks."

"Who? Who are you sending?" I asked, but he'd already hung up.

I DIDN'T WANT to go to work that evening. I couldn't find it within me to be bothered with the petty demands of the social drinker, and there was no way I was equipped to tolerate the inevitable jokes about Poppy's one-man show.

When I arrived and saw the stock truck lying on its side in the pub's car park, I knew it was a mistake to not have called in sick.

Muffled ovine chatter hummed through the closed back doors. I gritted my teeth, sealed my nostrils with my index finger and entered the pub looking like a C-grade Hitler impersonator.

Everyone turned expectantly, except for the sheep.

They nibbled on hay that lined the floor with single focus and filled every available gap between the stools and tables.

I took two steps towards the bar and skidded on a pile of sheep droppings. The "for fuck's sake" that on any other day might have been issued under my breath, fired off my tongue in a loud volley.

Manawa's head snapped up from whatever she'd been doing on the service bench. "What happened to you? You look homicidal."

"This," I said, pointing at the sea of woolly backs, "is the most stupid thing I've ever seen. Whose genius idea was it to fill a room people eat and drink in with shitting and pissing animals?"

Manawa shrugged. "Mitchell's."

God love Mitchell. "I've had enough arsing sheep antics for one day," I said, shocking myself into silence at how much like Poppy I sounded.

"The men are all under strict instructions to scrub this place to within an inch of its life once the show's over. I've brought in a stock whip to make sure they pull finger in a timely manner."

As a ewe emptied her bladder onto a thin patch of hay in front of us, I said, "You must really love him."

She threw the cloth she'd been cleaning the bench top with into the sink and leaned against the counter, crossing her arms. "You have no idea."

I cast my eyes around the room. The packed-in, wool-bound bodies had raised the temperature a couple of humid degrees, which had the effect of amplifying the smell. An acrid mix of the sweetness of lanolin, the nose-hair curling stew of bladder and bowel contents, and the faintest hint of armpit.

Nobody in their right minds would have agreed to

accommodating this. "I have a pretty good idea." The ewe's stream of urine continued and the hay lifted off the floor in the spreading pool. "You could have at least told me to wear my gumboots."

"I gave Callum a head's up. I hoped it would be over by the time you got here."

"I hope you put in a 1-1-1 call," I muttered.

Manawa raised a hand to my cheek. "I wish I could say you're cute when you're angry, but you look all Gordon Ramsay, and Lord does that man have a face like a smacked arse. Why don't you clear some tables? That way you don't have to talk to people and I might keep most of my patrons for more than one drink."

I grunted and turned to negotiate the maze of sheep, wishing I'd remembered to stuff my shepherd's crook in my pocket along with my phone.

Fifteen tongue clucks later, I approached my third table. The two men seated at it had their heads bowed together, deep in conversation. I reached past the first man to stack their empty beer glasses inside each other and his eyes darted towards me.

"Jesus Christ!" He jerked away and placed a hand on his heart. "God. You gave me a fright. You're like a she-hulk. No offence."

A professional way to respond to such a comment might have been something like, "Actually, that is pretty offensive. Putting 'no offence' after something offensive doesn't cancel it out." Unfortunately for my tenuous bartender career, what actually came out of my mouth was, "You're like an arsehole. No offence."

"Sadie!" barked Manawa. "Customer-abuse privileges belong to me. If he's behaving like an arsehole, *I'll* tell him. Settle your tongue behind your teeth."

I whipped around to return to the bar and kneed a sheep in its hind quarter. Hissing, "Get out of my way," didn't improve the situation. The flock closed ranks, blocking any path to the bar with their woolly backs.

I turned my face to the ceiling as if to ask whoever was up there, "Why me?" and closed my eyes as I imagined what an actual she-hulk might do to someone so unforgivably obtuse.

My eyelids fluttered as her fist disappeared through his skull, the impact jettisoning bone out of an eruption of pink mist.

A sheep nudged the back of my knees and I nearly collapsed onto the one in front of me. "*Fuck's* sake."

"You look like you're about to murderise someone," said Mitchell, plate of nachos in one hand, steak and chips in the other.

"I have several options for top of the hit list, beginning with people who commit grammar offences." I sidled my way between two sheep. "You'd better be very bloody nice to me for the rest of the evening. Starting with buying me some new Converse."

"I'm sure the uniform budget could stretch to shoe replacement." He reached the pub floor and negotiated his way through the sheep with the grace of a dancer.

"How on earth?" I scowled at his back. "*God*, that's unfair."

"He can Michael Jackson, alright." Manawa leaned on the service counter, watching him with a chin propped in her hand. "He's got this move, where he grabs my right leg -"

I *thunked* the glasses down on the bench. "Please, stop. I'm not coping with anything much right now as it is and I *really* don't want to hear about Mitchell's sexniques," I said, grimacing at my use of the women's magazine term. I plugged my mouth with my fist before I could launch into a diatribe entitled 'Mansplaining. Lol!'.

Manawa conscientiously obliged by edging away from that particular conversational mine field and straight into the crossfire of the front line by asking, "Is it true Dante Kerr's heart stopped when your grandfather hit him and they had to resuscitate him?"

"No!" I thrust the glasses into the steriliser. *Clank. Clank.* "He lost consciousness for about ten seconds." Then I muttered, "He's got a minor concussion. Apparently."

"I wish I'd seen it. Nobody can talk about anything else." She turned her face up to me. "They won't send Gerry to prison, will they?"

I thought of what the reality would be for an eighty-eight-year-old succumbing to confusion and forgetfulness. Of being in a place that was unfamiliar, uncomfortable, unforgiving. A fissure cracked across the surface of my heart with each of its beats. "We're going to avoid that at all costs. I'll fight tooth and nail to keep him out."

A man shouldered his way through the back doors and let out a loud bray of laughter at the scene, frightening several sheep into the area behind the bar. They pushed up the narrow passage at a run, forcing Manawa to jump on to the service bench at a kneel, while I was buffeted against the cupboards underneath, my knees striking the wood painfully.

"When the *fuck* is Callum getting here?" I said as he stepped through the doors.

A kaleidoscope of butterflies hatched and took flight in my stomach.

Callum's eyes flicked to me before they scanned the pub floor with a smile and a wave.

"I make it six fifty-three," shouted Manawa, before

sidling between the sheep and towards the Fuzz Cup score board.

"About bloody time," I said by way of greeting to Callum.

"Evening, Sadie. Nice to see you too."

I eyed him for a beat. "I know I should say I'm sorry, and none of any of this" - I gestured to the pub floor - "and the wider shit show in my life is your fault, but I am really struggling to be rational right now."

"Understandable. You're under stress."

I eyed him for another beat. "*God* you're nice. How can you be so bloody reasonable when faced with idiots and angry people every day?"

"If I didn't work on my calm, I'd have had a triple bypass by now. And I have an ulterior motive."

"What's that?"

"He wants to ride downtown on the Sadie line," said Mitchell, sidling past, as Callum said, "Guilt for charging Gerry."

I snorted at Mitchell's comment. It was mostly out of a lifetime of a habitual assumption that no one would want to ride on the Sadie line, even though there'd been the odd encounter to suggest the contrary. If I was honest, I knew perfectly well that Callum's recent behaviour suggested Mitchell might not be far off the mark. "That's not a good reason to be nice to an irrational person," I said to Mitchell's disappearing back. "He'll only end up regretting it later."

Manawa moved down the bar to serve someone, and Callum leaned against the bar, his eyes roaming the shuffling spectacle on the pub floor. "I'd have thought you'd have a finely-honed appreciation of the thrill of risk-taking."

"I'm a fucking mess, Callum. I have no idea what the appeal is, but you'd be better off keeping your distance."

He swung his body around to face me. "This stuff with Dante Kerr will blow over. Gerry will be sentenced lightly. It will be okay."

"No, it won't. Poppy has dementia." As I said the words, it seemed as if the whole bar came to a standstill. The acknowledgement, the voicing of it was as shocking as if someone had back-handed the words across my face.

"You don't know that."

"I know what I see and hear. You heard the lyrics to that song. It's a familial trait, apparently, and now I have a full understanding of the god-awful reality of it. If Poppy doesn't think he's a cowboy in a posse, he's a resistance fighter in World War Two, he mysteriously disappears all the bloody time, and who *the fuck* is Eddie?" I leaned towards him and tapped my finger against my temple. "I'm beginning to think this Eddie person is all in his head. Like an imaginary friend."

"He seems remarkably lucid to me."

"You're not round him all the time!" I put a hand to my forehead and closed my eyes, immediately regretting my raised voice. This wasn't Callum's fault.

"No."

"Look." I lowered my hand. "I'm fighting this on two fronts. Dad and Uncle Peter want to put Poppy in a home. I've told them over my dead body, but they think they have the right to make the call. I don't know how long I can hold them off for. Poppy's making it harder and harder."

Callum's forehead creased with a frown. "I'll do anything I can to help. Just let me know what I can do."

"Can you order this lot to get these fucking sheep out of here? It smells like a septic tank."

He smiled, swung around and clapped his hands

together like a teacher drawing the attention of a classroom of children.

AT CLOSING, I stepped into the near empty car park to drag my tired feet to Poppy's car. There were two other cars parked beneath the yellow light of the security light. Mitchell and Manawa's, along with a low-slung, spoiler-adorned Mazda bearing the number plate MO1ST.

I stopped, peered at the car, then turned and walked back into the pub.

"There's a patron's car out there. Have you checked the toilets?"

Manawa grunted while she skittered change across the service counter and into her hand. "Sent him home with someone else. Had far too much to be driving."

I watched her count six more dollars' worth of coins. "Okay." Four more dollars. "Night then."

"Ae. Kia pai tō moe."

THE VIRGIN WAS WINNING the battle of nerves.

I stood two feet away, staring up at her, willing her to break.

Her smile beat down on me and I shrank under the weight of its beneficence.

"Don't look at me like that. I've been called a 'big girl' and a 'she-hulk'. You wouldn't have any idea what it's like being made to feel a freak or unwomanly. You're perfect and adored."

One eyebrow twitched.

"They *moo*-ed at me."

Obi-Wan moved across the light cast by the bedside lamp and The Virgin's brows met in the middle.

"Fuck this." I reached for the blanket folded at the end of my bed and threw it over her.

"Come on Obi-Wan. We've got some vengeance to mete out."

CHAPTER ELEVEN

THERE WAS ONLY one security camera in the pub's parking lot. An antiquated rectangular box on the end of a short arm.

I sidled up to it, placed my step ladder on the grit-laced bitumen and climbed up. It didn't take me long to secure the thick jersey around it, tying it tight so no sudden gust could dislodge it.

Then I sauntered to the car and ran a hand over its pristine paintwork. Someone loved this car very much.

I turned to Obi-Wan. "Ready?"

She bleated, then leapt on the bonnet and clattered up onto the roof.

I pulled the key to Poppy's car out of my pocket and walked the length of the Mazda, the screech of the biting metal loud in the still night.

I looked down at the thin line now decorating the side of the car and up at Obi-Wan. "Oops."

She lowered her head and offered a closed-mouth bleat, its pitch rising at the end like a question.

"Heck, yes, I want you to dance for me. Show me the four-hoofed polka."

Obi-Wan spun to face the opposite corner and leapt around the edges of the roof in a series of sproings, like a lamb full of the joys of being alive. I'd had the forethought to avoid a second incriminating mishap and donned her in a rainbow unicorn nappy before we left the house. Her tail wagged from between the gap I'd designed in the fabric.

When she reached the centre, the steel crackled. A series of dents appeared where she landed, the pattern building in intricacy the more she danced.

I walked to the front of the car and pulled up a windscreen wiper. "Hey Obi. Don't these look delicious?"

She leapt onto the bonnet, the steel whining beneath her, and took the wiper into her mouth. With two shakes of her head, she'd ripped it free, spat it out and mouthed the other one.

"That's my girl." I took the can of spray paint I'd taken from the garage and gave it a shake. "What do you think of 'I'm a tiny-pricked arsehole'? Too puerile? Too generous?"

Obi-Wan said she had an opinion, but her mouth was too full to share it. She jumped down from the car, trailing a long black line of rubber window sealer behind her.

"What was that, Obi? 'The only love I can get for free is the tube steak boogie'?" I gave the can another shake. "I like it."

I WOKE to the gentle patter of rain on the tin roof. It made a nice change from my goat-bleat alarm clock.

I craned my neck to peer into the gloom of the curtained room. No Obi-Wan.

The Virgin Mary remained a ghostly, blanketed figure.

I let my head drop back against the pillow and felt around the closed Singer sewing machine for my phone.

11 am.

Most of the morning was gone. It was a very good sign. I had half expected to be jerked from sleep by the battering ram-crash of a dawn raid.

Maybe Callum had any number of offended women to work his way through before his suspicions turned to me.

I pushed back the covers, swung my legs out of bed and fanned my toes over the scratchy carpet. Today felt like maybe it would be a good one.

My bladder pressed against my lower abdomen and I stood to make my way to the bathroom, yanking the blanket off The Virgin on the way past.

It might have been the shifting shadows thrown by the folds of fabric running down and over her head, but I was certain her right eye offered me a wink.

I peered into her glossy pupils, willing her to confirm my suspicion. She gazed back at me, unblinking. I walked towards the door and turned suddenly, hoping to catch her out. Her face remained frozen in smug virtuousness.

SHUTTING the hall door on the gurgle of the toilet cistern refilling, I stumbled into the kitchen. It was empty. Poppy's breakfast dishes sat stacked in the rack by the sink.

I opened the back door. "Poppy?"

The garage door was open, my un-roadworthy car parked inside, his outside.

"Poppy?" I called louder.

A bleat drew my attention to the field behind Poppy's back fence.

I peered through the gauze of misty rain and a small figure on top of a low hill waved at me, a goat at his side.

Stepping down on to the porch, I put my hands around my mouth and shouted, "What are you doing?"

In answer, Poppy laid what appeared to be a piece of blue cloth at his feet and sat on it.

"Oh shit." I bent to retrieve the shoes I'd worn last night and kicked off at the door, hopping to gain balance while I pulled them on. "Poppy wait!"

I leapt off the back step as he lifted his feet and began to slide down the hill.

"Oh God. Poppeeeeeeee!"

I *thunk-thunk*ed across the wooden boards in the vegetable garden and wrestled with the rusty bolt on the gate, willing it, with a "come the fuck *on*" to come unstuck faster.

Poppy, it would appear, did not share any of my concern for his well-being, for brittle bones splintering under impact, of papery skin splitting, hands de-gloved, heads cracked open on wayward rocks.

His cackle chased him down the hill like the wake of a boat.

Obi-Wan ran alongside, chirruping a sequence of high-pitched bleats.

They both slowed to a stop long before I could intercept them.

"What. The. Fuck," I said, between pants, hands braced on my knees. "Do. You. Think. You're. Doing."

"Having an arse-load of fun." Poppy pulled himself upright with a long groan and plucked the material, which I could now see was a raincoat, off the grass. "Eddie soaped up the bottom. Makes it go way faster on the wet grass."

"Eddie did *what?*"

"Wanna go tandem?"

I righted myself, sucked in a large lungful of air and looked between him, the goat and the raincoat.

Then I shrugged. "OK."

AT THE END of ride five when both Poppy and I decided that the top of the hill was finally too hard a walk, I decided that this Eddie person, while slightly irresponsible and possibly non-existent, might just be alright.

In the desperate hope I could allay my suspicions, I suggested to Poppy that he invite Eddie over for dinner so I could meet him.

He looked at me quizzically. "Why would I do that?"

"So I can meet him."

Poppy stared at me like I'd said something wholly ridiculous. Then he shook his head and walked back towards the house.

I pulled my wet and muddied pyjamas away from my thighs with a *shluck*. "Don't you want me to meet him?" I called after him.

Poppy's step faltered before he found the rhythm of his stride again, but he didn't turn. "How about cheese scones for lunch? You go have a shower and I'll get them in the oven."

I ran to catch up with him, my strides wide-legged to prevent any risk of chafing. "But -"

"Then we should go and see what Mrs White's up to. The weather's clearing so she should be out in her garden."

"I'm not sure that's a good idea."

"You didn't think sliding down the hill on a soaped-up raincoat was a good idea either, but changed your mind pretty quickly."

"Winding up Mrs White is an entirely different kind of sport. I'm not sure I want to play that game."

"She loves it."

"I bet you anything she doesn't." I wrenched open the gate latch and held it open for Poppy and Obi-Wan to walk through.

"A cup of tea and something warm in your stomach will put you in the mood for some entertainment. Check the mail will you? I'll get dry then get the scones going."

I walked in my awkward gait to the end of the driveway, Obi-Wan clopping behind me. Mrs White was not yet in her garden. I hoped for her sake she'd got all her gardening done the previous day and Poppy would have to look for sport elsewhere.

The door on the mailbox squeaked open. There was only one piece of mail inside. A letter addressed to me in my father's handwriting.

I pulled it out with pincered fingers like it was toxic to the touch and glared at it through narrowed eyelids. I didn't need to open it to know what was inside.

Looking between it and the house to where Poppy was no doubt rubbing softened butter through flour, I wondered if I could smuggle it in unnoticed and write return to sender in capitals along its front.

A car drove up the street, Obi-Wan bleated, and I tore the envelope open.

There were three brochures for retirement homes, all of them glossy, the residents staged in various activities, expressions of delight on their air-brushed, white faces. A privileged vanilla-fest.

I held the brochures out to Obi-Wan to get her opinion. She "blah-ha-ha"ed a "happy old white people. Delicious" and tongued the first one into her mouth.

I had no idea what the ink might do to her system. Perhaps it would dye her turds primary colours so they looked like Skittles. It didn't matter. Obi-Wan had proved time and again her insides were made of Teflon-coated asbestos.

Within thirty seconds, the last set of glistening, pearly-white dentures had disappeared.

"No mail today," I called to Poppy as I headed to the bathroom.

AT TEN PAST TWO, Mrs White was, as Poppy predicted, in her garden. She clipped at the fresh spring growth on the small shrubs dotted around her front lawn with a pair of secateurs.

Poppy had just returned from one of his hour-long disappearances and I trailed behind him, my reluctance to be part of the game making my steps leaden. Obi-Wan, unaware of what was afoot, trotted alongside Poppy, her hoof steps clopping lightly on the road.

"Morning, Jean." Poppy extended a finger. "You missed a bit."

Mrs White ignored him and continued chopping.

"Just on this one here. Looks like the dags left on a sheep's behind after shearing."

She whipped around and pointed the secateurs like a gun at Poppy. "Don't you address me, you awful old man. You've deliberately come across the road to provoke me. You've got no business standing on this part of the pavement. Get back on your side of the street."

"You're quick to fire today. Bit of ol' hair of the dog?" Poppy turned to me and mimed slugging back a drink.

Mrs White gasped. "I do *not* debase myself by drinking spirits, let alone in the middle of the day!" Her nostrils flared, a small patch of white ringing each. "My morals are upstanding. Unlike you and your filthy granddaughter."

I raised my hands. "Whoa. Don't bring me into this warped love-hate game you two like to play."

"You," Mrs White said, her voice, and the finger she pointed at me, shaking. "Have got tongues wagging all over town with your whoring ways."

"Excuse me?" I said, as Poppy paled.

"I know all about your career in the porn industry." She said *porn* like it was made of ash and absorbed all the moisture in her mouth.

My stomach twisted. Callum.

He'd told people what he'd overheard in the backyard.

"And if that isn't disgrace enough, now you're pregnant out of wedlock to who knows which" - she flapped a hand about - "of those men."

My stomach released itself. Not Callum.

There was only one place where the words "porn" and "pregnancy" were issued in the same breath.

The haberdashers.

The smiling woman at the counter.

Before I could summon any type of indignation, Poppy put a hand on Mrs White's letter box to steady himself.

"Poppy?" I stepped over to him and gripped his shoulders. "Do you want to sit down?"

"Useless old man. That's what you get for maligning your neighbours. Someone's watching." Mrs White pointed at the sky.

"I..." Poppy mumbled something I couldn't hear.

"What, Poppy?" I had to lean in close to hear his words.

His voice was little more than a whisper. "Home."

He attempted to turn and stumbled.

I bent down and gathered him up in my arms. There was so little of him, it wasn't much of a struggle to pick him up.

I stepped out onto the road and headed back towards Poppy's driveway.

"You freakish girl. That's right. Get out of here. Go sully some other part of the country. Take your grandfather with you." Then she gasped. I craned my neck to see Obi-Wan standing in her flower bed, eating her dahlias.

"Get out! Shoo!" Mrs White yelled over a series of claps. "You come back here, Sadie Quinn and retrieve your animal."

I ignored her, my attention focused on how cold Poppy felt, how grey his skin looked.

Once in the house, I sat him in a dining chair and put the jug on. Then I called an ambulance.

"Here, drink this," I said, handing him a cup of strong, sweet tea.

"I think I'll go to bed." He attempted to get up, but his legs gave out from underneath him.

"There's no point. The ambulance'll be here soon."

Poppy's eyes lost their glaze. "Ambulance? What the bloody hell did you call an ambulance for?"

"You've had a turn, Poppy. For all I know, you've just had a stroke."

"Cancel the blasted thing," he growled. "I haven't had a stroke. I just want to be left alone for a while." He stood up, energised by his indignation and left the room. A few seconds later his bedroom door slammed.

I followed him and laid my head against the door, listening to the squeak of the bed as he sat on it. "Poppy? I'm not pregnant."

No answer.

"That's just a bit of nasty small town gossip because I happened to buy material to make nappies."

The bed groaned. I imagined him swinging his legs up onto it, the mattress depressing under his weight.

"I haven't had sex in months. Wouldn't know what to do with a penis now, let alone let it impregnate me." I lay my forehead against the door and grimaced. Too much information. "Poppy?"

No answer, no movement from within.

I left him and went to sit on the front steps and wait for the ambulance.

MY PHONE RANG JUST as the ambulance pulled out of the driveway.

Dad.

Once again, his timing was uncanny.

"Hi-i," I singsonged, attempting false cheer.

"Well, if it isn't my Amazonian throwback."

"Dad, *you* called *me*."

"I sure have. Your mother wants to know if you organised the Labour Party conference and what it felt like looking down on the most powerful woman in the country."

"Don't know. Didn't do it."

"Fair enough. *I* want to know what's happened to your grandfather."

The speaker distorted with a rush of air, like he'd planted his nostrils over the phone's mic. I scraped my toe across the concrete of the driveway, loosening a piece of grit with a *scrick*. "Nothing."

Snuuuu Dad exhaled.

I held the phone away from my ear.

"Then why have I just been informed that an ambulance is at the property?"

I raised my head and peered at the house over the road. The front garden was empty. "Mrs White is your informant?"

"I'm not at liberty to say, but I take it from your 'nothing' lie that the old bugger's still with us."

Suddenly I was very tired. I didn't have the mental and emotional space to shoulder my father's daddy issues. "He's fine," I said through gritted teeth. "There's nothing wrong with him. I over-reacted when I thought he looked unwell. The ambulance left empty."

Snuuuuu. "And what happens the next time he takes a turn and you're not there to call for help?"

"That could happen anywhere, Dad. They don't watch residents twenty-four hours a day."

Silence.

"Is he really OK?"

I pinched my nose between my thumb and forefinger. "Yes. The paramedics checked him over. Everything's normal, apparently. They think he went into shock, but nothing more serious."

"Shock. Why?"

"Mrs White accused me of being a porn star and being with child to one of my many well-endowed co-actors."

Dad's outward breath hitched, then stopped. After three seconds, the crackling of his exhale resumed. "You're not, are you?"

"No! She's just a nasty, self-righteous old woman who Poppy wound up a bit too far. You know her kind. They love to ride the swell of town gossip."

"Hmm. I didn't think anything could rattle your grandfather, let alone idle gossip. So, what on earth did you do to provoke the wagging of tongues?"

I would have liked to have given my father the benefit of the doubt that he didn't actually believe I had invited this upon myself, that I was in some part responsible for being the object of the local rumour mill, but I was, after all, and as he reminded me, a genetic throwback.

I moved to close the conversation and turned to walk back up the driveway. "I got the brochures."

"Good. What did your grandfather think?"

"He hasn't seen them yet. I've filed them."

"In the rubbish bin?"

"Something like that."

"Sadie, I need you to take this seriously."

"I am. Very seriously."

"But not the seriously I mean. Your grandfather's a danger to himself. You need to be objective about this."

"No I don't. This whole thing is an incredibly emotive process. Just because you've stripped all emotion out of it doesn't mean I have to."

A sigh. "Sadie."

"I have to go. I need to check on Poppy."

WHEN POPPY EMERGED from his bedroom several hours later, followed by a goat who had, unsurprisingly, got through all closed doors to keep him company, he wore his pyjamas and a grim determination.

"Let's bring forward number five."

Number five was *Rearrange the flowers in the bed outside the library into the shape of a naked lady*, which seemed like more of a job than Poppy and I could handle, let alone a seven-year-old.

"You really did that?"

Poppy shrugged. "It was all marigolds and pansies in those days. Easy to dig up and move around. We'll have to adapt it to fit what I've got in mind, but I've no doubt we can manage it."

"What *have* you got in mind?"

He peered up at me and rubbed his hands together. "Topiary."

A THICK FOG rolled in the following day, throwing the world into a hazy half-light and obscuring the view across the street to Mrs White's front yard.

After breakfast, Poppy lugged his leaf blower to the end of the driveway in an attempt to dispel the soupy mist. It swirled around him and resettled into a milky wall.

Working by torchlight the evening before had meant his creative vision relied on spatial memory. It had been impossible to tell if the hedge art had been effectively executed, and now Poppy vibrated with impatience, expecting his topiary masterpiece to be unveiled with the rising of the sun.

He thrust the leaf blower into my arms and declared he was going to play in his fort "until the day had the decency to start bloody properly".

THE FOG LIFTED while I'd been attempting to remove the plates of my ill-fated Barina, revealing a uniformed

Callum pacing at the end of the driveway, his attention across the road.

He took a few steps, leant to his left, then straightened up. Then he retraced his steps and leant in the other direction.

I slowly closed the garage door so as not to attract his attention, which would no doubt fall on the Warrant of Fitness-less car. The rollers *screeked* their way over a piece of rust and I froze, waiting for Callum to turn, to call me out. But he remained fixated on Mrs White's house.

The door issued a soft *thunk* as it settled against the concrete lip of the garage floor. "Hey," I called out. "Watcha doing?"

"Come look at this," he said, his back still to me.

I looked at the house as if I could peer through its walls and locate Poppy. Hopefully, he was still playing in the fort, unaware the fog had dissipated. If my luck was rotten, and Callum's voice had alerted him to the day's emergence, he'd give away our midnight antics in a heartbeat.

I walked as quietly as I could up the driveway, placing my running shoes heel first and rolling onto the balls of my feet.

As I drew to a halt beside Callum, he placed a hand on each of my upper arms and guided me to the right and onto the footpath. My skin burned beneath his palms. My step faltered and his hands squeezed my flesh as he attempted to keep me upright. "Careful." He dropped his hands. "There."

I knew what he was referring to, but I played dumb. "Where?" I said, my voice husky.

"Why are you whispering?"

I had to blink twice before the lie appeared on my tongue. "Poppy's asleep."

"I don't think talking at normal volume at the end of the driveway will wake him up."

"He sleeps very lightly," I whispered, as Callum's arm appeared over my shoulder and he pointed at Mrs White's garden. "The tall conifer. The one that's tapered at the top." Callum's voice was a low rumble. It reverberated through my breast bone and vibrated in the pit of my stomach.

"Uhuh." I swallowed. It sounded far too loud in my ears. I was sure it would give me away, betray the thought flitting over my mind that all he had to do was turn his head and his lips would press against my neck.

"And see the small bush across the drive way? The one that's been rounded?"

I nodded. He could have asked me to interpretive dance the national anthem and I would have agreed to it.

"There's another one in front of the conifer and three feet to the left. All fairly normal and innocuous. Now." He placed his hands on my arms again and guided me to the left, to the other side of the driveway. "What do you see?"

I stifled a snort. Poppy's vision had worked. From this perspective the three lined up in a neat sequence.

"A cock and balls."

Callum grinned. "It's totally a cock and balls."

Then I couldn't hold it in any longer. I allowed myself a single guffaw and slapped a hand to my mouth to suppress the snigger building in my throat.

"She can't know."

I shook my head, the tears blurring my vision.

"Do you think I should do my civic duty and tell her?"

"Please no. Ignorance, they say, is bliss." I laughed again. "Poppy's going to love it."

"You mean to say you guys had nothing to do with this? I'm not going to find a pair of smoking hedge clippers in the garage next to the car you've failed to provide a Warrant of Fitness for?"

I laid a hand on his arm. "Please don't tell her. It'll put a spring in Poppy's step every time he walks out the gate." I wiped my eyes. "Why are you here?"

The smile slipped off Callum's face and it was like the sun's light had been extinguished.

"I need to talk to you about an incident."

Shit. The car.

I made an "uh-oh" face and clamped my sphincter closed before my bowel could drop out of it. I glanced across the street, looking for a pair of eyes in the hedgerow, the twitch of a curtain. I didn't need Dad to know about my vandalism, let alone hear it from a prying neighbour. "Come inside. I'll make us tea."

CALLUM SAT DOWN HEAVILY in a dining chair, his stab-proof vest scraping against the wooden spindles.

I flicked the jug on and clattered around in the cupboard, searching for the biscuit tin. I prised it open and placed four chocolate chip cookies on a plate. "What's the incident?"

"Someone vandalised the MO1ST car."

I shoved a biscuit in my mouth to stop myself from any impending blurt and turned to place the plate in front of Callum. The cookie plugged all available space and trapped my tongue beneath it. As long as I didn't chew, I should be safe. "Ungh?" I said, feigning interested surprise.

He pulled his phone out of his pocket, thumbed open an app and swivelled the screen around so I could see a series of photos.

"I want to check you know nothing about this."

The white Mazda was in a much worse state than when Obi-Wan and I left it. The windows and lights had been smashed out, the seats carved up like someone had taken a pickaxe to them, and someone had spray painted a target on top of the roof. Underneath the target was written, "Scud bomb here", only the 'd' had been crossed out and an 'm' written above it.

The biscuit, soggy from absorbing my saliva, collapsed and freed my tongue to push it towards my teeth, where I instinctively set to chewing.

"Done night before last. Sometime after your shift at the pub."

I swallowed and tried to block all memory of my moment of madness, which, of course, only served to shove the recollection to the front of my brain in vivid technicolour, the chemical astringency of the spray paint fresh in my nostrils.

I pointed to the target, the words *I didn't do that bit* racing between my synapses and my tongue when Poppy burst into the kitchen.

He stood framed against the morning light, a gun in his hand. "Put your hands on the table, son. Nice and slow where I can see 'em."

CHAPTER TWELVE

"POPPY!" I shouted, as Callum said, "Take it easy, Gerry."

Then Poppy stepped into the full light of the kitchen, revealing the gun in all its childish fabricated glory. It appeared to have been crudely carved out of wood, its trigger guard made from a Bakelite cupboard handle.

"Ha! Got you good. You *almost* looked like you shit yourself." He sat himself down at the table and helped himself to a biscuit.

I stood up and, offering Callum an apologetic half-smile, turned to make the tea.

"Probably not the best game to play with a police officer, Gerry."

"Why? You're not armed."

"The risk isn't me shooting you. It's me arresting you for threatening a police officer with an imitation firearm."

"This isn't imitation." Poppy picked up the gun and stroked it, a smile playing on his lips. "This was the very first prototype."

I tipped milk into Poppy's cup. "Prototype for what?"

"My ray gun."

"You played with ray guns? Didn't they come out of 1950s science fiction comics or something?"

"1920s. I developed the very first *real* ray gun in 1945. Was powerful enough to vaporise a whole building." Poppy shifted his eyes to me. "You know the concave section at the side of the garage? Looks like it's been melted?"

"No."

"Ray gun. Second prototype. Not very powerful."

I rocked in my seat and raised my eyes to meet Callum's.

He held my gaze for the space of two of my blinks, in which time I tried to interpret what his careful lack of expression communicated. I'm amused yet concerned? Good luck, Sadie. You've got your hands full?

He turned to Poppy. "You mean to say, you could have vaporised me when you burst through that door if you'd wanted to?"

Poppy chuckled. It bubbled in his throat. "Nope. Never got this one to convert enough energy to fire so much as a fart. It's eighty years old now. Surprised it didn't fall apart in my hands."

"Where on earth did you find it, Poppy?"

"Eddie found it for me. Under the bed."

My eyes flicked back to Callum. "*Eddie* found it," I said as if absently echoing Poppy's words. I turned to Poppy. "I've been here all morning. When was Eddie here?"

Poppy shrugged. "Does it matter?"

I opened my mouth to retort *No. Actually, it doesn't matter because two thirds of the people at this table know Eddie isn't real. Though one of those people desperately wishes an Eddie would materialise - blood, bone and beating heart - so that person (me) could then ray gun the shit out of the burning nugget that's anchored to her stomach lining and eyeing up her heart with metastatic fervour.*

I plugged my mouth with my teacup before my thoughts spilled out into the air.

Callum placed his hands on the table, readying himself to get up. "I need to keep moving. Thanks for the biscuit, Gerry. Delicious as always. Sadie -"

I tried to move my eyes from the cup of tea in my hands, and meet his, but I had a fair idea of what was coming, and if I looked at him now, the truth would rush out of me like the innards of a gutted carcass.

"- I want you down at the station at 3pm. Don't be late."

"Okay," I said to the grey and cooling surface of my tea.

THE POLICE STATION was closed when I arrived at 2.57 pm, which was understandable, given I was three minutes early and Tokawai's only police officer wasn't afforded the luxury of office staff.

I sat on the bench outside, Poppy's car keys and phone in my hand, and watched cars drive past for after school pick ups.

At 3.10 pm, Callum still hadn't shown up. I thought it unlikely that he'd have forgotten. It was more probable he was out attending to an emergency.

I wondered if I could slope off, say I'd been, but he wasn't there.

I eyed Poppy's car, its keys hot in my hand.

Then I sank back into the curved wooden slats of the bench. There was no point in avoiding the inevitable. It wasn't like Callum didn't know where I lived or where I worked.

At 3.17 pm I shifted on the seat, lifting one bum cheek, then the other, to find a more comfortable position on the hardwood.

At 3.22 pm, I stood and paced along the front wall of the small station, inspecting the cracks in its brickwork, the lichen taking root in its tiny crevices.

At 3.31 pm, a car pulled in next to Poppy's. It wasn't a police car and the woman driving it was not in uniform.

She climbed out, her yellow Hello Kitty T-shirt garish against the beige of her sedan. She eyed me with a small frown and twitch of her mouth, and stayed poised outside the driver's door, one foot in front of the other in a half step.

"He-ey," Flick singsonged at half her usual verbal power-level. There was no "gangsta!", no finger gun salute. Instead of behaving like a puppy greeting its owner after the work-day absence, she looked like she'd been growled out for chewing shoes. "You, like, my support person?"

"No." I sat upright, my muscles tensing as if ready to spring into the midst of a fight. "Why do you need a support person?"

Her eyes shifted from me to the closed sign on the door, then she tipped her wrist and peered at her large turquoise watch. "Is he coming back soon?"

"No idea. I was meant to meet him at three." I stood up from the bench seat and took a step towards her. "Are you okay?"

She whirled towards her car, as if contemplating the same options as me, before turning to look at the station again, her cheeks puffed out. She exhaled with a little pop of her lips and sauntered past me to the bench seat.

"Probs best to wait." The seat rocked as she let her weight fall onto it.

I sat down beside her.

"He'll be out busting some ass. Doing some Sherlock shit."

"Flick?"

She planted her hands under her thighs and swung her legs forward, her gold Nikes scraping on the pebbled path. Then she stood up abruptly and shook her hands out.

"What's going on?"

Flick turned to me, her eyes large, her brows cinched up to meet in the middle. Then she blinked - a curtain lifting on the next act. "Holy shit, sister. Your grandfather pulled some crazy ninja shit on the Dante. Took out four Kerrverts." She slapped a palm on top of the other. "Crushed like origami cranes. It was savage. Is he, like, in jail now?"

"No," I answered, then amended it to a "not yet."

"He'd be a badass in there, wheeling and dealing his way to kingpin. Age is like to the power of five in the 'who gets to wield power' formula. Muscles are like, times three. If I go to jail, I've only got my cunning and my mouth to protect me. Cunning's pretty good. To the power of two. But mouthing off's, like, divisible by three on account of it's a sure-fire way to get stuck." She mimed plunging a knife into what presumably was a stomach. "Do you think I can go to the same jail as your grandfather? He could offer me protection."

"Ah," I said, guessing the answer before I asked the question. "Why would you be going to jail?"

She sat back down on the seat, leaned forward and placed her elbows on her knees. "No reason. He cain't prove sheeit."

I bit my smile between my lips, laid a hand on her back and gave it two pats.

She turned her face to look up at me. "What if he cracks

me? He might be proficient at verbal water torture. You know, the cop equivalent of an after-dinner mint. Sweet on the outside. Himmler on the inside."

"Okay. One, chocolate and mint is a delicious combination."

"Yeah? There's a reason why no fool's produced chocolate-flavoured tooth-paste. If that flavour abomination worked, no parent would have to tell the teeth-falling-out lie."

"Two. Callum's all chocolate. Maybe of the lightly salted variety, but I don't think you've got much to worry about."

Raising a finger at me, she shook it. "Uh uh. Chocolate's more effective. Lull you into a false sense of security, get your trust, then BAM." She smacked a fist into her palm. "They ambush your arse and you're spilling your guts before you realise your mouth's even open." She stood up again and paced two steps away.

"But you're Flick."

"I know that." The gravel *skrikk*ed as she pivotted.

"The woman with the badass name, who can take on a grown man in a paper cut fight *and win*. When the heat's on, you'll do what's necessary." I didn't need to add whether that be lie to Callum's face or confess to the truth, which was exactly the battle raging inside me.

Flick placed her palms over her eyes and exhaled through pursed lips.

"You're making me nervous. Please sit down."

She dropped a chin and peered down at her T-shirt, as if seeking permission from the cat. Then she resumed her seat next to me. "Asshat deserved it anyway."

"Which bit did you do?"

Flick swivelled her entire body to face me. She eyed me

for three seconds. Then she raised her arms into the air and shot her finger guns into the blue above. "Holy shit, gangsta. Did you bring some reckoning to that pig mobile, too?"

"Shhhh." I flapped my hands in front of her and looked out on to the street. "Lower your voice. Your mouth's a megaphone."

Flick followed my gaze, then leaned towards me conspiratorially. "Which bit did *you* do?"

"I scratched it up a bit, broke a few pieces off. And I spray-painted the bit about the small prick. But, wow, you went to town. What did you take to the seats with? A chainsaw?"

Flick shook her head. "I didn't touch the inside. I just did the target. So the stealth bombers knew where to land their arsehole-seeking missiles."

"The stealth bombers?"

"I got contacts."

"Okay. So, if neither of us did the inside, who did?"

A compact, duck-egg blue hatchback pulled into the station's driveway, its indicator winking.

The driver's knuckles were as white as the pinched face behind them.

Mrs White.

She pulled in next to Flick's beige sedan, stepped out of the car, and like Flick, peered at her watch. Then she strode toward the station entrance, steadfastly ignoring us and the sign on the door. Gripping the door handle, she attempted to move it. When she couldn't, she shook it as if she could rattle the door loose from its frame. "Oh, for goodness sake, I know I'm twenty minutes early, but it's still business hours."

"I've been waiting forty minutes, Mrs White. He asked me to come at three, Flick at three-thirty."

She let her hand drop from the handle and sighed disapprovingly. "I just want to get this blasted thing over with."

Flick glanced at me, then jumped off the bench seat. "Yeah-ya. We got ourselves a new sister in the fight against sexist tyranny." Flick shimmied her way over to Mrs White and held both her hands in the air, palms outward. "Don't leave me hangin', chica."

Mrs White took a step backwards, her eyes wide, lips parted.

Flick reached forward, grabbed one of her hands and slapped her palm into it. Before she could do the same with the other, Mrs White pulled her hands into tight balls and pressed them against her chest.

"Get off me. What are you doing?"

"I'm showing my appreciation. You are down, dawg!"

She pulled her purse around from her hip and held it in front of her as if it might shield her from Flick's exuberance. "Did you just call me a dog?"

"Mrs White," I called. "We could be waiting here a while. Why don't you come and have a seat?" I slid along to the end of the bench to give her plenty of space.

"I don't...I don't think so." She gripped the door handle and shook it again.

I lowered my voice. "Look. Officer McLintock wants to speak to me and Flick in relation to some vandalism sustained by a car parked in the pub's car park a couple of nights ago."

"Well, I wouldn't put that past you, Sadie Quinn."

I took a deep breath, forced a smile, and unclenched my tongue from between my teeth. "I don't suppose he's asked you here for the same reason?"

"My reason for being here is none of your business." She

turned and headed back towards the small car park. "I'm going to wait in my car."

"Well, Flick and I are going to help each other out over this thing. See if we can avoid anything nasty like a prosecution."

Mrs White stopped walking.

"You're welcome to join us."

She peered over her shoulder at the locked police station, then at Flick, and finally at me. Then she turned and marched towards the bench seat and sat down. "I'm not lying for you," she said to the cars passing on the street.

"You hacked up the inside of someone else's car but you can't force a lie across your tongue?"

Flick moved away from the door and edged herself in between the wall and the back of the seat. Leaning over, she whispered into the ear hidden from Mrs White, "Sis, this witch is cold. We don't need her. Li-a-bil-it-y."

"We're stronger as a united front. Mrs White will do just fine."

Flick leaned out past me and surveyed Mrs White through narrowed lids. Then she righted herself, shuffled sideways and tilted her body over the back of the bench between us, her breasts anchoring her upper body over the top of the seat.

She laid an arm over my shoulder, then Mrs White's. "Alright, lady G's. What's our story?"

CALLUM LEANED back in his chair and crossed his arms, the blue of his eyes barely visible between his narrowed lids. "So, you expect me to believe that you and Flick and Jean White were playing a game of *quidditch* between 11:30 pm and 2 am?"

"Cribbage."

He drew his mouth into a thin line and emptied his lungs twice before saying, "Well, I don't."

"Why can't you believe that?"

He held up his hand and counted off on his fingers. "Firstly, you guys hanging out with Jean Caustic White? The woman you stealth topiaried, no doubt to get even about something she'd offended you or your grandfather over. Secondly, cribbage? What on earth would anybody below retirement age, no, the previous generation's retirees, know about cribbage? Thirdly, who plays anything between eleven-thirty and two am, unless you're a Fortnite addict? None of those things lend themselves well to your story. And collectively?" He shook his head with a little laugh. "I'm offended you think I could swallow something like that. In fact, it's *such* a bad lie, I'm beginning to wonder if it's true."

I shrugged my shoulders. "Try us."

Callum eyed me for five very long seconds. Then he threw his hands up in the air. "Jesus. The school bus driver couldn't have picked a worse bloody time to attempt a three point turn on a narrow highway."

"Wheel stuck in a ditch?"

"Blocked the road for an hour while we tried to haul it out. Giving" - he stabbed his finger at me - "*you three* ample time to cobble together an alibi."

"It's no alibi. We've formed an exclusive club to share our love of the beautiful game. We play when I finish my shifts because it beats staring at the ceiling counting sheep."

Callum raised an eyebrow. "All three of you are insomniacs?"

"Yes. Anyway, if I was guilty, I'd have incriminated myself by now."

"No, no. That's not the way you work. You incriminate yourself when you're taken by surprise. You were given time to prepare for this." He stood up and pointed a finger at me. "You stay here." He left the room, leaving the door open and reappeared a minute later, carrying a chair. He placed it opposite me, next to the one he had vacated. Slapping a pack of cards down on the table, he locked eyes with me and called, "You two, get in here. Prove to me your unlikely story has substance."

Flick sauntered in, whipping her head from shoulder to shoulder like a boxer warming up for a match, and flicked her hair over her head to reveal her 'mean strip'.

Mrs White squeaked behind her in her orthopaedic shoes, her rigid spine displaying a confidence wholly undermined by her darting pupils. She placed her handbag on her knee and sat primly with her knees pressed together.

I smiled at her, widened my eyes and gestured with my eyeballs for her to put her bag on the floor.

With a little "oh" that had me wishing I could have anyone else, Rudy Guiliani, on my team right now, she did as my eyes requested.

"Okay ladies," I said, as I began to shuffle the cards. "Who's scoring?"

"Me!" Flick flipped open the casing on her phone. "I'm all about the numbers. In school they called me Denominator due to my ability to convert fractions into percentages. And my sweet right hook." She thumbed open an app on her phone. The app she and I had downloaded before Callum arrived one and a quarter hours late to my appointment.

Mrs White didn't have a cell phone, due to it, she said, being "a devil's plaything". To which Flick said she thought that was penises and Sharon Osbourne. "He's really got it in for her."

I placed the pack on the table, cut the deck, and the game began.

AFTER THREE HANDS and a turn each at being dealer, Mrs White had pulled ahead, having pegged a growing 72 points. Tallying the cards in her hand, she placed a jack of diamonds next to the start card, a three of diamonds.

"Say it, sister," said Flick.

Mrs White paused, pursed her pale lips, then said, "One for his nob," as evenly as she might have said, "I prefer margarine to butter."

"Damn right, one for his nob," Flick said.

I caught Mrs White's eye and grinned at her. She returned my gaze, then her shoulders began to shake as she emitted a girlish giggle completely at odd with her usual prim manner.

The laughter jumped like wildfire leaping a road. It caught hold of Flick, then me, the release of tension echoing around the interview room.

Mrs White's laughter turned into a series of "hoh"s. "Oh my goodness," she said, dabbing at the corner of her eyes with her finger tips. "I'd forgotten how fun this is to play."

Three pairs of hands stilled.

I raised my eyes and met Flick's, my grin still plastered on my lips.

She glanced at Callum behind me, then at Mrs White.

Mrs White attempted to suck her lips inside her mouth and rearranged the order of the cards left in her hand.

"I know," I said slowly. "Two days can drag by. It can feel like an age since the last game."

Callum cleared his throat.

Flick drew her chair closer to the table, the linoleum shrieking in protest.

I placed my cards face-down one by one. Then thought better of it and picked them up again.

The walls of the small room inched towards the table, closing in on us like a vice.

Behind me, the clock on the wall loudly counted off the seconds until our inevitable implosion. *Click. Click. Click. Click.*

"I cut my knuckle shaving." Flick thrust out a fist and circled the table with it so each of us could see the scab of dried blood on the middle knuckle of her ring finger. "Thought I was going to bleed out. It was like, *ffft ffft ffft*." She mimed blood spraying from her fist. "Who'd have thought fingers required arterial blood?"

I bit my bottom lip and laid a pair of eights on the table to be pegged.

"I only shave them once a week. On Sundays."

Mrs White, her eyes wide, looked between the bloodied finger and somewhere above my head, presumably at Callum.

"Uh huh," I said, as if she was talking about walking her dog.

"Got my wookie hands from my Dad. My Mum's Tongan. Like, *no* body hair. My Dad's a throwback to an ice-age Celtic warrior or some shit. You know, where they had to sprout back hair to keep their kidneys from frosting over? Messy genetic mash up."

A snort issued from behind me. Flick grinned, and I wheezed out a laugh.

Mrs White started sniggering into her hand of cards. "I've got a -" Snigger. "Skin tag on my -" She whistled two quick notes and darted her eyes downwards. "- I call Winston."

The room crackled with laughter. Flick threw her head back and had to catch herself on the table as her chair teetered on its back legs.

"Can't you get those removed?" I asked, my voice thrown an octave higher by my constricted windpipe.

"I have." Mrs White dabbed at her eyes with a handkerchief. "Keeps growing back like a lizard's tail."

I chortled and slapped my hands on the table, disturbing the small piles of cards and sending several skating towards the table's edge. "I get nasty gas from my support briefs. They're meant to control the fleshy bits of your stomach and thighs, but they just mould my intestines into a walnut. Poppy calls me Captain Thunderpants."

Another round of laughter ricocheted around the room.

I sniffed and wiped at my cheeks with the backs of my hands. "Callum. Your turn."

"Not on your life. I'm not going to be lulled into your desperate diversion tactics. Don't think I didn't notice your slip up."

Mrs White huffed. "I wouldn't reveal something so personal for a *diversion tactic*." She pointed at Callum. "It's you. Standing over us and frightening us into stupidity with your hard-nosed cop routine. Sit down or go away." Then she turned her glare on Flick and me. "Don't you dare breathe a word of that to anybody. He's watching." She pointed at the ceiling.

Flick crossed her heart and offered Mrs White a Vulcan salute.

"Course, I won't tell, Jean," I said, testing the intimacy she'd just established between us. "Anything said under duress doesn't count."

"*Duress,*" Callum grumbled.

Flick let out a final snicker and Mrs White glared at him. "Well?"

Silence.

Then a sigh. "Fine. *Fine.*" He reached his long arms across the table and gathered the cards towards him. "The evidence is in your favour."

"In that you have shit," said Flick.

"Which is just as well because I could drive a tanker through your collective alibi." Several cards skittered across the glossy surface and hit the floor with a *snap*. He bent to retrieve them. "What do I really care anyway? Kid's let his insurance lapse."

He reappeared and his fingers danced as they worked the cards into a neat pile. "If I can't charge anyone with clear proof, it'll take him months to save for a new car. You've actually all done me a great big bloody service."

I shoved my fist between my teeth before I could say anything incriminating, like, "You're welcome".

Flick leant forward and offered her hand to Callum to shake. "Been nice doing business with you, son." Then she winked. "Told you we'd make a kick-ass team."

"In a purely hypothetical sense," I added before Callum could take her words as an admission.

Callum gestured to the door. "Please go so I can enjoy my paperwork hell in peace."

ONCE OUTSIDE, Mrs White wordlessly strode towards her car and stood shivering beside it, rummaging in her handbag. After two failed attempts to put her key in the lock, Flick blocked her access.

She folded her arms and leaned against the driver door.

"You're not getting away so easy, sister. We got some heavy shit to debrief on."

Mrs White took a step backwards. "I'm not interested in either your inability to speak without cursing, or dissecting the last two awful hours. I want to put the whole thing behind me."

"Fact." Flick's face lit with a slow smile. "I'm talking a debrief with our old friend, Glen of the Fiddich."

Mrs White said nothing for a beat, then she made another attempt to slot the key home. "Get out of my way." Her words might have packed potency were it not for the chattering of her teeth.

I stepped up behind Mrs White and slid the keys from her hand. "Come on. I'll drive you. Flick can bring up the rear."

"THREE OF YOUR FINEST, barrel-aged whiskeys, please bartender," I asked Manawa, hoping there was a dusty bottle hidden somewhere behind the ranks of standard-brand liquor.

Manawa eyed me and pulled a bottle of Jack Daniel's from the shelf above the glass-fronted fridge.

I shrugged my shoulders. "All tastes the same by the end of the night."

"You celebrating something?"

I wasn't sure. On the surface, we had reason to - bluffing our way, however, cack-handed, out of arrest - but I didn't think any of us felt the elation of it. It was only the car owner's continual pushing of Callum's patience and his resulting lack of sympathy that had gotten us off. It had little to do with our ability to pull the wool over his eyes. "Mostly refortifying."

Manawa nodded at the table Flick and Mrs White had sat themselves at. "Interesting choice of refortifying partners."

I followed her gaze. "Yes."

When she raised her eyebrows, I said, "We're a club. Mrs White happens to be a crib card sharp. She just read us our pedigree."

"A cribbage club?" She eyed me for three beats, then filled our glasses. "Not much surprises me anymore, not even Mitchell's" - she raised two fingers to form air quotes - "'business initiatives', but *that?*" She shook her head. "I wouldn't have picked it in five millennia."

I thought back to the moment Mrs White drove into the police station carpark, the certainty and accompanying incredulity that she was the other perpetrator. "Me either. Who knows? It could be the start of something great." I had my doubts, but there was no denying the fact the three of us forming a united lying front to cover mirrored acts of vigilantism was something remarkable. That because of a shared outrage and need for justice, tenuous bonds had already stretched out between us and found a hand hold.

I pulled out my debit card.

"On the house. To mark the occasion of your club. Besides, I'm hardly going to be mortgage free by the end of the night. It won't make much difference."

I looked around me. The pub was Monday-night quiet. Australian football flickered on the tele, four hardened drinkers attempted to wear their arse grooves down a little further into their stools, and a group of three women looking like they'd come in for a quick one after being released from the work day, sipped wine and laughed.

Flick had sat Mrs White down at a table near the gas-lit and faux-wood open fire, and was engaged in an enthusiastic one-way conversation. Her fingers fluttered and her arms danced as she worked her mouth and body together to impart a story Mrs White looked wholly disinterested in. Her features were gathered in their usual scowl, and her eyes shifted feverishly between Flick's face and the blue flames of the fire.

As I approached them, balancing our glasses within the triangle of my hands, Flick punctuated the end of her story with a two-handed slap on the table top and Mrs White jumped.

Flick looked up at me as I set the glasses down. "I think I've just recruited my first taker in my betting league. Jean agrees on the superiority of a competition based on statistically informed odds, rather than the arbitrary whims of someone who could give a shit."

"Right." I eased myself into a chair. "I see you've mastered the power of telepathy."

"The body talks. It's not all about the verbals."

If I was in any doubt, Mrs White took it upon herself to demonstrate just how good she was at making her body talk. She brought her whiskey to her nose, closed her eyes and inhaled like she was sniffing the soft skin of a newborn baby. With her eyes still shut, she drew the glass to her mouth and pressed it to the hard little beak of her lips. The muscles in her throat undulated as she swallowed.

Then her eyes snapped open and locked onto mine. "Don't think because I'm recuperating in your vicinity, I think any more of you, Sadie Quinn."

I suppressed the laugh that bubbled at the top of my lungs. "Oh, I don't. However, I'm happy to admit this afternoon's events mean I think a little more of *you*." I winked at her and whispered, "Car slasher."

Mrs White dropped the hand holding her glass onto the table with a *clunk* and darted her eyes around the room. "Don't address me like I've earned some great honour." Her gaze fell on her glass. "It was a moment of madness. I lost control."

"Yes, and I'm not going to judge you for it." I raised my glass as if toasting her. "You could do with practising at that."

"Losing control?"

"Not judging others."

She eyed the glass in my hand and raised an eyebrow.

I sighed. "I'm not pregnant, and I've never been involved in the porn industry."

Flick, who'd been sucking the Jack Daniel's out of the ends of her hair after a mis-directed hair toss, slapped her palms on the table. "Hold up. What?"

"Mrs White has been paying heed to unsubstantiated tongue-wagging."

"It's not unsubstantiated, Sadie Quinn. That policeman said it."

"Oh, you heard him say it, did you?"

Silence.

"So, you'll use a machete to protest against the tyranny of misogyny, but you'll uphold the destructive forces of the rumour mill?"

Mrs White's lips remained pursed, but her eyes dropped to her drink. "It was a kitchen knife. And a hammer."

Flick folded her arms. "Here I was thinking you were a solid representative of the sisterhood. I'm thinking of revoking your membership."

I sipped my whiskey, let the burn track across my tongue and down my oesophagus to sit warming the emptiness of my stomach.

Mrs White placed both hands around her glass, but she didn't drink from it.

A bray of laughter from the table of women penetrated our mute stand-off.

I knew an apology or an acknowledgement of her ill-judged behaviour would not be forthcoming, but I also knew her silence was as good as one.

Flick looked at me, rolled her eyes, and uncrossed her arms. "Body-spoken apology accepted."

I leant into the table and dropped my head until I was in Mrs White's eyeline. "So. Why'd you do it?"

She blinked at me. "They..." She rotated her glass, then picked it up and swilled it. Taking a large swallow, she returned the drink and her eyes to the table, her mouth a tight, pale slash.

"Let's start with an easier question. Where'd you learn to play?"

She raised her eyes then. "I'm old. I know all the games."

"I bet you do. You a piece of hot sauce. One lick of you and VWOOM." Flick raised her hands in mimicry of a rising flame.

Mrs White looked from her to me. "I have no idea what she's talking about most of the time. Can you interpret what you think I need to know? Leave out the fluff?"

"Sure." I eyed Flick and said nothing.

"Well?" asked Mrs White.

"That was all fluff."

"That was not all fluff. That there was some fancy verbal footwork. I even squeezed in an extended metaphor."

I snorted. "Yes, you did."

"Where'd you learn to play?" Mrs White asked Flick.

"My nan taught me when I was, like, six? Seven? I liked putting the pegs in the little holes, and then it was because of the maths, and then the strategy. I was a fool for it before I'd cut my first adult tooth."

"I played with my uni friends" I said. "One night my flat-mate brought out a crib board and pack of cards and taught us. We were hooked by the second game."

"Fact." Flick raised her hand for a fist bump. "Pulled on to the path to cribbage ninja-ry."

"What do you think we'd have to say we were doing if we didn't all know how to play?" I asked.

"Dogging," said Flick.

I laughed.

Mrs White looked at me questioningly.

"One hundred percent fluff."

A plate of wedges slid across the table to rest between our glasses. "Herc you are ladies. Courtesy of the otherwise idle kitchen. Try and get some food into this one." Manawa nodded at me. "I have yet to convince her she needs feeding to sustain her shifts. See if you have better luck." She turned and headed back towards the bar.

Flick reached for a wedge of potato, and slid it out from beneath a pile of sour cream. A string of melted cheese connected it to the rest of the stack.

As the smell of fried potato teased its way up my nostrils, my stomach, which had been neglected since a late breakfast, listed forward in a slow, painful roll.

"They give you free food on your shifts and you turn them down? Are you loco?" She held the wedge above her head and caught the string on her tongue.

"I eat before I come to work," I lied.

"You haven't eaten since I've been with you this afternoon," she said through her mouthful. "And it's pretty much dinner time. You gotta be a bit hungry."

"Wedges with sour cream and cheese are approximately 240 calories a portion."

Mrs White took a wedge from the side of the plate and dipped it into the small bowl of sweet chilli sauce.

"I know you think I should know what that means, but all I hear is wa wa." Flick raised a hand and opened and closed it like a talking mouth.

"It *means* I can't afford to take an energy hit that big."

"Why?" Flick reached for another wedge.

"Look at me," I hissed.

Flick leaned back in her seat, her chin low and her brows bunched together. "I see you, girlfriend. You look just fine to me."

"Well, I don't feel fine."

"I know you've got this whole 'circus freak' thing going on, poisoning your sense of womanhood. You think skipping meals empowers you?"

"Yes." It was the one thing I could control when I had absolutely no say over my genetics.

"And how's that working out for you? Does being hungry make you feel less big and ugly?"

I didn't say anything.

"Didn't think so. That there - your lack of tongue movement - is some loud-ass body talk."

Mrs White sat upright, her face slack with incredulity. "You're not ugly. You're not remotely ugly."

"You know what the moist crew called me?" I looked each of them in the eye. "A transvestite. They *moo-ed* at me."

Flick halted her chewing.

Mrs White sucked her cheeks in, pushing her lips into a

tight white circle. "I might have committed the worst sins of my life in the last forty-eight hours, but you know what? I have absolutely no regrets. If He doesn't understand that," she said, pointing at the ceiling, "I'll give Him another think on Judgement Day."

"Amen, sister!" Flick raised a hand for a high five and Mrs White eyed it suspiciously. Undeterred, Flick removed one of Mrs White's hands from around her glass, pulled it into the air and slapped it, before carefully returning it to the glass.

Then she turned to me. "The sooner you love the body you're in, the sooner shit like that will slide off you like Teflon."

"Thank you, Oprah. I'm well aware of the theory. The application's difficult when you've been told your whole life you're abnormal."

"*I* haven't told you that."

Mrs White opened her mouth, then closed it again, no doubt recollecting having called me a "freakish girl."

"Omission might as well be the same thing. Every single comment thrown at me has been negative. It's either judgement, veiled judgement, or silence. No one, nobody at any point in my life has explicitly made me feel that I wasn't wanting in some way."

Almost no one. Callum's words at the Ag Day echoed in my head. "I see a woman with flesh in all the right places." I knew he meant it, even if I couldn't quite believe that he did. The knowledge of it sat glowing behind my breast bone, warming the swirling fog of disdainful words and looks I'd collected over the years. I ignored it, choosing to poke at the wound I'd carried for almost a lifetime.

"Self-love is something I'd love to be able to just turn on. Flick a switch and *boom* - positive body image - but I've got nothing to work with. I'm coming from a place that's less than zero, and all that self-affirming energy *I've* got to create. It's not so bloody easy."

"I call bullshit. I don't think you're even trying. Covering up your body in black dresses? Telling yourself you're too big to deserve to eat? I bet you've never stood in front of the mirror and told yourself you're beautiful, that you're perfect the way you are." Flick leaned forward and placed a palm on either side of my skull. Lowering her voice, she said, "I see inside your head, sister. You reflect that negative shit back at yourself like you some kind of dumb parrot."

Indignation flared under my scalp and crackled along my skin, its potency sharpened by the sudden and certain realisation that she was right.

I leaned away from her, sliding my head out of her reach. How dare she reach into my mind and read it better than I had myself? "You have no fucking clue, Flick."

"Yeah?" She took a sip of whiskey, her eyes never leaving mine. "I had a brief stopover in Idiotsville a couple of months back and bumped uglies with one of Layton's friends. Layton's the douchebag that owns the car. And cause he owns a car, and cause I was willing to sleep with one of his boys, he expected me to sleep with him. I said hail no, cause he's a troll with chronic halitosis. And then I was a fat-ass slut. Said I was so ugly he couldn't even crack a fat. Said it would be like trying to stuff a marshmallow into a piggy bank."

I was quiet for a moment. "We should have set fire to the fucking thing."

"Yeah. Those stealth bombers really let me down."

"Your pube sonar not send you accurate information?"

"My pubes ain't got no freaky bat sonar. They got sixth sense. Sixth sense don't work with heat seeking missiles."

I wondered if my pubes would stand on end when in close proximity to Callum's heat seeking missile, and with a fluttering of my insides I had absolutely no doubt that they would.

Mrs White smacked her lips as if readying herself to say something, and I guiltily cast the thought from my mind.

"Those -" she paused and said "boys" like she'd swallowed a teaspoon of earwax, "- followed me home one afternoon after I told them to mind their language. They were in the car park of the supermarket, and cursing left right and centre." She looked up from her drink, her tone defensive. "There were children around. I was within my right."

I nodded encouragingly.

"Word, sis."

"I'd walked to town that day and on my way back, they followed me, driving along behind and calling me awful, vicious names, yelling out things they wanted to do to my -" she leaned over glass and whispered, "- 'haghole'. I have never been more humiliated in my life."

"You know what?" I said. "Maybe we deserve a toast. Maybe what we've done has made them review their life choices and we've saved other women from being subjected to that horrific behaviour."

"What should we toast to?" asked Mrs White.

"Divine intervention," said Flick. "I look around me and all I see is strong specimens of divine womanhood."

I nodded in assent and we raised our glasses, chorusing, "Divine intervention."

After a silence punctuated with a masculine cackle from a table across the room, I said, "Mrs White, can I ask you a question?"

Her eyes widened slightly in alarm, and I rushed the words out before she had pause to say "no".

"Has Dad asked you to spy on Poppy and me for him?"

She blinked. "Spy? Why would he want anybody to spy on you?"

"I take it that's a 'no'?"

"I haven't talked to your father in over ten years. And spying is not a very Christian-sounding pastime."

"No," I agreed. "Somebody living near Poppy is doing it, though, at my father's bidding."

"Why?"

"Because Dad thinks Poppy has dementia and he's evidence gathering so he can put him in a home."

"And does he?"

I sighed. "I don't know. Maybe? I think 'yes', but I know a rest home or a hospice is not where he needs to be."

"I'm so sorry to hear that. My Dennis had early onset. It's a terrible, terrible thing. But, you know you can help slow its progress?"

I raised my chin to look at her more squarely. "No."

"Get some stuff into him that's good for the brain. Omega 3 foods, like fish, and keep him mentally active. Crosswords, creative stuff like drawing or making something."

"OK," I said, thinking that Poppy was already plenty creative. He played all the time. But perhaps hanging out with an imaginary friend wasn't the right kind of creative.

Before I could ask her more about fending off a mental decline, the town's air raid siren, re-purposed to alert the volunteer fire brigade when there was an emergency, wound up to a full-throated whine.

One of the women at the table of three, pulled out her phone, peered at it, then sprinted for the door.

Flick's eyes widened and her lips parted slightly as she followed the woman's progress across the room. "Awesome," she breathed. Then she stood up and shouted, "You got a membership, sister," as the double doors swung closed.

"Sadie?" Manawa called from behind the bar. "You need to get going." She pointed into the air and flicked her eyes to the ceiling to indicate the now winding down siren. "The address they're heading to is Gerry's."

I didn't need to give any thought to how Manawa knew, considering the extent of her pulse-fingering in the town. My lizard brain had me out the door, keys in hand, before my sapiens one caught up.

CHAPTER THIRTEEN

THE FIRE TRUCK pulled into Poppy's driveway just before I did.

Above us, thick black smoke billowed in folds and whorls into the powder blue sky.

I tracked its path to the source and released the breath I'd been holding since I'd wheel-spinned my way out of the pub car park.

It was the garage.

Six firefighters swaddled in protective gear shifted and danced around each other in their attempt to reel out hoses.

Inside the glowing structure of the iron-clad garage, my car rocked under the force of water. It was already blackened, its windows cracked and blown, the paint charred and blistered.

A wave of pity for its undignified end crested under my breastbone, only to be replaced by a frigid backwash of fear. The car, the garage was empty of humans and goats, wasn't it?

My "Poppy?" cracked on its release from my throat.

One of the fire fighters turned. "He's in the house with

instructions to put towels at the bottom of external doors. Make sure he's closed all his windows, will you?"

I ran towards the back steps and stopped on a "wait!".

"Is there any fuel in that car?"

I shook my head and continued up the steps. As I pushed against the back door, the towel at its base *shlicked* across the vinyl floor.

"Poppy?"

"Ring-side seat," drifted from somewhere within the bowels of the house. "Bring the popcorn with you."

I headed for my room. Its only window was the closest one to the garage and despite its camellia-obscured outlook, would have the best view.

Poppy knelt on the spare bed, his elbows on the window sill and his cheeks propped in his hands.

Obi-Wan stood beside him. When she saw me, she bounded from the bed with a bleat and gently butted my hand.

"Bloody good entertainment. We should make this an annual event. Next year it's your turn to set the garage on fire."

The Virgin peered at him. Her expression flickered between disapproval and bridled amusement with the shadows thrown by the shifting figures of the fire fighters.

"How did you set the garage on fire, Poppy?"

A sigh. "It was the marbles."

"Which marbles?"

"Obi-Wan and I turned your car into a secret clubhouse, because she can't play in the fort, but your car's already dogmeat, so I figured you wouldn't mind if she chewed it up a little more."

"A clubhouse?" I positioned myself beside him to watch the progress outside. Obi-Wan pushed her head into my palm and I scratched behind her ear. "What do you do in there besides eat upholstery?"

"I can't tell you. It's *secret*. It's a club members only thing."

"Right." I leaned towards him and whispered, "I take it you play with marbles?"

"No." Poppy looked at me like the marbles in question were ones I'd lost. "You can't roll a marble in there. I had my marbles lined up on the dashboard with the toe breaker cat's eye Eddie gave me at the start of the line up, going all the way down to my pee wee milky way."

"And the garage door was open?"

Poppy shifted his gaze to the window again and said with resignation, "The garage door was open. It's the hottest day we've had since winter."

"Yep." I ran a hand across my face.

"Sun would have hit the cat's eye and refracted off the others."

"I take it you weren't in the car the time?"

Poppy shook his head. "Must have been smouldering away for a while."

I knew exactly how this would look to people on the outside. A befuddled elderly person not remembering to be careful, to turn the element of the stove off, to keep the kerosene rag away from the kerosene bottle. It was just the kind of thing Dad and Uncle Peter needed to happen to get what they wanted.

My back pocket vibrated. I didn't need to look at it to know who it was. Dad's informer would have rung him as soon as the fire truck swung into the drive.

I let it ring out and when it immediately rang again, I took it out of my pocket and turned it off.

An explosion rattled the window frame and the figures outside hunched reflexively.

Poppy "yee-haw"ed like an elated cowboy. "There goes the jerry can. It'll be the paint cans next. They'll blow like a pot of popping corn."

I imagined the inside of the garage awash with the vibrancy of a Jackson Pollock painting and placed a hand on my brow as if my inability to find any of this fun or exciting was the result of a malady. "Thank God you had the foresight not to have an inbuilt garage."

Laying a hand on Poppy's bony shoulder, I nodded towards the fire truck. "They might be here a while. I'll make some dinner. You want anything else? Stiff drink?"

Poppy smacked his lips. "Bring me a can of bitter from the fridge. There's soup on the stove. Just needs heating."

BY THE TIME Poppy and I had sipped the soup from our mugs, the sky had edged into indigo and the fire had reduced to a smoulder.

A figure slid past the truck and stopped just outside the beam of the truck's lights to talk to one of the fire fighters. "Who's that?" Poppy asked.

My heart registered it was Callum before my brain did and it galloped like a bolting horse. I could tell that gait anywhere, the fall of his long, lean limbs, the ease with which he carried himself.

"Why is *he* here? Poppy growled. "This isn't a bloody police matter. No reason to turn it into a complete arsing spectacle."

"I'll go out and talk to him," I said, turning for the door.

"Tell him to bugger off. Save the drama for something that deserves it."

"I'm not telling him to bugger off, Poppy. He's probably just concerned. Keep Obi-Wan in here, will you?" I pushed her nose away from me as I edged around the door and she bleated in protest. "I'll be back soon," I promised her. "No walking through walls."

I stopped on the top step of the back porch as an un-uniformed Callum approached the bottom one. He peered up at me, his expression apprehensive. I wasn't sure if it was as a result of concern, or uncertainty about being near me so soon after our last encounter.

"I thought you'd be wanting at least a hemisphere of space from me after today."

He quirked his lips under a frown. "There was a bit of chatter on the radio tonight. I can still be concerned about you even if I want to throttle you."

I descended the two remaining steps. "I take it you're talking about the emergency frequency, and Gerry Quinn's garage catching fire is not all over Talk Back."

Callum snorted and turned to watch the progress of the fire fighting. "No doubt it'll be all over Tokawai's version in about -" He pulled his phone out of his back pocket. "- Five more minutes. Everyone will have heard the siren."

"Shall we get deck chairs and watch from the comfort of the lawn?"

"I think they've got it all under control now. Just making sure there's no hot spots." Callum swivelled his head towards me. "Grant tells me Gerry thinks his marbles on the dash of your un-roadworthy car did it."

"Guess you won't be arresting me for not having a WoF now."

"No. Though I'm sure it won't be long before you find something else for me to arrest you for. I'll give you forty-eight hours."

I nodded as if his assessment was fair. "It *is* only Monday."

Callum's face broadened into a smile.

The garage groaned and cracked and a portion of the roof collapsed onto the car.

I took an involuntary step backwards, forgetting there was nowhere to go but up, and grabbed Callum's arm as he reached out to prevent me from falling. The warmth of him seared into my palms and I let go before the fabric separating our skin burst into flames.

Callum shifted his eyes from mine to the garage and asked, "How's Gerry?"

"Wholly unconcerned. Thinks this is a great lark."

"Do you want me to speak to him?"

"No. He thinks you're unnecessarily getting involved. Though he didn't put it quite so politely."

Callum put his hands in his pockets and chuckled into his shoes. "I won't disturb him, then. How about a cup of tea and you can tell me all about where you learned to play crib?" He turned and lowered himself onto the top step. "I'll let you know if you miss anything good."

I saluted his back and went inside to put the jug on.

Poppy was in the bathroom brushing his teeth, while Obi-Wan watched from the bathtub.

"Are you calling it a night already?"

"Nothing left to see," he said through a mouthful of foam. "I'm gonna head to bed. It's been a big day."

As I bid him goodnight, he spat the remainder of his toothpaste out and requested I do "the thank you thing", like it was some kind of performance reserved for the initiated.

I assured him "the thank you thing" was something I

excelled at and went in search of a blanket, a small goat hot on my heels.

When I returned to the back step, Callum sat facing the backyard and the dark expanse of hills behind. He patted the concrete beside him without turning around.

Spring may have been steadily advancing towards summer, but the night was clear of any insulating cloud that might keep the heat of the day in. The blanket was to keep the parts of us warm the tea couldn't spread its heat to.

It worked. A little too efficiently. The fissure of air between our bodies steamed and crackled in the growing warmth. I wanted at once to shift away from its intensity and to press my side against his, to step straight into the flame.

I couldn't bear the thought of Callum retreating. Knowing he appreciated the way I was made was enough. I didn't want to do anything that might risk having that affirmation ripped out from under me.

I sipped my tea and waited for him to ask the inevitable questions that must have arisen during the course of this afternoon's events.

They didn't come. At least not yet. Callum appeared to be waiting for something, too.

Obi-Wan appeared around the corner of the house, returning from bleating at the reversing truck, like a dog seeing off trespassers.

She made a bee-line for me, head bent for a scratch, and tried to nuzzle her way between us. "Get off," I laughed. "Go bury a stick or something."

She bleated her disappointment and headed out onto a lawn made grey in the starlight.

"Don't go in the garage."

On the other side of the house from the blackened

remains of the garage crouched Callum's childhood home. The windows glowed wanly, the curtains long since drawn against the cool of the night.

I raised my cup in its direction. "Do you ever miss living there?"

Callum turned the handle of his mug from him and nestled the body of it between his palms. "Nope. The house has been done up now, but it was a bit of a shit hole when we lived there. Landlady wasn't aware of her obligations, but the rent was cheap, I guess."

"Why'd you come back?"

"To Tokawai? Believe it or not, I like this place. I like the pace, the fact that everybody knows each other, looks out for each other. Most of the time. It'd be a good place for raising kids, if I wanted some."

"You're not sure?"

"I like the idea of it, but the other person has to be on board too. I wouldn't consider it if I didn't have a rock-solid relationship. I've seen first-hand how hard it is to be a solo parent." He brought the cup to his mouth and sipped at it twice before asking, "You want kids?"

"I don't know." I looked away from him. "Parenting is not a strong suit in our family. From what Dad says, Poppy wasn't much of a father, which meant Dad didn't have a good model to work off." I left the rest unsaid, knowing Callum had already been privy to a part of that picture. "I have no confidence I'd be able to raise children in an environment that won't strip away their self-esteem."

"That's why you need a solid partnership. You work on being good parents together, support each other through negotiating the tricky stuff."

I offered a non-committal grunt.

"What about your mother? Did she balance out your dad's failings?"

"A bit. She's loving, but sees material markers as proof of success - academic achievement, being in the top sports team, having a profitable business - not happiness. She's gentrified. She's never known anything else, so I don't really blame her."

"I'm sorry you missed out on that. My Mum's a big proponent of 'follow your heart'."

Having momentarily forgotten, I was again acutely aware of the lack of distance between us. That if we both turned our heads, all we'd need to do was lean forward a fraction and our mouths would meet.

I dared not look at him. A small flicker of hope that his last statement was a loaded one flared behind my belly button, but I didn't want to read in his face that I was wrong.

I pulled myself out of my awkwardness by changing the subject to arguably more dangerous territory.

My near arrest.

"Why'd you pick on us three? There must be numerous women the moist boys have offended."

Callum snorted. "Educated guess."

"*Wild assumption*. How could you be educated about it if you had no evidence as to who the perpetrators were?"

"Because -" he counted off on his fingers. "- It happened at your place of work, you had the opportunity, and you had motive."

"What motive?" Surely my brief comment to Callum about the offence they'd caused me wouldn't have been enough to suggest a violent level of loathing.

"They upset you, and you've been under a lot of stress in

the last few days. *And* you're wholly unpredictable. Perfect combination for some revenge-seeking."

"Tenuous."

"Educated."

"What about the others? I mean, Flick, maybe. But *Mrs White?*"

"They're the only ones who've laid a formal complaint about that crew."

I was quiet for a moment. "God. Why are women so afraid of making a fuss?"

"Because that behaviour has been normalised. The old wolf whistle from the construction site, the slut-calling to women in short skirts, the whole 'you asked for it' mentality. Women have been conditioned to accept it, regardless of whether it offends them. To be honest, those guys had it coming. If it wasn't you, it would have been someone else."

Obi-Wan bleated from somewhere in the vegetable patch and he raised his head at the noise. "Can I ask what they did to you?" he said, still looking into the darkness.

His jaw flexed as I told him.

Eventually, he turned his head to meet my eye and said, "It's not very often I feel this way, and I would *never* say this to anyone else, Sadie, but -" He paused and drew a breath. "- I don't blame you. It's incredibly unprofessional of me to say so, but I don't."

I offered him the flicker of a smile and reached across our knees to squeeze his hand.

Then I played my part. "But it wasn't us, officer."

He looked away then, breaking the spell. "Ha! To be fair it was pretty much guesswork, but when you came up with that crib story, all doubt disappeared to the same place as your honesty. You wouldn't have needed to scrape together any alibi, let alone one that farcical, if you all had nothing to do with it."

"It wasn't farcical."

Callum leaned back and peered at me, his brows pushed together in an expression of dubiousness. "Of all the people likely to hang out, and over a game that hasn't been played this side of the Napoleonic wars? Come on!" He shook his head. "And yet I still couldn't pin it on you. Outplayed by a prospective assassin, a sheep stylist, and a pensioner."

"I want to agree with you, but you might use it against me later."

Callum leaned over and nudged me with his shoulder. "Where did you learn to play?"

"Believe it or not it was a game we played in our flat at Uni. We couldn't afford board games, so we played card games. One of my flatmates knew how to play."

"So it's not a dying art. The crib gods will be proud of your representation this afternoon."

"Are you trying to lull me into a false sense of security so I'll confess? Flick thought that was your game plan. Said you were like an after-dinner mint. Sweet on the outside, Himmler on the inside."

Callum threw back his head and laughed, which pulled the blanket taut and me into him. Our shoulders bumped and the tepid remains of his tea slopped onto my thigh.

"Oh God. I'm so sorry." Callum lay his hand over the patch of damp fabric. The heat from his palm zip-lined to my groin. "Don't make me laugh and I won't soil you."

"Okay. How would you like me to be? Dull, or serious, or both? I can do a passable impression of Severus Snape."

"You know what? Can you remind me of the story of

Jean White's labial skin tag? I really enjoyed that the first time around."

It was my turn to shake the blanket with laughter.

Callum put the heel of his cup-free hand to an eyeball. "No matter how hard I try, I can't unimagine it."

"You pulling us into the station at the same time was worth it if just for that. It proved she's human underneath the sour exterior."

"Aha! So you admit you haven't hung out together before."

"We hang out for the game. Not the company. It makes beating her easier."

Callum "mm-hmm"ed doubtfully and I raised my head to peer up at the night sky. "You know one of the things I love about being here?"

"Inflicting pain on me?"

"The lack of light pollution," I said, ignoring him and he, too, raised his face to the stars.

"You never get a sense of the volume, the depth of the Milky Way in the city. Here, it's like a solid ribbon of stars you could reach up and pull from the sky."

Callum turned his head to look at me. "Are you...thinking of hanging around?"

I shrugged. "There's nothing to go back to, and Poppy needs me more than anything."

"You know, I never thought Gerry would need protecting. He's impervious to everything." Then Callum grunted and leaned forward, pulling his phone out of his pocket. The screen showed a number. No name.

"I'm so sorry. I better take this." He pressed the screen to accept the call and held the phone up to his ear. "Callum McClintock." He listened for a few seconds, threw a glance at me, then said, "How did you get this number, Alan?"

All the cold of the night air seemed to rush in around the edges of the blanket.

Dad.

I shook my head at him.

"I see. This is a private number. I'd prefer it not be used for police business. In future, please call the station number and you'll be connected with Turangi dispatch. They can take care of your query from there. However, I have been to check on the property in question. Everyone's fine. It was a minor garage fire. Nothing to worry about."

He listened for a few more seconds. "That's right. Have a good evening, Alan." He hung up and looked at me. "I'm guessing there's a good reason your phone's turned off."

I sighed. "Dad's got someone - a neighbour - spying on us, letting him know if there's anything about Poppy's behaviour he should be worried about. Or rather, some evidence he can add to the Poppy needing to be in a home argument. I just couldn't face talking to him, or having another argument about it."

"But you think Gerry has dementia?"

"It doesn't mean it can't be managed in his own home. Where he's happiest."

"You know, I love that about you," Callum said, and my heart flip-flopped before I knew the context for his affection. "Your concern for Gerry's state of mind, his level of fulfilment in his old age. I don't love the paperwork you make for me."

"If I can help make his final years happy ones after what I suspect was a lifetime of depression, then of course I'm going to do that."

"Even if it means running in with the law?"

"I figure I've got nothing left to lose."

Callum swayed away from me momentarily and resettled a little closer. "Jesus. Things are that bad for you?"

I looked into my cup as if the milky dregs held an answer. "I've stopped thinking of it that way. I now see it as giving me a whole lot of freedom."

He frowned. "But the church thing. You looked terrified when I had you up about it."

"He was going to do it anyway. If I was there, it meant I had some control over how it played out."

This time when Callum turned his head towards me, he didn't move it back to create a small amount of personal space. His breath feathered my cheek. "What is it about Gerry that makes it impossible for you to say 'no' to?"

I swivelled my head to face him. Now our words were issued in the space of a shared breath. "The fact that I think I'm the only one of his family who loves him."

He held my gaze for eight of my rapid heartbeats, then his eyes shifted to my mouth and he leaned towards me and touched his lips to mine.

They were softer than I imagined them to be and the kiss seemed fragile, something that might be taken away as quickly as it was given. My entire being focused on this precious press of skin and my world became the warmth of his breath, the cinnamon of his shaving cream.

The sound of liquid hitting concrete brought me to my senses.

Callum withdrew his head with a smile and I righted my teacup.

"I didn't think anything could unsettle you. Apart from the threat of arrest."

"Don't look so smug. I'm just out of practice."

"Oh, it's just lack of practice that had you so out of your mind you forgot how to hold a cup of tea?"

"Right." I removed his cup from his hand. "I think that's all the practice I need. Don't forget to collect your ego before you head home."

With a laugh, Callum took both cups from me, placed them on the ground, then cupped my face.

I was ready for the next kiss. Ready for Callum to part his lips, to draw his breath in and feel the cool night air rush to fill the vacuum between our mouths.

I leaned into him, sealing the gap, tasting the tea on his lips.

When our tongues met, the stars above us swarmed through my veins to form a constellation low in my belly. They swirled and regrouped, expanding and contracting with my pulse.

Callum placed a hand in my hair and ran the fingertips of his other lightly down my back. The heat of the stars shifted to settle heavily between my thighs.

I laid my fingers against his cheek, the stubble prickling my skin. I traced his eyebrow with my thumb, ran a fingertip over the hollow of his eye socket, tracked the hard edge of his jaw with the back of my fingers.

Callum smiled against my lips. "You're so tender."

I wanted to ask if the unsaid half of the sentence was *for such a big girl,* and immediately regretted it. Callum was not that man. Callum looked at me and saw someone with curves he wanted to run his hands over.

The idea, the hope that I turned Callum on so much, he wanted to have sex with me, was heady enough to send moisture wicking through my knickers.

I tried to shift closer. I needed to press my body against his, feel his heat.

My kneecap *clack*ed against his and he grunted.

"You're too far away," I groaned against his lips. "Stupid knees."

"You know there's an easy fix."

"Amputation?"

"Moving to somewhere a little more comfortable." Callum traced the curve of my neck with his lips, the touch like a feather.

My nipples tingled. "I can think of somewhere," tumbled out of my mouth in a rush.

"Is it the same place as I'm thinking?"

"Well, the back seat of my car's out of the equation, and the lawn's covered in Obi-Wan landmines."

"I think we can upgrade on both of those options." Callum found the hem of my dress and shifted his hand beneath it, running it up the length of my thigh.

I shivered. "My bed. Let's go to my bed."

"Awesome suggestion."

I placed a final kiss on his lips, then I stood and pulled him up after me. "This way," I said, moving towards the back door.

Callum remained where he was. "I just -". He ran a hand through his hair. "Can you show me where the toilet is? I need to recalibrate and get a little more blood pumping into my brain."

THE VIRGIN GAZED down upon me, her curved mouth redder, fuller. I eyed her suspiciously, not trusting her lack of censure.

As if reading my mind, her eyebrow twitched.

I raised a finger. "I don't need your approval." Grabbing a blanket off the spare bed, I threw it over her. "And I definitely don't need you cheering from the sidelines."

The toilet flushed.

I turned around and faced the room, feeling large under the glare of the room's central light. I turned on the lamp beside my bed, faced it away so that I wouldn't be spot lit, and flicked off the main light.

Callum poked his head around the door, smiled and closed it softly behind him. "Gerry's not going to come bursting through the door with a gun?"

"I doubt it. He sleeps like the dead, but it's probably best to lock it."

Callum turned and flicked the small knob under the door handle.

When he faced me again, he pointed at the shrouded figure. "What's that?"

"A statue of the Virgin Mary."

"Huh." He cocked his head to one side.

"Don't ask. I have no idea. It's been in this room for as long as I can remember."

"It's creepy."

"It's creepier without the blanket. I have to sleep with her watching me every night. I draw the line at having her watching me have sex."

"You brought me in here to have sex with you?"

I walked over to him, grabbed his hands and pulled him into the centre of the room. "I can teach you to play crib if you'd prefer." I raised one of his hands, undid the button on his cuff, and, rolling back the material, kissed his wrist.

"Tempting," he said, as I raised the other hand. His fingers curled around my cheek as I kissed the pale skin. "What's the thing you say when you're scoring the jack?"

I stepped closer and undid the top button of his shirt. The blonde hair beneath his clavicle shimmered in the glow of the lamp. "One for his nob." I pressed my lips against the freshly exposed skin.

Callum drew in a shaky breath. "I had a suspicion crib was kinky."

The next button revealed the neckline of a white singlet. I set to work on the rest of the buttons and pushed his hands away when they crept into my hair at the base of my skull.

"I think Mrs White is one person. Jean is entirely another." I walked around him, tugging his shirt free of one arm. I ran my teeth over the smooth skin of his shoulder, kissed a mole at the base of his neck, and freed the shirt, trailing my fingers over his other shoulder and slipping them beneath the fabric of the singlet to feel the hot skin of his chest, just above his heart. He smelled of wood smoke and Sunlight Soap, like he'd hand washed his clothes and hung them to dry over the fire.

"God, this is torture. Can I touch you yet?"

I pulled the bottom of the singlet free of his trousers and ran my fingertips from his belly button out towards his hips. "No."

"I'm going to have to at some point, you know. That's kind of how sex works."

"I thought you wanted me to teach you how to play crib." I tugged the singlet over his head and enclosed a nipple in my mouth. Nipping it between my teeth, I ran my tongue across it and inhaled, sucking cool air over its tip.

Callum hissed and his hands were in my hair again. "Sadie?"

"Hmm?"

I trailed my fingers down between his breast bone towards his belly button and followed with my tongue.

"You have to tell me so I can stop feeling sexually inadequate."

"Tell you what?"

"What 'a momentary lapse of judgement' means."

Ah, yes. That old elephant. I stopped and straightened up.

Taking Callum's hand, I brought it to my breast and stepped forward to kiss him. His hand squeezed. "I was never in the porn industry," I whispered between kisses. "You misheard."

Callum's fingers relaxed, but the heat from his palm seared across my nipple. After a moment he whispered back, "What did I hear, then?"

"I'll tell you one day. I have other things I want to do with my tongue right now," I said, pulling at his belt buckle.

A little "ah" escaped Callum's lips as I freed the tongue of the belt from the prong. The belt pulled from his belt loops with a *shwip*. I dropped it to the floor behind me.

Callum stepped forward, wrapped his arms around me and pulled me into the hard front of him. "I need to touch you all over. If you keep teasing me, I'll explode."

"Metaphorically?"

"I can't guarantee that." His fingers worked at the bow at the back of my dress, freeing the ties that cinched in the waist. "Let me see you."

A hand gripped my heart, forcing it into stillness. "I don't..." I stepped out of his reach.

Callum stared at me for a beat before stretching forward and pulling me back to him. "You don't want me to see you?" He said into my hair.

I shook my head. "I've never been completely naked in front of anyone."

"But you've had sex?"

"Yes."

Callum's chest expanded and contracted three times before he said, "I don't want to push you, but it's okay to be vulnerable right now, to trust me. There's nothing under your dress that's going to stop me wanting you. In fact, I guarantee everything under there is going to make me want you more."

I wanted that. God how I wanted that, to feel that my body was desirable, to have him touch me everywhere.

"Trust me, Sadie," he whispered into my ear.

I raised my head and met his eyes.

Then I lifted my arms.

Callum smiled and dropped his mouth to mine as he gathered the fabric at my hips to pull the dress free.

The cool air of the room cloaked my skin. I fought the urge to wrap my arms around myself, to turn away, but Callum's stillness prevented me. He looked down at me, all of me, his chest heaving. When he eventually raised his eyes, they were dark with desire. "You still have too many clothes on."

I clasped my hands to my belly as if to keep my support briefs in place. My flesh looked different without them, more, rounder, fatter. I wasn't sure I was ready for anybody to see the truth of my body, not even Callum.

He ran a finger up the length of them. "Is this your Captain Thunderpants uniform?"

I grimaced, knowing how extraordinarily unsexy they were. It wasn't like I'd had a better option had I the benefit of seeing an imminent sex-coloured future when dressing that morning. I'd never worn a pair of lacy knickers in my life.

Callum pulled at the waistband and released it so that it slapped against my skin. "Kinky."

"Don't tease me."

"Oh, I'm not. These pants are doing curious things to my blood circulation."

"I call bullshit," I said as I undid the top buttons on his jeans.

"I can think of a very good way to find out." Callum moved his mouth from my lips to the swell of my breast, kissing his way to the edge of the bra fabric. As I released the final button on his fly, he pulled the strap down, exposing my nipple. He ran a thumb over its pinched end and bit my neck on the soft skin beneath my ear.

I had intended to roll his jeans over his buttocks, but all sense, all thought, all coordination left me as he released the other breast.

Shifting his hands to my back to undo the clasp, he moved his mouth to my right breast, taking in a large mouthful and running his tongue around my areola. I gasped as he sucked, a pull that was at once an ache and an electric charge.

Freeing the bra of my arms, he moved to the other breast, flicking the nipple with the end of his tongue, tugging it with his teeth while his hands moved under the waist of my underpants and over my buttocks, exposing them.

"Wait," I said, pulling him back to my mouth. "Let me see you." I tugged at the top of his jeans, pushing them down his thighs and he stepped out of them. The front of his trunks fought to contain the swollen flesh beneath and I wanted to feel the thickness of it in my hands, hold it in my mouth.

As if sensing the urgency of my need, Callum took my hand and slipped it between the elastic of his briefs and the feverish skin of his stomach. Guiding me to his cock, he stuttered out a breath as I wrapped my fingers around its girth, slid my palm up the hot skin, stroked the tip with my thumb.

I sucked Callum's rasped, "Jesus," into my mouth. Placing my lips and tongue against his, I invited him to reciprocate. To explore my hidden places with his fingers.

I gasped when he found the swollen nub of my clit. The contact was a shock, a delicious charge of energy. He slipped his fingers deeper, dipping them into my wetness before extracting them, and using my arousal to slide against my sensitive flesh.

With an "uh", I threw my head back and the movement pressed my breasts against his chest, our bodies skin to skin for the first time.

"I want to taste you," Callum whispered against my neck.

I didn't have the brain power to offer an articulate reply, but it sounded good to me. "Yes," I exhaled with a hiss.

He pushed my underwear down and I stepped out of them as he climbed out of his and stepped away from me.

Callum's eyes swept over me, his features soft, the want clear. His chest still heaved when his gaze returned to my face. "You are so beautiful, Sadie. Don't let anyone else make you think otherwise."

A tsunami of warmth crested and crashed over me and with every beat of my heart, light pulsed in my chest. In that moment, I believed him without a shadow of a doubt.

And Callum? Callum was glorious. His muscles and sinews were etched against olive skin made milky by a winter-long lack of sun. His lean frame was long enough to wrap around me, his hips narrow enough to fit perfectly between my thighs.

"I am so going to break you."

"I very much doubt that, but I'm happy for you to do your best." Callum's gaze fell to my single bed. "This is what we've got to work with? I can't pull my signature move on such a small canvas."

I eyed my bed and entertained a vision of us pin-balling off the wall and on to the floor, waking Poppy. "You're right. It'd be like trying to make love in a coffin."

I leaned over and began to pull the bedding off. Turning, I spread the blankets over the carpet. Callum did the same with the bedding from the spare bed, laying the duvet over the top.

When the blankets were smoothed down, I grabbed the pillow from my bed, lay down and propped myself up on one arm. I watched Callum arrange the pillows on his side.

"What?" he said as he mirrored my pose.

"I'm waiting for you to make your signature move now you've got a larger canvas. Are you gathering your strength?"

Callum offered me a slow smile and ran his eyes down my body. "I'm considering my options."

"Oh, you have more than one?"

"I have a whole library. Just working my way through the index."

I threw my head back and laughed. "You are so full of shit."

Callum's smile turned to a grin. "Yes I am." Then the grin dimmed. "I'm actually a little nervous."

My voice dropped to a whisper. "Me too."

We eyed each other for one, two, three seconds. Then we scrabbled to close the distance, our mouths pressing, tasting, savouring, our bodies finding purchase, legs on hips, hands on shoulder blades.

Callum's erection pressed against my pubic bone and I shifted my hips forward, pinning him between my legs.

He rocked his pelvis in response, his shaft pushing against my clit. With the fourth grind, Callum croaked, "Condom."

I licked his throat. "I've got some." Bite. "In my toilet bag."

Callum groaned as if he'd been told to swim to Australia. "Where's your toilet bag?"

I ran my tongue over his bottom lip. "In the drawer under my bed."

"Do you think you can get one in five seconds?"

"No. But I'll try for ten."

Callum kissed me. A slow, melt-your-legs-into-pools-of-nothingness type of kiss. Then he pushed me from him. "Go."

As he started counting, I got to my hands and knees and swivelled to face the bed.

Callum hissed in a "two" as I turned and revealed my centre to him.

I yanked the draw open, pulled the toilet bag towards me and unzipped it.

On "five", the pressure of a hand on the inside of each of my knees encouraged me to shift them apart.

On "six" I unzipped the compartment with the squares of blue foil and the hands moved to my hips, tugging me downwards.

Callum's "seven" whispered across my folds of flesh in a hot rush and I lost all ability to think beyond that single point of exquisite sensation. As his lips enclosed my clit, I gasped out an "oh", dropping the condom I'd retrieved and gathering the sheet covering the bed's mattress in my fists.

His tongue circled the swollen flesh. He sucked at the hood, blew across the tip. Then he placed the flat of his tongue over my nub, before rolling it upwards in a long lick.

When the end of his tongue met the tip of my clit, he flicked it. Another lick, another flick.

If this was his signature move, it was a pretty fucking good one. I knew without a shadow of a doubt, he wouldn't need to pull the move for long to make me come. I hadn't had an orgasm in weeks, the will to try severely curbed by the unnerving presence of a watchful messiah-bearer.

I picked up the condom and pulled myself out of his reach. Using my fingers, my lips, my tongue, my teeth, I traced a path down his body, eliciting hisses and groans, the flex of his fingers, the arch of his back.

I trailed my nipples across the tip of his cock and dipped my head to run my tongue up its length from base to tip. When I reached the end, I pulled it into my mouth and ran my tongue around its head.

Callum emitted a series of tiny "uh"s as I slid him in as far as he could go, but when I wrapped my hand around the base of his shaft, he gripped my wrist and stilled it.

"No more. I need to be inside you." He pulled the condom from my grasp, tore the packet open with his teeth and handed the sheath to me. "You've got four seconds this time."

I managed it in three.

Straddling him, I said, "This is where I break you."

"You can't break me, Sadie," he said softly. Then he clasped my hips and tugged downwards.

I lowered myself onto him, slowly letting him fill me.

Callum's lips parted as I nestled onto him. "God, you feel amazing."

The low rumble of his voice sent a shiver coursing up my spine. With his ice-blue eyes made soft by desire, his mouth open with want, he was heart-achingly lovely.

I reached forward, ran a finger from his eyebrow to his

jaw bone and brushed the backs of my fingers across his cheek.

"You okay?" he asked.

I leant forward, grazing my nipples along his chest, and kissed him by way of answer, tasting my tang on his lips. Then I gently rocked my hips.

"Immf," he said against my tongue.

I rolled my hips again and Callum threw his head back, exposing his neck. Kissing his Adam's apple, I thrust again, the shift of my clitoris against his skin an ache.

As Callum rolled his head forward to meet my lips, his eyes darted over my right shoulder and he started. "Jesus. How did she get in here?"

I turned my head. Obi-Wan stood on the spare bed staring down at us.

"Ignore her. It's her bedtime. She breaks in every night."

He remained frozen in the act of rolling my nipple with his thumb. "No. It's too weird."

"I'm not stopping. Do you really want to stop?"

Callum eyed me for a beat.

I flicked my hips.

He grunted and shook his head. "I had a cat once who used to sit on the end of the bed and watch through narrowed eyes, like he was scoring us. He got rocked and jerked around, the odd accidental kick, but it never put him off."

"So, you're used to it, then."

His eyes shifted back to Obi-Wan. "She's looking down on me, like some evil, goat-shaped chaperone."

I leaned over him and switched the light off, and Callum enclosed a nipple in his mouth, sucking hard.

"See?" I gasped. "She's not that much of a deterrent."

Callum placed his hands on my hips, raising his own

slightly and pulling me down in a long, hard grind. Then he put his hands over my breasts and pushed me to sit upright. His fingers kneaded as the pace of my rocking quickened.

I barely had time to draw breath before my first orgasm hurtled through me like a bullet train, rolling out from my centre in a current of molten light. The second orgasm built before the first had receded and as the tension left my muscles and my spine curved with the daze that rushed in on its heels, Callum rasped, "Don't stop. God, I'm close. I'm so close."

His hands slipped to my hips again, pushing me down and into his thrusts. As his breath hitched and stuttered, I leaned forward, catching his long, low groan between my lips. He shuddered into breathlessness and I pressed my chest to his, laying my head on the pillow beside him and encircling his head with my arm. His hair tickled the skin in my inner elbow.

He turned his face towards mine, our rapid breaths shared. "That was...fast."

"Is speed your signature move?"

A laugh. "No one's made me come that quickly since I was just out of my virginity. I find you very fucking sexy, Sadie Quinn."

He kissed me slowly and tenderly as if the last few minutes were not proof enough of his words.

CHAPTER FOURTEEN

I WOKE when Callum pulled his arm out from underneath me.

"I have to go." He kissed me softly.

"OK," I whispered, the syllables strung out with disappointment.

"Next time let's go to mine."

"You want a next time?"

"I want a lot of next times. I'm only at 'C' in my signature move index."

I snuggled in closer, pushing against his erection. "Your penis tells me it doesn't want to go."

"Strangely enough, my penis does not dictate my working day. That honour is held by the clock on the wall of the Turangi police station and I need to be online by 7.30 am and check in."

I brushed the hair off his forehead. "Callum?"

"Hmm?"

"Why are you doing this? With me? Isn't your professional conscience blaring a klaxon? *Run away*."

Callum laughed. "Maybe a little bit, but my intuition has the louder voice. I don't think I have much to worry about." He shifted his head to kiss me and I thanked Mary his words weren't posed as a question. Propping himself up on an elbow, he looked down at me and hitched one side of his lips up. "Maybe I just like bad girls."

"I imagine that would be a conflict of interest you'd have to declare at police college."

"It didn't come up in the forms," he murmured as he kissed me again. "Is the goat still here? I'm too afraid to look."

"She's here. She's curled up on the bed, pretending not to listen."

"How do you know?"

"Her eyes are closed, but her ear's turned towards us."

"See? Just like a cat." Callum stretched, his long arms exposed to the cool morning air. "Christ, that was uncomfortable. I'm too old for sleeping on floors."

"You're a year younger than me. If I can do it, you're not too old to doss on a floor."

"You have more padding than me."

I bunched my lips.

"It's not a criticism. It's a fact. I love your padding." He ran a hand over a buttock and cupped it, and dipped his head to bury himself between my breasts.

I laughed.

A door whined open and feet shuffled in the hall outside the door.

"Shit," Callum said. "I'm going to have to run the gauntlet."

"You'll be fine. He's all soft and squishy in the morning."

"Gerry? Soft and squishy? That's like calling a shark cuddly or a scorpion cute."

I laid a soft kiss on his lips and murmured, "Woman up, McLintock. I'm going back to sleep."

"MORNING, POPPY." I smacked a kiss on his soft, whiskery cheek.

Poppy pulled his head away a fraction of a second too late. "Steady on. What was that for?"

"Just, you know, letting you know I'm happy to see you and I love you."

"Huh," Poppy growled. "So that was the reason Callum appeared in the kitchen earlier. I thought he was changing up his routine, giving you some early morning interrogation to keep you off balance. I take it he didn't leave after visiting last night?"

"Nope," I smiled.

"Good on you, girlie. You could do much worse."

I thought back to the tender way Callum had encouraged me to open myself up to him, his understanding, his acceptance. Perhaps, in fact, I couldn't do much better.

After breakfast, I all but skipped into town. I said good morning to everybody I saw. And then I had to concentrate very hard to remember why I'd made the journey.

I'd never had three sets of multiple orgasms in one night before, and I sure as hell was never turned stupid the next day by the reel of sex flashbacks running intermittently in my head.

My equilibrium was off. I felt unbalanced and dazed, yet I hummed with a golden energy. I imagined the retail assistants of the shops I went into flinching from the glow emanating from my skin.

I returned home with a bottle of omega 3 tablets, a couple of jigsaws and some juggling balls. I was met at the door by Obi-Wan, who told me she wanted to check the quality of my new purchases by chewing them.

I informed her that her only quality control responsibility was the lawn outside and carried the bags into the kitchen. "Poppy? I've bought some things for you."

"I'm in the living room playing with a Jevoha's Witness."

"Ah, now, Gerry," a woman's voice said. "We've talked about this already. I'm not a Jehovah's Witness."

His "bring a bowl of chips in with you, Sadie. This is getting good" was met by a forced laugh.

"I'm not entertainment. You need to treat what I'm asking you seriously."

My insides turned to liquid and I dropped the box of juggling balls onto the kitchen table with a *thunk*. Then I marched into the living room.

Poppy sat opposite a woman wearing one too many batik scarfs for the temperature in the room.

"Who are you?"

"Leonie," Poppy said with a grin. "God sent her."

"God didn't send me, Gerry. I'm here to assess you, remember? I'm a clinician from Zeta Health."

I crossed my arms. "*Dad* sent her. He wants a dementia diagnosis so he can put you in a home."

The woman smiled first at me, then Poppy. Given the situation was not a remotely happy or amusing one, the effect was somewhat patronising. "I've been asked to conduct an *objective* assessment of your cognitive abilities. Check the health of your brain."

"You know." Poppy shook a finger at the woman. "You remind me of Eva Gauthier. Something about the way you open and close your mouth. Sort of fish-like. She was a double agent working for the Gestapo. Not that we knew that at the time -"

"Right." I stood in front of the woman, blocking her view of Poppy. "I think you've outstayed your welcome. Off you go."

"But I haven't completed my assessment."

"You need his consent. He hasn't given it, so you need to leave. The boundless depths of my father's credit card does not automatically give you the right to be here. Pack up your things and go."

"She's alright, Sadie. I haven't had a visitor to play with since Jean came over to accuse me of gluing the lid of her letterbox closed."

I whirled around to face Poppy just as he winked at the clinician and said, "I had, of course."

"This isn't a game, Poppy. Dad and Uncle Peter are trying to force you into a home so they can pass on their filial responsibilities to someone else. Remove an inconvenience in their lives. Do you want that? Do you want to leave your home? Rot away in a mausoleum for the old and forgotten?"

Poppy winked at me. "Eva and I -"

"My name's Leonie, Gerry."

"- were just starting to have fun. You can stay and enjoy the tete a tete, or you can clear off."

I narrowed my eyes at him. He narrowed his back and I knew this wasn't something I would win. Poppy could out-stubborn me blind-folded and gagged.

I closed my eyes. "Fuuuuuuuuck." I open them and turned to the woman, pointer finger extended. "I want a full copy of the report."

She beamed her brittle professional smile at me. "Oh, I'm sorry. This information is confidential. It will be shared with the client and the patient, and seeing as you're neither..."

I gave her my best "fuck you" eyes and turned to Poppy again. "Just don't do or say anything you're going to regret later. This shit is real, Poppy."

Needing to not think about what hole Poppy was currently digging himself into, I climbed into the car and stamped on the accelerator, reversing up the driveway with a whine of the engine.

I did a circuit of the town and thought about calling in at the pub and unburdening myself to Manawa. But I didn't want to be overheard. The Tokawai rumour mill was lubricated enough without me feeding it fresh material.

On my second pass of the main street, I saw the patrol car was parked at the police station. No other car sat alongside it.

I pulled in, called out hello on my way through the door and was answered by a "in the office. Doing paperwork".

I locked the door and turned the sign to "closed".

When I arrived at his office, Callum leaned back in his chair, waiting for me.

I hesitated in the doorway, reached under my dress and pulled off my knickers. Stepping out of them, I approached the desk.

Callum didn't say anything for the first couple of steps. When words emerged, they were gruff. "This is an unexpected surprise."

I closed the distance, placed a finger on his lips and undid the zip on his trousers.

"Did you lock -" Callum's question was lost in my kiss.

"Yes." I leant over him and turned the louvres on the Venetian blinds closed, then I lowered myself down.

"Not the chair," he murmured. "Desk."

I pushed the monitor and keyboard aside, hoisted my bottom onto the wood and pulled Callum by the hips towards me. "I want you to take me so hard, the desk is barricading the door by the time we're done."

Callum eyed the distance in question, his brows raised.

Then he grinned at me. "Challenge accepted."

When I eventually returned home having given *Leonie* what I felt to be a reasonable window of time to determine the fate of my grandfather, a jigsaw was on the table. It was neither of the jigsaws I bought, and both.

The outlying pieces were of a kitten yawning, an ostensibly cute and benign picture. Except Poppy had swapped out the mouth pieces for those of the T-Rex puzzle. The kitten's maw was laced with razor-sharp teeth and its lips scaled. A pointed tongue protruded in the midst of a roar.

It was grotesque and decidedly disturbing.

"You like my creation?"

"No. It's horrible," I said, omitting an admission of the genius of it.

"Jigsaw companies often use the same pattern. Eddie showed me how to mix them up to make wacky versions. When we came out for a cuppa, Eva saw the boxes and asked me to do a jigsaw for her."

I placed a thumb on each of my eyeballs and pressed, not sure if the fact he kept calling her Eva, or that he created this monstrosity for her was worse.

"Poppy, what else did you do? You didn't show her the list did you?"

"Course I bloody didn't. She did ask lots of questions about why I clocked Dante Kerr, though."

"What did you say?"

"The amplified crack of the microphone connecting with his skull was the sweetest sound I've ever heard."

I took a deep breath. It would be fine. Everything would be fine.

As long as the report gets lost in the mail.

And Poppy hasn't done anything stupid like give Power of Attorney to Dad or Uncle Peter.

I DECIDED to walk to work. If I couldn't turn back time and vaporise Leonie before she'd had a chance to knock on the door, some fresh air was a poor, but more obtainable alternative to finding calm.

It was a beautiful late spring evening. The air was still, the lowering sun bleached the western sky, and it *almost* allowed me to forget the last five hours had happened.

I approached the pub from the opposite side of the street and halted as I put my foot out to step down from the curb.

Two men were having a tussle on the roof.

One ducked as the other threw a punch. Straightening, he shoved the punch thrower, who staggered backwards, and before he could regain his balance, the shover dropped his shoulder, tackled his opponent around his waist and drove him towards the back of the building. He released him and with a push to the chest, sent him disappearing off the edge of the roof.

I slapped a hand to my mouth, my "oh my God" distorting through my fingers.

The pusher looked over the edge to where his adversary

had fallen, and began to wobble. He wind-milled his arms, then he too disappeared.

"Holy fuck." I re-engaged my frozen limbs and crossed the two lanes as quickly as I could. Bounding up the steps to the front door, I burst into the pub's foyer and pushed open the double doors into the pub proper just in time to see another body hurtling from the roof.

And landing on a bouncy castle.

It was Fuzz Cup night.

I strode to the window, rapped furiously on it and shouted, "You fuckers! I thought I was going to have to scrape up man pizza from the car park."

When my heart returned to its normal rhythm, I turned and glared at Manawa. I pointed out the window. "*That* is unforgivable. I don't care how much fun their tiny lizard brains are revelling in right now, I thought I saw two men *die*."

Manawa threw her hands up in the air. "Not arguing with your derision, Sadie. I'm still wrestling with the self-professed genius of Mitchell's latest initiative, let alone the spectacle out the window."

She turned to watch Mitchell, clad in a tight blue jump-suit, wander from table to table and by some kind of physics-defying magic, attach empty glasses to his body.

He leant over a table top to retrieve a pint glass and a punter slapped one on his buttock, much to the hilarity of the rest of the table.

"Suit's Velcro." Manawa picked up a glass from the bench top and held it in front of me. A narrow band of furry material had been fitted around its circumference. "Some-times I wonder at the success of our species."

"You've changed your tune."

"Touching him is like rubbing up against a Brillo pad.

I've had to put my hair in a bun so he doesn't rip half of it out on his way past."

I turned from her and reached for the bottle of Jack Daniels on the liquor shelf. The day had gone down the toilet several hours beforehand. If I didn't fortify myself, I'd be left feeling like that lonely, buoyant turd circling the porcelain with each new flush.

The first punter didn't help matters by making a request for "a beer".

The Tokawai pub, being an alcohol-serving establishment dealing primarily in beer, stocked over a dozen different brands.

"*Which* beer? This isn't your fridge at home. Or is this a fun game of 'make the bartender read my mind'?"

The man looked from me to Manawa and asked if he could order a beer from her.

When I wished aloud that I'd worn my *OF COURSE there's such a thing as a stupid question* T-shirt, Manawa reached up and pinched my lips together while she poured the man *a beer* with one hand.

The next punter (five foot nine, seventy kilos, dress size 14. Four fifths of a Sadie) approached the bar, allowed her eyes to travel from my hips to the top of my head. "Whoa," she said, "how...?", the sheer awesomeness of my size apparently rendering her incapable of finishing her question.

"I was breastfed until the age of eighteen. I still go round to mum's for a nightcap before bedtime."

"Sadie!" Manawa barked from where she was filling a glass from a beer tap.

"Well, come on. If she'd asked someone from Nigeria how they got to be so black, you'd call it racism."

Manawa eyed me for a beat. Then she said, "You're right." She turned to the woman and turned the full might of her unimpressed face on her. "Tash. Sit your sizeist arse down. Come back when you're ready to apologise."

As Tash dragged her feet to her table, Manawa turned on me. "What is *wrong* with you this evening? You're scaring all the punters into drinking sensible levels of alcohol, which while good for their livers, is terrible for my bottom line."

"My Dad. He's being a prize tool."

She crossed her arms and leant against the bar, cocking a leg. "What's he done?"

"He's trying to force Poppy into a home, and as fast as I can build a defensive wall around him, Poppy rides a wrecking ball through it. It's like trying to plug the leaks in a sieve."

Someone stood at the bar and cleared their throat.

Ignoring them, I continued, "I can't be everywhere. He's probably at home right now, stapling the furniture to the ceiling because Eddie told him it'd be a fun game."

"Excuse me."

I turned to glare at the customer. "We're talking and this is important. I can't imagine you're about to drop dead from thirst any time soon. You can wait another minute."

"Manawa?" the patron asked.

Without looking at him, she said. "No, she's right. Waiting won't kill you." Then she nodded at me to continue.

"He set the garage on fire yesterday playing marbles. How does anybody do that?"

"Maybe he was trying to get your attention so he didn't waste away from neglect," the disgruntled customer volunteered.

I pulled a Steinlager from the fridge, popped the top, slapped it into his left hand and pulled the ten dollar note from his right. "Go and whine your first world problems to someone who cares." I pointed at an empty table. Then I shrugged my shoulders. "I guess that would be no one."

After that, Mitchell said I was metastasising into Gerry more and more each day. I presumed he meant metamorphosing, but his word choice could equally have been deliberate. A metaphorical disapproval.

"Why are people happy to put up with your rude and not mine?" I asked Manawa.

"People have a rude-acceptance level. I've trained them to expect mine, but there's only so much they can take. Rude in stereo is demoralising and emasculating if issued by two women."

"Since when have you been worried about emasculation?"

"I have a business to run. I want the punters to return. I strike a fine balance."

"Chica!" A My Little Pony T-shirt danced into my peripheral vision. "You are *glowering*. It doesn't suit you. Makes your eyes into mean little slits. Come here for a hug." She pulled herself onto the bar, shimmied across it on her knees and wrapped her arms around me.

My nose pressed into the bony bit between her breasts, flattening my nostrils. I opened my lips to draw a breath and sucked in a mouthful of rainbow-coloured cotton. I tried to pull away, but her arms cinched tighter around my head. God she was strong. I was going to die and go to My Little Pony hell. "I can't breathe, Flick."

I was saved by Manawa shouting, "Get off my bar".

Flick released me and jumped back on to the patron side.

I gulped at the stale pub air and rubbed feeling back into my nose.

"I've got a new T-shirt order coming in." She winked at me. "Got a little something for you."

"A new set of manners, I hope," said Manawa.

"Nuh." Flick backed away from the bar, both hands extended and fingers pointed at me. "Something *way* better than that. Later, sis." She disappeared through the doors to the garden bar and a *THUNK* against the back wall of the pub drew me into an instinctive hunch.

"I can't look," I said to Manawa. "Is he in one piece?"

Manawa peered round me to look out the window. "He's just peeling himself off the wall. Must have ricocheted off one of the turrets."

"*God.* When is Callum going to get here?" I said as the door cracked open.

The pub held its breath, and as Callum entered, Manawa called out, "I make it 7.56 pm."

He raised his hand to deliver the obligatory wave as cheers echoed around the pub floor, but despite the alarming hurtle of bodies past the large sash window, his eyes were on me.

I was spot lit. My clothes felt too hot, too heavy, my limbs cumbersome.

He walked towards me, side-stepping someone who had approached to talk to him. His eyes never left my face.

Stepping up to the bar, he laid his hands on the wood. "Hey."

"Hey," I replied, lost in the blue of his eyes.

Callum grinned.

All thought, all words, fell out of my brain and I grinned back.

In my peripheral vision, Manawa swivelled her head from side to side, looking from my face to Callum's, and our bubble burst with a *pop*. "Jesus," she said. "Would you two like to use the storeroom?"

"Yes," I said as Callum said, "A bed. I'd really like a bed next time."

"Next time? When did you guys graduate from ogling each other? I am the heartbeat of this town. The pulse doesn't so much as flutter under anybody's thumbs without my say so. How can I not know this?"

"It just...happened," Callum said, his eyes still locked on mine.

"It didn't just happen. This has been brewing for weeks."

"No." Callum finally broke our wordless conversation and looked at Manawa. "It just happened as in 'last night' just happened."

"Ohhhhhh." Manawa's smile faded into a frown. "Then why is Sadie a grumpy shithead and not swinging from my deer antler candelabra? Did you not take her to the opera?" Manawa leaned forward and whispered, "I can get Mitchell to give you a few pointers on female anatomy, if you like. How best to tend the tulip tip?"

Callum held up his hands. "I tended Sadie's tulip tip just fine, thank you very much."

"Well, it seems like she could do with tending right now. She's a pain in my arse and been the Mistress of Misery all evening, not helped by the lunacy of this lot."

Callum's head jerked towards the window. His eyebrows rose in surprise and his mouth made a loose 'O' before the edges curled up into the beginnings of a smile. "That'll be the report of someone falling off the roof of the pub, then."

"Oh, you've only just noticed? Perhaps if you hadn't disappeared into telepathic love land as soon as you stepped through the door, you might have seen the commitment to idiocy made in your honour."

"It's not for me, Manawa. They do this for their own entertainment. I'm incidental. An excuse."

The next man to fall screamed the length of his descent and I crushed the can of Red Bull I'd picked up just before Callum entered.

I ungritted my teeth and surveyed the damage. The blast radius encapsulated a square foot of the service bench and the entirety of the fabric under my breasts.

I held up the can and shook it. "I'm going to stuff this in that dude's scream hole."

Manawa sighed and waved a hand in the direction of the door. "Take her home."

I raised an eyebrow at Callum, picked up my bag and coat and raced him for the door.

THE NEXT FEW days passed in a sex fog. I'd drive to Callum's after work, where we'd have sex (at least twice, as requested by me) in his bed (as requested by him).

Callum operated on three hours of sleep. I managed to sneak in a couple more when he left for work, and then we'd do the whole thing over again the next night.

I was too tired and too happy to be worried about the impending report on Poppy.

Two things ground it to a halt. Callum momentarily falling asleep at the wheel while on highway patrol. And a neglected Obi-Wan expressing her feelings by eating half my bedding.

I swapped beds, relegated Obi-Wan to the one she'd

ruined in her tantrum-throwing, and removed the blanket that had shrouded the statue all week.

The Virgin looked blue from lack of air, the shadows on her brow deeper than normal.

Then, with the equilibrium restored to the room, I sunk into a deep slumber born of sleep-deprivation.

When I woke eleven hours later, my world imploded with the force of a megaton bomb.

CHAPTER FIFTEEN

I STUMBLED into the kitchen to find a uniformed Callum seated at the table, cup of tea clamped between his white-knuckled hands. His eyes remained on the steam rising from the cup. A muscle in his jaw ticked.

"What's wrong?" I asked, plucking a wayward piece of sleep goo from the corner of my left eye.

Poppy turned from the cupboard he'd been rummaging in and placed the cake tin on the table. "You're going to need this."

My breath caught in my throat. Poppy was well aware of my aversion to anything with a high calorie count. Offering cake for breakfast? Things must be *really* bad.

I pulled a chair out and slowly lowered myself onto it. Flicking my eyes between a taciturn Callum and a scowling Poppy, I aimed for the least dire option of all possible mute-rendering scenarios. "Did you get a court date?"

Poppy didn't answer. He opened the tin, cut a slice of carrot cake and placed it on a plate. He slid it towards me. "I'm making you coffee."

A resounding no, then.

That was when I noticed the piece of paper lying on the table bearing the letterhead Zeta Health.

My heart tried to exit my body through the soles of my feet. I picked the letter up, the shaking of my hand making it impossible for me to read. "What do they say?"

"It seems I had a little too much fun with Eva. Probably shouldn't have called her fish-like."

I scanned the letter. The words swam and blurred into each other. I flipped over to the next page and the heading *Suggested care plan* told me everything I needed.

"They can't do anything with this Poppy. They can't make you do anything you don't want to."

He turned from the bench, jug in hand. "Yes, they bloody can. I've been medically declared unable to make safe decisions for my own well-being."

"What does that mean?" I looked to Callum for an answer, but his eyes remained fastened to his cup. "I don't know what that means, Poppy."

He lowered the jug and returned to his chair. Slumping into it, he slid a hand down his face. "I gave Power of Attorney to your father and Peter when your grandmother died."

I knew the process. They could declare Poppy mentally incompetent and file to become his legal guardian. All decisions would pass to them, just as Dad wanted.

I reached across the table and gripped Poppy's swollen hands. "I won't let that happen. I'll do everything I can to stop that from happening."

"You won't be able to do much from jail." Callum's breath scraped across the words. A cracked half-whisper.

"What do you mean from jail?"

He looked at me then. "Jordan Simeon has been in touch with the Auckland police."

An arctic wind gathered strength under my breast bone and swirled around my organs in a category one cyclone.

"Of course, you were never in the porn industry, because you were in a pawn *shop*."

I opened my mouth, wanting more than anything to defend myself and knowing that I couldn't. At least not in any way that might be excusable. My actions were reckless and desperate and vengeful. A terrible combination. I settled for redirection. "That heartless mother fucker."

"Jesus." Callum shook his head. "They have CCTV footage in those places, Sadie. They have to, to protect themselves from being prosecuted from receiving *stolen goods*. What the fuck were you doing trying to pawn stolen goods?" A reel of emotions flickered across Callum's face. Anger, bewilderment, heartbroken disappointment. "*Christ*, this is humiliating. I've been tasked with charging you, the woman I've -". He broke off and ran a hand through his hair.

The woman I've - what? Been poling? Fallen for? Just what exactly have I royally screwed?

"Callum." I stretched a hand out towards his and he withdrew it, placing it on his lap. I sat upright and stared down at the cake, not really seeing it. "To be honest, I don't really know how I got to that point, to break and do something like that. It all seems a bit of a bad dream."

"I can show you the footage if you like. Jog your memory." Callum's voice was sharp with bitterness.

"Please know I never would have put you in this position if I thought -"

"You'd be caught?"

"- Jordan would take issue with it. I really believed he would be, I don't know, understanding."

Callum dropped his chin and said slowly, "Understanding of you stealing and pawning his stuff?"

"Yes," I whispered.

He eyed me for two beats before slapping his palms on the table and pushing himself to standing. "Right, well that clarifies everything. I'll be on my way so I can start filling out the exoneration forms."

"Callum." I stretched out my arm, reaching for him again.

He placed his hands in his pockets. "You know what this means?"

I did know what it meant and the walls of my chest inched towards each other in inevitable collapse.

I didn't want to face that reality. Anything but the certainty that whatever tender thing Callum and I had been nurturing was destroyed. My default position of deflection through sarcasm shifted into gear with a *clunk*. "Poppy and I get to be court-date twinsies?"

Callum closed his eyes on an exhale and gave his head a small shake.

"I get to test Flick's theory? See if having a smart mouth really does negate size-factor ten in the prison hierarchy?"

"No, Sadie. It means, *quite obviously,* that I can't see you anymore." He turned for the door and muttered, "You ruined us before we even began."

Before the back door closed, he called out, "Come down to the station so I can do this officially."

My phone rang as my chest caved in on itself.

Dad.

Jesus Christ, could this day get any worse?

I swiped my phone to answer the call, bit my tongue before a "fuck you" could rush out, and said, "I'm applying to be legally recognised as an orphan."

"Oh, ho ho, Sadie, no need to be dramatic."

"There's every bloody need, Dad. You are an underhanded shit. *God*, I have never been so disgusted in the behaviour of a member of my family. I'm right here!" I shouted. "I'm right by Poppy's side, helping him lead the life he wants."

Dad employed a patronising calm, which only succeeded in raising my infuriation levels. "Take a breath, Sadie, and look at this objectively. Your grandfather consistently calls a medical professional after a woman he says he met while fighting for The Resistance, despite being a child during the war and having never left the country. He disappears for ten minutes and she discovers him standing on top of his wardrobe. When she asks him how he got there, he says 'Eddie helped me'. No other person entered the house after you left. Then he bellyflops onto the mattress he'd pulled from his bed to the floor. An eighty-eight-year-old! And if that weren't evidence enough of the danger he is to himself and the confused state of his mind, there's a long list of questionable, dangerous and destructive behaviour before that exhibition. He's set the garage and car inside it on fire, he's had to be rescued from a building top, he attempted to kill someone, he's broken into the church, and he's had a turn that required a 1 1 1 call. He's a total liability to himself, Sadie. Surely, you must see that."

I did. Christ, it sounded *terrible*. Poppy's list of infractions was light years away from being in his favour.

"You being present hasn't prevented any of that from happening. In fact, all of it's happened under your supposed watch."

He was right. He was a total arsehole for pointing it out, but I couldn't deny that I'd been there for all of it.

"He's *happy*, Dad. That trumps everything."

"Oh, yes. Is that the defence you're going to use when he's defending his violent actions in front of a judge?"

I didn't say anything. I couldn't.

There was only one way out of this conversation. I hung up.

Pulling the plate of carrot cake towards me, I hunched over it and shovelled two big forkfuls in. I lifted my head, met Poppy's rheumy stare and said through my mouthful, "What do we do now?"

"Barricade the doors and have ourselves a showdown. I'm not afraid of going out in a blaze of glory. You in?"

I was in.

Anything was better than being helpless and allowing Poppy to decay in misery. Plus, I didn't want to go to jail. Orange wasn't my colour. It made me look like I was in the final throes of kidney failure.

"What do we do about Obi-Wan?" Poppy asked.

"Flick's going to love her."

I DIDN'T END up calling Flick and asking her to adopt my goat. I ended up going to the police station as requested.

"A PAIR of Razor Edge roller blades, an assortment of LPs including a special edition Grateful Dead album printed on blue vinyl, a K2 puffer jacket, a Casio G-Shock watch, a pair of five kilogram dumbbells and a set of eight kilogram dumbbells, an unused car cover still in its packaging, an XPress coffee plunger, a pair of wireless Apple earbuds, a Back Country one-man tent, a Back Country goose down sleeping bag, a DeLonghi bread maker. Is that correct?"

Callum sat opposite me in the interview room, reading

from a sheet of paper. His lips were pale and he drew them into a thin line when he finished reading.

"I don't know. Those few hours are pretty hazy."

He tapped his pen on the paper and raised his eyes to mine. "Not the most impressive list of stolen goods I've seen. Certainly not worth the trouble it's causing now."

I wasn't sure if he meant just trouble for me or trouble for him as well. Trouble for us. "The repossessors had taken all the good stuff."

"Was this spurred by some kind of petty revenge? Because it has 'petty' written all over it."

"No. I don't know. He left me with nothing, Callum. Less than nothing."

Callum, now cognisant of the chain of events that had led to my bankruptcy status, frowned and gave a minute shake of his head, as if to say, "That excuses you?"

"I'll never get a loan to start another business, a mortgage to own a home. My world had caved in on me and I guess I kind of flipped. I was overcome by a panicked desperation to leave, to find a safe place to curl into a ball. I only needed enough money to get transport for me and my gear out of town. I didn't need much. It seemed like a just solution."

"Couldn't you have gone cap in hand to your parents?"

I snorted. "Believe me, this was the better option."

Callum folded his arms and looked down his misshapen nose at me.

"At the time, it *felt* like the better option."

"Now it seems as stupid and reckless as it's proved to be?"

I didn't say anything.

"So." Callum looked down at the piece of paper. "You split the goods and took them to four different pawn shops around the city."

"I...if that's what the evidence says." I exhaled through pursed lips. "It's all a bit of a blur. I wasn't exactly thinking straight that day. I forgot to put on underwear, for goodness sake."

"I see." Callum looked down at the papers in his hand again. "And you counted on your business partner not reporting you?"

"He'd taken so much from me. The least he could do was give me this. This chance to find a place to lick my wounds. I assumed, wrongly as it happens, he'd respect my actions. See it as small compensation for what he'd done."

"That's a lot of trust to show a man who hid a gambling problem and stole from your business."

"Yes," came out on a sigh.

Callum rubbed his eyes as if attempting to erase the last few awful hours from his memory. Then he lowered his hands and blinked at me through red, bleary eyes. "Burglary. You're being charged with *burglary*."

"The injustice of it is not lost on me, Callum. He steals thousands from me, ruins my financial future and gets away with it. I steal a handful of goods for a couple hundred bucks, and I'm the one who gets the conviction."

"Why didn't you pursue a legal case against him?"

I rubbed at my brow. "Because, despite having a master's degree in business, I didn't do my due diligence. We didn't set up a legal agreement that would provide protection for both of us or outlined our profit and asset share. Technically, he was entitled to everything and he took it. I meant to do it, but things took off so quickly. I didn't get a chance."

"So, you might be very smart, but you're an idiot." Callum pushed the paper around for me to read. "Something I've seen in you time and time again since you arrived back in Tokawai."

I understood Callum's anger and he was right. I had been unbelievably careless about my business. Too high on the quick success of it, too busy figuring out how to run it. I absolutely should have known better, but it wasn't those words that hurt. It was the ones that came next.

"Up until now it's been endearing."

I peered at the paper not seeing what it said. "You need me to sign something?"

"At the bottom. And date it."

I moved the pen across the paper on autopilot and stood. "Well, Callum. Thank you for your time. It's been nice seeing you again after all these years." *Thanks for the, frankly, fucking incredible sex. Thanks for making me feel beautiful.*

"Sadie." The syllables may have expressed chagrin, or what might have been hurt.

I turned. "What else is there to say, Callum?"

When he didn't answer, I continued on my way.

I HAD to knock when I got home, as Poppy had locked the door.

"What's the password?"

"I don't know, Poppy. You didn't give me one before I left."

Silence. Then a grumble, followed by a bleat as if Obi-Wan attempted to help me out by passing on the code. The lock clicked, the door opened, and he flapped a hand, waving me in. "Quick, before the Gestapo come by."

I stepped past him and into a kitchen that had the sweet yeasty smell of hot bread. My mouth watered.

"I made cheesy pull-apart bread. You want some?"

Cheesy pull-apart bread had a calorie count that tipped

the chart. But fuck it. Hot, cheesy bread was the last thing I needed to worry about. "I'll put the kettle on."

We drank the first cup in silence. I dipped my bread into the tea and rolled my eyes in pleasure as the sodden bread disintegrated on my tongue.

Poppy's right hand kept disappearing under the table.

I sipped at the greasy surface of my tea, pretending I didn't know he was feeding Obi-Wan.

On the second cup, he said, "You going to jail?"

I shook my head. "I don't think so. The crime's too petty."

"You're going to be sweeping streets with me?"

Reaching across the table, I placed my hand over the back of his knobbly one. "Let's hope so."

I excused myself, told them both I needed to lie down for a bit and stopped short when I entered my room.

There was something different about the Virgin. Her eyes were glossy with unshed tears, her mouth no longer curved in serene happiness.

I couldn't believe I hadn't seen it before, that I'd mistaken her expression for smug-wrapped judgement. The Virgin Mary wasn't immortalised in an eternal contentment. She was immortalised in an unbearable sadness, and no wonder after the heartbreak she'd lived through.

I couldn't bear it. I pulled the covers up over my head and lost myself to the blackness.

MY PHONE WOKE ME. The room was dark. I'd been asleep for hours.

I picked it up and blinked at its brightness, letting the name swim into focus. Then I swiped to answer it. "Mum?"

Her "Sadie" sounded as if it was issued on a sigh. It

might have been disappointment, but it was the kind of disappointment that wraps around you, hugs you tight. A disappointment born of a deep love.

I didn't know whether to bristle or cry.

I had no idea how she could possibly know about the events of the day. Surely, Dad's informant wasn't *that* well-informed.

"You are the most stubborn child. It's fierce. Always has been. Used to drive me up the wall, but it made me proud of you, too."

I sat up, tucking the covers under each armpit. "Mum, have you rung to fight Dad's battle for him?"

"Partly. I know the diagnosis is only going to make you dig your toes in even more, especially now you don't have a business to run."

My breath lodged in my throat and I didn't say anything.

"Yes, I know about that. Working remotely for an events business for weeks on end began to get a bit suspicious. It didn't take too much detecting to work out the business was no longer running, but we can talk about that later. Poppy's well-being is the most important thing now."

"Mum," I said, but she continued.

"Poppy will listen to you. You must see he needs more care than you can give him."

I groaned. "I don't want to have this argument with you as well."

"Nobody wants an argument. We're going to send the brochures again, so he can start thinking about where he wants to live."

I threw my free hand in the air and looked to the darkened ceiling. "I'm not doing Dad and Uncle Peter's dirty work for them. They can front up to Poppy themselves instead of hiding behind clinicians and brochures."

"You know that won't work. Communication would break down the moment your father made his presence known."

"What would you have done if I wasn't here? Straitjacketed him and bundled him into the back of a van?"

Mum lowered her voice. "I'm not sure what happens in those situations, Sadie. I don't really want to think about it."

"So, if I left, you'd have no leverage. You can't use force."

"We have the leverage of Power of Attorney."

"But you can't. Use. Force." My words edged their way between my clenched teeth.

"We won't have to, because you'll help him to see where he needs to be now."

"I'd rather leave," I said, my voice thick with holding back emotion.

"Where would you go?" Mum replied quietly, knowing those four words had the power to undo me, because where did I have to go? I didn't have a home any more. I couldn't go to Mum and Dad's under the present circumstances. My sister lived in Sydney. I thought of Flick, wondering if she had a couch, or a spare room.

"I'll find somewhere."

"Sadie, sweetheart, why didn't you tell us about your business going bankrupt?"

"Because, *Mum*." I shut my eyes against the crack in my voice. "Because of the abject disappointment you'd hurl at me."

"No, we wouldn't. We'd have -"

"Yes, you would. You've always put pressure on me to succeed. When my brain proved to make up for what I lacked physically, you leapt at the opportunity to prove to the world your ugly duckling was worthy, and you set your expectations very high. Always. God, I *slaved* to get Dux at school. Something you and Dad wanted. I wanted to be a normal teenager, but I didn't want to disappoint you. I tried so hard to please everyone because I had so much disapproval thrown at me due to how I looked. You included."

Mum sucked in a breath. "We didn't - we don't - disapprove of how you look, Sadie."

"Dad calls me his 'Amazonian throwback', makes comments about how I should be wading through life, bulldozing the hard stuff out of the way with my broad shoulders. You call me your 'big girl'."

"Well, you *are* my big girl."

"Mum, has it ever occurred to you what the cumulative effect is of having your abnormal size commented on all the time? You guys joke about what a genetic anomaly I am. That your real baby is being raised by another family."

"It was never put like that."

"It certainly felt like that. I had it from all angles. Strangers on the street, kids at school, friends even. And to have it at home too, like it's acceptable behaviour. There are times when I am *crippled* with shame about my body. Dad wonders why I'm at Poppy's. It's because my family home is too filled with judgement. It's not a sanctuary. It's not somewhere I'd *ever* go to lick my wounds. Poppy's always loved me without judgement, and now -" a sob escaped, abrupt and deep. "Now you want to take that away too."

"Sadie, my sweetheart, you have to see that the decision about Poppy is not about punishing you. It's about looking after Poppy."

Another sob escaped and I sniffed wetly.

Mum didn't say anything for a few seconds. When she did, her voice was thick with tears, too. "I am so sorry if we made you feel abnormal, or judged. It breaks my heart to think we might have damaged you, that we've pushed you away. You must know that I would have loved you even if you were green and had four ears. I would never *ever* have wanted to hurt you." She sniffed and huffed out a shaky breath. "And your business? Companies fail, my love. That's the nature of a capitalist system. You dust yourself off, and you start again."

"Not like this, they don't."

"What do you mean?"

"My business partner siphoned all the profits into his gambling habit. That business failed so spectacularly I was declared bankrupt when we couldn't pay off the suppliers."

"Oh, Sadie."

Like my tears, the rest tumbled out in a hot rush. "And now I've been arrested for burglary. I needed enough money to get to Poppy's with my stuff, so I stole some things from my business partner and sold them for less than two hundred bucks and the bastard reported me."

Mum gasped.

Before she could ask the obvious questions, I said, "I'm so fucking scared. I'm probably going to lose my job. I've lost Callum, and I'm going to lose Poppy. It's like I never deserved any of it. A career, love. Just like I've never deserved to feel normal because I've been constantly reminded that I'm not."

"Oh, my love. You deserve so much. I wish you could see that. Would you like me to come and visit, look after you and Poppy for a bit?"

"Yes," I sniffed. "But Poppy would see that as a flanking manoeuvre. You'd be sent on your way before you got a foot in the door."

"What can I do for you then?"

"Just...let me and Poppy be."

"I don't have control over that. It's not up to me."

"Well, can't you withhold sex or something, like those Greek women did to stop a war?"

Mum laughed. "I'm not sure that would be terribly effective these days. It's going to happen, Sadie, but I'll try and cool their heels. Give you some time."

———

I CALLED in sick the following night, and the night after that. And barely left my bed.

Obi-Wan gave up on me pretty quickly and spent her days with Poppy - a much more willing playmate.

Every few hours, Poppy would put his head around the door and offer something to eat. I'd say I wasn't hungry and try to find the escape of sleep again.

I felt weighted to the mattress. A terrible heaviness pressed down on me, and my mind and limbs operated as if bound in fog.

A beam of light, broken by the shifting leaves of the camellia, penetrated the gap between the curtains and stretched its milky fingers across the room. The illuminated Virgin Mary extended her hands towards me in what might have been an offer of comfort, the promise of an embrace.

I lay in the dark and watched her, willing her to say something, anything. Tell me how I could go on from here.

She kept her thoughts secret.

On day three, when my limbs and head finally felt light enough to move, and the stink from my armpits drove a fierce need for a shower, Poppy burst into the room followed by Obi-Wan.

He threw open the curtains, and turned and clapped his hands. "Right. Enough bloody sleep time. It's play time."

I pulled my head back under the covers at the thought of another item on the misdeeds list and offered a rasped, "I can't."

The end of my bed depressed and the covers were pulled from my face. Poppy stood on top of the blankets looking down at me. "Yes, you sodding-well can. Let's play 'the floor is lava'."

He was dressed in a pink T-shirt that read "Riots not diets".

"What are you wearing?"

"Some slang-talking, shaved-headed girl came round. Said it was for you. Figured *I'd* wear it seeing as you can't find your way to vertical. So come on. You get up, you can have it."

"Flick came round?"

Obi-Wan jumped up beside Poppy, sending him stumbling against the wall. Unfazed, he said, "First one around the room and back to here without melting their legs off gets first dibs on the pancakes."

My stomach moaned, the need for it to be filled more urgent than the need for me to be clean. "You made pancakes?"

"Not yet. Gotta wake up and play first." He stepped over me. "Come on. The lava's bubbling up. It's about to consume your bed."

Obi-Wan leapt past both of us and sproinged up onto the sewing-machine bedside table, before jumping down onto my still chewed ex-bed.

Following, Poppy clambered onto the sewing machine on hands and knees, and crawled across its top. When he put his arms down onto the mattress of the spare bed, they gave out. He tucked his head in before he face-planted and executed a clumsy forward roll.

I gave a hoot of laughter.

"That's the spirit, my girl. Let's get some more of that sunshine in you."

As I took a tentative step up on to the sewing machine, not convinced it wouldn't collapse beneath me, Obi-Wan leapt the span between the end of the bed and the chest of drawers on the other side of the doorway. "I think we're going to have our arses handed to us, Poppy. We should have started with a handicap. How are you going to get from the bed to where Obi-Wan is? Your grappling hook?"

"I'm old. My feet have had a good innings. Reckon I can manage to wobble around on stumps."

"Grim," I said, as Obi-Wan attempted to push her way past the statue.

The Obi-Wan of several weeks ago might have been able to tuck herself in behind The Virgin, but the Obi-Wan of now had not only grown into teenager proportions, her well-fed stomach was a tight, round ball. A ball she had no lateral awareness of.

She pulled her body past and the statue tipped on its front edge.

"Obi-Wan!" I called, risking my ability to ever walk again by jumping into the lava pit and lunging for the teetering statue.

She toppled forward and I dived. The carpet bit my elbows and knees, and I caught her just as her outstretched hands grazed the floor.

I had broken her fall, but I couldn't hold her weight, and she slid forward, overturning in a slow somersault from the axis of her hands. I scrabbled to catch her again before the weight of her base crashed against the wooden bed end.

There was a *schlick* behind me and several *fwaps* as a something, a number of somethings, hit the floor.

I turned. A pile of yellowed black and white photos lay scattered on the carpet at the foot of the dresser.

Poppy emitted a slow "ah" of discovery as Obi-Wan jumped down to nose them.

I craned my head to peer at the underside of the statue. It was hollow, a hole in the bottom the size of a grapefruit. I looked up at Poppy.

His face was soft, his lips parted in the ghost of a smile.

I pulled myself up to kneel and picked up the closest photo. It was of a smiling boy. He was small, maybe six or seven, a school satchel at his hip, socks pulled to his knees, hair parted on the side. I knew instinctively it was Poppy. The boy had the same curled over tops of his ears, the same devil in his wide smile.

Beside him stood a smiling girl. A teenager. She wore her hair in plaits on either side of her head, and a school satchel was slung across her body in mirror of Poppy's.

"Who's this?"

He climbed down from the bed and groaned into a sitting position beside me. He placed a fingertip on the girl's face. "Eddie."

CHAPTER SIXTEEN

A CHILL RAN up my spine as if someone had walked on my grave. "I don't understand," I said haltingly as I picked up another photo. The same girl, a few years younger, squatted next to a tin tub in the grass, a chubby naked toddler sitting in the water. His blurred hands were raised to strike the surface.

Eddie was real.

Eddie was a girl.

I picked up another photo. Poppy and Eddie under a Christmas tree, each holding a wrapped present. "Poppy? Who's Eddie?"

"Eddie," Poppy's voice dropped to a whisper, "is my sister."

My heart jumped in my chest and thrummed a rapid drum beat. "But..." I fingered the pile of photos. They were all of Poppy and Eddie. "But you're an only child."

He didn't answer straight away.

I looked over at him.

His smile shifted to curve ever so slightly downward. "I was made an only child when she died."

A sourness flooded my cheeks, its cold flushing out the blood. "You've been...playing with a ghost?"

"It was time."

I paused before saying, "I'm scared to know what you mean."

He bunched his knees and shuffled backwards to lean his back against the bed, the photo still in his hand. Closing his eyes, he said, "I never got to mourn her."

I drew myself in close to Poppy. Curling my knees towards him, I wrapped my hands around his in a reversal of our usual sandwich. "Tell me."

He drew a deep, shuddering breath and told me how much his sister, older by seven years, loved him, looked after him, played with him when his parents, busy with the bakery, couldn't. How she was his best friend. That she and him, often parentless and left to their own devices would entertain themselves by doing naughtier and naughtier things. When he was ten years old, she was sent away and a few months later he was told of her death. Told that she'd brought shame on the family and he was never to speak of her again. All trace of her existence was removed from the house. Before they disappeared, Poppy managed to safeguard some photos and kept them hidden inside the statue he and his sister had stolen from the church.

"I think she knew she was going to be sent away. That statue was her last act of defiance. We hid it in the garden." Poppy drew a rattly breath. "I wrapped the photos in waxed cloth and put them in a tin so the snails and earwigs wouldn't get them, and brought the whole lot in here when my parents died."

I looked up at the now reinstated statue. Her smile seemed deeper, her cheeks rosier. For years I had resented her domineering presence, when all along she was a shrine to Poppy's sister.

I gave his hand a squeeze. "She got pregnant?"

Poppy's voice was low, the anger bubbling behind the bite of his consonants. "I had no idea what happened to her. I didn't know about sex and where babies came from. She was taken from me and I wasn't allowed to grieve for her when she died. Wasn't even allowed to talk about her. It was...confusing and isolating. It wasn't until I was a much less naive young bugger that I worked out what had happened."

"Did she really die?"

He gave a single nod. "I found out where they'd sent her and visited. I was taken to her grave in the home's grounds. She died from complications after the birth. They wouldn't tell me what happened to the baby."

Now his reaction to Mrs White made sense. Hearing those accusatory words hurled at me, of supposed licentiousness, of a shameful pregnancy, would have been deeply upsetting and unsettling.

"You know I've swallowed my stubborn pride and been seeing someone to help me work my way through this?"

I shook my head. "All those times you disappeared you were seeing a counsellor? I thought you were sneaking off for a nooner with Mrs White."

Poppy's laugh held no humour in it.

When he finally looked at me, the whites of his eyes were criss-crossed with blood vessels. "I'm so old, Sadie. I need to be at peace with this. It's been a bugger to live with for nearly eighty years. Would be a bloody shame to die with a bitter heart."

With a clarity borne of hindsight, the parts *thunked* into place like I'd won a level of Tetris.

Poppy wasn't suffering from dementia. He was coming to terms with his grief in his own way - playing the games he used to play with Eddie, reliving the misdeeds he'd done with her when their parents were absent. Her ghost in this critical time of his need, was very real. It needed to be. After eighty years of forcing her into forgetfulness, he needed to bring her back to finally be able to mourn her.

It was no wonder he was a grouch, a distant father. He'd been shouldering an awful burden his whole life. He'd had his only source of the kind of love that nurtures taken away from him.

"What was her name. Edwina?"

Poppy smiled and squeezed my hand. "Sadie."

Warmth bloomed in my chest.

"I couldn't say 'Sadie' when I was wee. The closest I could come to was 'Eddie'. It stuck."

"But if no one knew, if Dad didn't know about her, how did I get her name?"

"I suggested it when you were born. They wanted to call you Hannah. Something about the way you gripped my little finger like you wanted to snap it off, the way you held my eyes when they wandered unfocused and cross-eyed the rest of the time, reminded me of her fierceness, her larger-than-life-ness. I told them it was a family name and your mother happened to like it."

He gripped my hand on top of the sandwich stack and shook it. "I'm really happy you got to bear her name. You're different, but no less...wonderful."

I smiled and leaned across, kissing his temple. "Was what Dante Kerr sang about true?"

Poppy's mouth turned down at the mention of Kerr's name and it took him several seconds to gather his answer. "The knowledge they sent my sister to a lonely death without family around her, eventually ate away at my parents. The grief, the guilt, turned them half mad. I couldn't give them any sodding sympathy." He shook his head. "They'd brought it on themselves and ceased to function like proper humans from then on, including in their obligations to me." Running a hand down his face, he let out a long sigh. "What your father and Peter are doing now, is to be expected, I suppose." He looked at me then. "I didn't know how to father, Sadie. I'd never been shown. Your father and your uncle have every reason to resent me."

"You were carrying this awful thing around with you."

"Doesn't excuse me from being a bad parent."

"No, but talking about it with them will help build the bridge."

Poppy looked up at the statue. "I'm not ready, yet. I've got one more thing I need to do."

"The final item on the misdeeds list?"

A nod. "It has to go."

The broken profile of the shed, hidden behind bushes in the back yard, swam into my mind. For as long as I could remember, Poppy had forbidden his grandchildren from going anywhere near it. It was dangerous, a small person death trap.

"What was the shed used for? Why have you been so adamant we don't go near it?"

"It was the wood shed. My parents used to shut us away in it if we'd misbehaved." He shrugged. "We were out of control, left to our own devices while they worked long hours. They didn't know how to handle it. We'd be locked in total bloody darkness for hours. It was terrifying, not being able to see my hand in front of my face, hearing cockroaches scuttling, mice scratching. Eddie -" a smile flickered across his face. "- Was put in there more and more not long before she was sent away. It didn't scare her. She laughed at my parents, which made her stays longer. I used to sit outside and talk to her through the wall, upset on her behalf, missing our freedom." Shaking his head, he said, "Bloody awful thing. I haven't gone near it since I was too big for my parents to force me in it."

I gave his hand a pat. "Well, Poppy. We have absolutely nothing left to lose now. Let's do it for Eddie."

I stood up, then lowered a hand to help him up. "I smell like a sewer. Let me shower and then let's plan this thing."

"I'll get the pancakes on."

When I emerged from the bathroom smelling significantly sweeter than I had ten minutes before and the aroma of the cooking batter sending my saliva glands into overdrive, there was a new centrepiece on the table.

At its base were two small sets of electrical componentry and protruding upwards behind them were what looked like long antennae.

"What's this, Poppy?"

"A Jacob's Ladder."

I was none-the-wiser. "What does it do?"

"Creates an electric spark that jumps between the two wires."

"Huh. Why is it on the table?"

"It's programmed to work remotely. I need you to test it. You can control it with your walkabout phone."

"Through an app?"

Poppy grunted and flipped a pancake, which I took as confirmation. "Okay, we can test it out." The photos, I noticed, were stacked neatly on the sideboard. "You've dismantled the shrine?"

"It's time. Eddie wants to be acknowledged. To take her rightful place back in the family."

I got up and picked through the photos. She had the same mischievous smile as Poppy, hair a shade or two lighter, his wiry frame. She bore absolutely no physical resemblance to me.

"Did it make you sad having another Sadie in the family?"

Poppy ladled batter into the pan before answering. "It helped me. My heart needed softening. I could love you as freely as I loved my sister." He turned and looked at me. "You, my girl, were a blessing."

THE SHED HAD, naturally, experienced some decay over the years of neglect. Holes appeared where boards had split and cracked, or simply rotten. The floor slumped on one side.

I was given the task of screwing in sections of ply board over the holes and running beads of gap filler where the boards had shrunk and parted from each other. The shed was to be made as air tight as possible.

As the light began to fade on the western skyline and the first of the stars emerged on the eastern, Poppy handed me a pair of goggles and a respirator.

"Shake the bags out. Get as much of the stuff circulating in there as possible."

I did as instructed and emerged from the shed a ghost, flour shedding from my hair and clothes in little puffs.

Poppy patted me down, getting the worst off, and asked if I was ready.

I pulled the mask off and said, "Affirmative, Commander."

"Did you plant the device?"

"Device planted."

Poppy nodded once. "Let's go." He turned and headed for the gate in the back fence.

I took three steps after him, then halted. "Poppy, wait. I need to do something first." I returned to the house and put on Flick's T-shirt. Then I retrieved my collection of control briefs from the drawer at The Virgin's base.

As I rose to stand, her left hand brushed the top of my head as if she'd reached out and stroked me.

I looked into her tranquil face and mirrored her smile.

Back at the shed, I eased the door open enough to slide in an arm and threw the underwear into the dark interior.

Poppy waited for me at the gate with a torch and I joined him to climb the hill. Obi-Wan trotted ahead of us.

When we reached the top and turned towards Poppy's backyard, we fell into line, Obi-Wan on one side of me, Poppy on the other. Before us, the town stretched out in a criss-cross of street lights, the houses small squares of curtain-shrouded light.

Poppy's house and the backyard were sheathed in darkness.

I pulled out my phone, thumbed open the Jacob's Ladder app and took Poppy's hand in my free one.

I looked down at him.

"Spark it up."

We swivelled our heads towards the house. My thumb hovered above the app. Then I tapped the screen.

The shed exploded with a retina-searing surge of light and an almighty *BOOM.*

A minute later the town's air raid siren went off.

"Here comes the cavalry."

CHAPTER SEVENTEEN

WE WAITED until the fire truck reversed out of the driveway before making our way down the hill.

Obi-Wan leapt and skipped down the slope, and by the look on Poppy's torch-lit face, his heart was doing the same.

The remains of the shed were a watery, charcoaled pile of splintered wood. Bits of shed decorated the roof of the garage. A few pieces were scattered on the lawn.

"Veggie garden's probably shrapnelled to buggery," Poppy said. "Just when my tomato plants were getting to a decent height."

"It's still early enough to replant if you need to." I laid a hand on his shoulder. "We'll have a look in the morning."

A movement by the back door brought Obi-Wan to a standstill with a bleat.

Callum stepped out of the shadows and the security light came on. In his hand was a singed-looking Jacob's ladder, the antennae bent at right angles. "I didn't think you'd be far away."

Poppy stepped up to him and plucked the device from his fingers. "I'd thank you, but I wouldn't really mean it and you don't look in the mood to accept it." Then he opened the back door and disappeared inside.

Callum turned his head from the back door to me. His eyes flickered down my front, reading the text. "What are you doing, Sadie? Getting charged for burglary wasn't enough of a rush? You have to start blowing things up now?"

"It was a controlled explosion."

"*Controlled*. There are pieces of wood embedded in the steel of the garage wall. I should be charging you both for reckless endangering. It's only luck you haven't damaged neighbouring property or hurt anybody, though there's always time. Who knows what the adjacent properties will reveal in the light of morning. God." He ran a hand through his hair. "I feel like I've aged ten years since you came to town."

"Well, you don't have to worry any more. We're done."

"What do you mean '*we're done*'?"

"No more misdeeds. The list is complete. Poppy's done what he needs to and I won't be a problem for you anymore."

"What list?"

"Poppy's list of misdemeanours from when he was a boy. We've restaged them all."

"*That's* what you've been up to? Humouring the dangerous whims of a geriatric so he can die happy?"

"Something like that."

"Jesus. You Quinns."

I bristled and Poppy's devilish grin slid across my face. "I know, right? Hell of a way to process our baggage."

"Oh yeah? And how's that working out for you? Two family members about to be the proud bearers of a criminal record."

I shrugged my shoulders. "I don't like it, Callum, but I have to accept it's happening. There's nothing else I can do."

"How about trying to avoid another conviction by being a responsible human being? It's like you lost your common sense when you lost your business."

I pointed at the house. "He's gained so much. It's all been worth it."

"What could he have possibly gained that was worth risking you for?" Callum's voice cracked.

My heart flip flopped. I stepped up to him, tipped myself on my toes and delivered a soft kiss to his lips.

His breath shook as he inhaled against my lips.

"Ask him. It's his story to tell if he wants you to know." I gave him a small smile. "Goodbye, Callum." Then I stepped past him and headed inside.

IT WAS eight o'clock the next morning when I got the call from Mum to say the convoy was en route to Tokawai for an intervention. Her and Dad, Uncle Peter, Leonie the clinician, and a nurse.

I'd figured the news of the explosion wouldn't have taken long to filter through Dad's spy channel and that it was likely to push things to a head, but I had no idea how things would play out.

On one hand there was the truth - a startling one, that would test the tenuous bonds between Gerry Quinn and his sons. On the other, there was a determination by my father and his brother to make their lives easier by not having to worry about a troublesome father, a determination supported by clinical evidence and a legal mandate to dispense with their parent how they wished.

The truth might not change anything if they didn't want it to.

I figured having Mum and a couple of objective medical professionals present would weight things in our favour, but when I asked Poppy how he wanted to approach the situation, a slow grin spread on his face.

"Eddie would never have gone down without a fight."

"You want to take the offensive?"

"Too bloody right I want to take the offensive. If they haul me away today, I want to have done Eddie proud."

"I don't think it'll come to that, Poppy."

"I'm not taking the risk. We've got five hours to set up a defensive perimeter. Let's take stock of our arsenal and call in the posse."

DAD DROVE the first car to pull into the driveway. Uncle Peter sat in the front passenger seat, Mum in the back.

Poppy's car was parked in front of the burned out garage, and the property was still and quiet with Poppy and me ostensibly waiting inside, warming the teapot.

A goat emerged from the rear of the house and clip-clopped up the driveway. Then it stood a metre from the front fender and eyed the occupants.

Like all carefully-laid plans, they were pulled into the diversion, their attention on the small, gangly, round-bellied creature blocking their path to the back door.

Uncle Peter's lips mouthed, "Why is there a goat in the driveway?"

"Waaait," Poppy said from a cluster of bushes near the bumper of Dad's car. "Not until they crack their doors."

Three seatbelts were removed, a few words spoken, a yawn stifled, and then doors were released.

"Hold," Poppy said again. "They need a foot on the ground."

Uncle Peter was the first to throw his door wide. He leaned back in his seat, hands clasped on the frame of the door to give himself leverage for his large belly.

My fingers twitched.

Then, as Mum and Dad leaned into the swing of their doors, Poppy shouted. "Fire!"

The ornamental conifer charged forward and issued a white missile. It exploded against the window of Dad's door with a poompf, the force of it driving him back into his seat.

The camellia issued a quavering scream and delivered a projectile through the rear door. It hit Mum in the chest. Her head disappeared in a white haze.

"Yes! Take that, beeyotches."

Uncle Peter, having left himself wide open, never stood a chance. My flour bomb caught him on the chin. He turned his head sideways and lost balance, falling back into the car.

Dad's door twitched forward a couple of inches.

"They're regrouping," the conifer shouted. "Ready round two. And fire!"

My next shot hit Dad in the back of the head as Poppy's hit him in the face.

The second car arrived just as Flick's bomb landed and flour splattered against the inside of the rear window of the first car. A wide-eyed Leonie sat behind the wheel with a young man beside her in the passenger seat.

The three doors of Dad's car hastily slammed shut. A swell of muted shouts and unintelligible words rose from within.

The young man beside Leonie laid a hand on her shoulder and released his door. I helped remind him of his place by landing a bomb on his window at the exact position of his head.

He clicked the door to again.

"Rear gunner," Poppy shouted. "Advance."

A hydrangea with a beakish set to its lips appeared from the back of the house, hose in hand.

Dad and Uncle Peter exchanged furious words, then Uncle Peter unlatched his door and pushed forward, his arms wrapped over the top of his head, chin tucked down.

Mrs White hit him in the ear with a jet of water. "I wouldn't do that if I were you. Not unless you want to be glued to your seat for the duration of your return journey."

He flopped back into his seat, once again pulling the door closed.

A third car pulled into the driveway, it's red and blue lights flashing.

My heart stuttered and I stepped back into the weeping bottlebrush, becoming one with it again.

"Will we get arrested if we nail Callum's arse?" asked the camellia.

"Retreat," yelled the conifer. "To the second defensive perimeter. Cover us, rear gunner."

We ran down the driveway to the backyard as Mrs White fired a final volley, pelting the windscreen of Dad's sedan.

Once we had settled into position, our camouflage melding into the backyard greenery, we waited for the invaders to send their advance guard.

Nothing happened.

Two minutes went by and no heads appeared around the corner of the house. Nobody dive-rolled over the exposed section to the shelter of Poppy's car.

"What's happening?" Mrs White whispered.

Another minute of nothing passed.

"Sadie, do a recce," Poppy said. "Get us some intel."

I ran around the far side of the house towards the front lawn and hunkered down behind a pittosporum.

Callum stood beside Leonie's car in conversation with her and the nurse, while Mum argued with Dad and Peter.

"I'm not playing his game, Deborah."

"Oh, come on, Alan," Mum said, dusting off a sleeve. "It's all harmless. He's just trying to make a point."

"What point? What point could he possibly be making apart from confirming that he's totally doolally."

"What I want to know," said Uncle Peter, "is why the police are here."

Dad grunted and turned around to face Callum. "You there! Why are you here?"

Callum turned his face towards Dad. "I presume, Mr Quinn, you're talking to me?"

"Of course, I'm talking to you. I know why the other two are here."

Callum eyed Dad for beat, shifting the balance of power back towards him. "I'm here because I received a call that someone was being forcibly removed from their home. I have a duty to investigate, and to protect the interests of my community."

I smiled and looked back over my shoulder towards the backyard as if I could see the faces hidden there. I had no idea who'd made the call. I could only assume it was Flick or Mrs White.

"*Forcibly removed?* We're not going to straitjacket him."

"Seems like you've brought quite a team to make sure it happens."

"The stubborn old bugger clearly needs some convincing, and the urgency is real."

"He blew up a shed last night," added Uncle Peter.

"You saw that sideshow we were subjected to. He's crazy. They're the actions of a child. How he's roped in others to fight for him -"

"Mrs White!" My uncle sounded scandalised.

"We won't be pandering to his whims, officer," said Dad. "He's dangerous."

"You won't be forcing him to do anything he doesn't want to, either."

Silence.

Dad took a step towards him, straightening his cuffs. It was the kind of gesture made by someone who considered himself of import - a self-made man entitled to recognition of his status. The effect was somewhat undermined by the remains of a white blast radius covering the front of his smart-casual jacket. "Was it you who arrested him?"

"Yes."

"So, do you admit he's dangerous?"

"He's had a few lapses of judgement."

"Oh, *come on*. He used some sort of explosive last night. An explosive!"

"Flour."

After a beat, Uncle Peter said, "I beg your pardon?"

"He ignited flour. It's hardly dynamite."

"It blew up a shed!"

"Seemingly reckless, yes, but nobody was hurt and no property damaged." Callum moved past Dad and down the driveway towards the back of the house. "If you want to have a conversation with Gerry, now's your chance. Take it, or I'll escort you off the property."

Dad and Uncle Peter looked at each other, then turned to follow Callum. The others followed in their wake.

I ran back to my position and hissed, "They're on their way. Be ready."

Callum rounded the corner of the house and stopped at the beginning of the path to the back door. The group halted behind him.

"Do you think they're in the house?" asked Mum.

"Not on your life," said Uncle Peter. "They'll be lying in wait in the garden."

"Gerry?" Callum called. "There are people here who want to talk to you about your future. Could you please come out?"

When Poppy didn't answer, Dad growled, "For God's sake".

"We need to draw them in," whispered Poppy. "Get them into the hot zone."

Leonie stepped forward to stand by Callum's side. "Gerry? Would you like to come out and talk? Everyone's here out of concern for you."

Poppy emitted a "ha!" and the eyes of the group shifted to the conifer crouched behind the plum tree.

"He's not coming out," said Dad, turning to face Leonie. "I won't pander to the whims of a child. This is just more proof of the instability of his mind." He whipped around to face the lawn again. "Sadie? You get out here now. This is utterly ridiculous."

I shouted, "I'm not a child, Dad. I don't have to jump to your command," and winced, knowing I had in no way helped the situation

Uncle Peter rumbled out a laugh. "This is crazy. Are we just going to stay here all day in this absurd stand off?"

I looked at Poppy and whispered, "What do we do?"

"We shoulda laid a honey trap," said Flick. "Lulled their unsuspecting arses."

"We're not approaching anywhere within firing range," said Dad. "So, you might as well come out now."

The plan, which seemed flawless this morning during our strategy session, now looked set to unravel. We couldn't initiate our second and most vital offensive if they weren't in range.

"Fuuuuuck," I muttered into my branches.

A bleat at the far end of the yard drew my attention. Obi-Wan clattered her way across the boards on the vege garden, strolled past the defensive line of shrubbery and crossed the lawn to the waiting group.

She stopped in front of Callum and regurgitated something on to his shoes.

"Is that a photo?" asked Uncle Peter as Callum bent to pick it up. He flicked the saliva off, looked at it for several seconds, then passed it to Dad.

Mum and Uncle Peter crowded around, peering at it.

Dad frowned and turned the photo over. "Gerald and Sadie 'Eddie' Quinn in front of their secret clubhouse. 1947." He turned the photo back over and looked at Uncle Peter. "Who's Sadie? I don't know any relative of ours with that name, except my Sadie."

Peter took the photo off him. "She looks like Dad." He looked up and stepped towards the conifer. "Dad? Who's this in the photo with you?"

"Peter, wait." Mum rushed to follow, her arm stretched forward to grab his shoulder.

"In range," said Mrs White.

"Execute Combatant One," Poppy yelled.

I pulled on the string labelled *One* and a large rectangular piece of cardboard popped up from its hide of grass clippings like a human target in a shoot-out simulation.

Mum yelped and jumped backwards.

Uncle Peter turned around to face Dad. "Here she is again, Alan."

As he turned back to the enlarged photo and the rest of the group shuffled forward to join him, Mum read, "Gerald and Sadie 'Eddie' Quinn, French Resistance fighters. 1946."

"Execute Combatant Two."

Flick pulled on one of her strings and another rectangle popped up from out of its camouflage.

Dad read, "Gerald and Sadie 'Eddie' Quinn, cowboys. 1945."

"Is this...is this the Eddie Dad said helped him up on to the top of the wardrobe?" Uncle Peter said. "That was an Eddie, right?"

"Combatant Three."

Another string pull, another enlarged photo. Dad, Uncle Peter and Mum approached it as Callum, Leonie and the nurse stepped up to view the second photo.

"Gerald and Sadie 'Eddie' Quinn, washing line swing. 1940," Uncle Peter read. "I don't...I don't understand. Who is this person?"

Callum swivelled his gaze from the photo to the collection of bottlebrush leaves I had strapped to me. "Somebody pretty important if Gerry's gone to this much trouble to show her to you." Then he stepped towards the third photo as Poppy shouted, "Four."

There were eight photos in all.

Gerald and Sadie 'Eddie' Quinn, ray gun inventors. 1945.

Gerald and Sadie 'Eddie' Quinn, playing marbles. 1943.

Gerald and Sadie 'Eddie' Quinn, grass sledding. 1941.

Gerald and Sadie 'Eddie' Quinn, blanket fort. 1943.

And finally, *Douglas, Rose, Sadie and Gerald Quinn, outside Quinn's Bakery, 1946.*

When the last one had been revealed and the back lawn descended into silence, I ran the gauntlet to Poppy's position, knowing full well everyone could see me. I crouched beside him and whispered. "It's time, Poppy. Are you ready?"

"Gerald Quinn," Dad boomed. "For goodness sake, come out and explain -"

"Shut up, Alan," Uncle Peter hissed. "This isn't your boardroom. You can't snap your fingers and shout and expect people to cow to your whims. Just *shut up*."

I grinned at Poppy.

"Dad?" Uncle Peter continued. "I really want to talk to you about these photos. Alan does too, he just doesn't know how to do it without being a pushy bastard. Will you please come out?"

I raised my eyebrows at Poppy and he gave a single nod.

Standing up, I pulled a piece of paper out of my back pocket and read, "Here's Poppy's conditions. You will listen while seated. You will not interrupt until Gerald Quinn's representative, Sadie 'The Younger' Quinn has finished speaking and Gerald has offered concluding remarks. You will consent to Gerald Quinn's GP doing a second evaluation of his mental state. All decisions on Gerald Quinn's future will be made collaboratively and consensually. You will investigate alternative options to rehoming him, if such an investigation is required, and you will respect his choice. Do you agree?"

Uncle Peter looked at Dad.

Dad glared back. "He doesn't know his own mind," he hissed. "How can we *collaborate* with him. He's incapable."

Mum stepped forward to create the third wall of their huddle. "It can't be any worse than the current approach, Alan."

"He'll make it absolutely impossible, as per usual. And I doubt very much his GP will be unbiased."

Uncle Peter shifted closer to Dad, their faces inches away. "Of course he'll be unbiased," he said in a fierce whisper. "Doctors are professionals. They behave professionally, which means *no bias*."

"Not doctors who have known their patients for most of their lifetimes."

Uncle Peter's jaw clenched. His chest rose with a deep breath before he placed his hands on Dad's shoulders and lowered his voice. "How can you not want to know what this is all about? What the story is behind these pictures?"

"I want to know." Dad jabbed a finger in the conifer's direction. "Just not all on his terms."

Uncle Peter dropped his hands and eyed Dad for several seconds. Without shifting his gaze, he called, "Yes, we agree. At least I do. Alan can speak for himself."

Dad opened his mouth, closed it again and looked at Mum, who nodded and flapped her hands in a shooing gesture.

He turned his head towards Poppy, sucked in a breath and expelled it through pursed lips. Then he tipped his head back to throw his words into the air above him and raised his palms as if imploring whatever he saw up there. "OK, fine. I agree."

I lowered my hand to Poppy to help him up and said, "Please go through to the living room and take your seats."

After they'd disappeared inside the house, Flick emerged from her position, shedding branches. She "boo-ya"ed and ran from conifer to bottle brush to hydrangea, raising her hands for a high ten.

When she got to Mrs White she was met by a steely glare. "Don't you think about slapping me. Come on." She gave Flick a push in the direction of the driveway. "Our job is done."

Flick stumbled. Turning, she wrapped a hand around Mrs White's upper arm, giving it a squeeze. "Oosh, gangsta, you got some iron in those breadsticks."

"I eat all my spinach." Mrs White pointed up the driveway. "Get! They've got the hardest bit to do, yet. Let's get out of their way."

Flick looped an armed through Mrs White's, told her she wanted to be like her when she grew up, and they disappeared around the corner of the house.

I smiled at Poppy, helped him out of branches, and with a deep breath headed for the back door.

When we stepped through to the lounge, everyone turned their faces expectantly towards us. Dad glowered on the couch beside Uncle Peter, Callum perched on its arm beside Mum, and Leonie and the nurse sat in the two armchairs.

I placed the dining chair I had brought in with me in front of them for Poppy to sit in. Then I positioned myself behind him and placed my hands on his thin shoulders.

Poppy drew a long, rattling breath and told the story of a loving relationship, full of adventure and mischief, between a sister and her much younger brother. He told them the tragic end of her story and the family's descent into dysfunction.

When he'd finished and haltingly apologised for the way that his parents' treatment of his sister and of him, and the forced boxing-up of his grief, had turned him into a difficult man, and a distant father, Dad stood. "This is a lot." His voice was thick. He swallowed, then walked out of the room.

"I'm seeing a counsellor," Poppy said to his disappearing

back, his voice low with humility. Then he looked at Uncle Peter. "I want...I want to make things better between us."

Uncle Peter regarded Poppy, then he leaned forward in his seat, hands clasped, elbows on knees. "Dad? I appreciate you doing that, seeing a counsellor. That's a brave thing to do. You need to know it might take me and Alan a while to work through this to reach understanding, but we will. You're going to have to be very patient, particularly with Alan."

Poppy nodded and looked at his hands in his lap.

I cleared my throat and brought out another piece of paper from my pocket. It was crumpled, the ink smudged. I smoothed it out on the coffee table.

Everyone leaned in to read it. "Misdeeds list," Leonie said and looked up and into Uncle Peter's face.

"Lace the communion wafers with laxatives," Mum read. She gasped. "You put laxatives in the communion wafers?"

"These were the naughty things Poppy and Eddie did when their parents were absent. Poppy wanted to relive them, to help him finally process his grief by remembering these experiences with her. We changed them to work in with what was possible now."

I could feel Callum's eyes on me. "You changed the wording on the church sign instead."

"So, the crazy stuff you've been doing, Gerry, were items on this list?" asked Leonie. She pulled the list towards her and read, "Burn down the wood shed."

Poppy's voice bubbled in his throat. "Eddie and I never quite got to that last item. She was taken away before we could destroy the blasted thing."

"But you made sure you destroyed it this time around," said Callum.

Poppy's smile lacked mirth. "That thing has been a reminder my whole life of that awful time, of how she looked out for me for all of my childhood and I couldn't protect her. It needed a savage end."

Callum nodded. "I can't condone what you did, but I understand."

Mum slapped her hands on her knees and stood up. "I don't know about you lot, but I could do with a very big cup of tea." She started for the door. "I'll make a pot. Sadie, come and help me?"

Before I could follow her, Callum stood up. "I'll be on my way. You don't need me here any longer. Gerry." He reached out and shook Poppy's hand. Then, with a glance at me that had my heart tumbling through the emptiness in my chest, he turned and left the room.

WHEN MUM DROPPED me off at the pub that evening, a Tokawai Drag Race sign, erected above the entrance to the car park, greeted me. The lot was filled with cars adorned with racing stripes and numbers.

My step faltered. It had to be Fuzz Cup night, which would mean seeing Callum. I had no idea how that would go. He now had a complete picture about the reason for my recent behaviour, but that didn't alter the fact I was facing burglary charges. No amount of backyard theatrics could change that.

I read the *Tokawai Drag Race* sign again. How on earth were they going to pull off an illegal drag race in the car park? Surely they wouldn't go so far as to race in the street. Not only was it dangerous, it kind of defeated the purpose of the game, which was to draw Callum into the pub.

Perhaps I wouldn't be seeing him after all.

When I opened the back doors, I understood.

Every single Fuzz Cup competitor who might otherwise be dressed in a combination of rugby or plaid shirt, jeans or fleece pants, work boots or socks, was adorned in a dress and a wig.

Ru Paul's Drag Race had come to Tokawai.

The mood was buoyant, the men more animated, the laughter louder.

"Proof," Manawa said when I voiced my observation to her, "that men love dressing up as women."

Something else was different about tonight. The pub was fuller than any previous Fuzz Cup events. Not all the women were in ball gowns or wearing garish lipstick.

"Why are there *actual* women here?"

Manawa held up a glass and eyed it before filling it with wine. "One of two possible reasons. Tonight's Fuzz Cup's the final, so they could be here in support. But I put my money on two. The spectacle value. Who wouldn't want to miss this glorious display of womanhood?"

A skinny man in a cream satin and lace gown leant against the bar and asked for a lager.

"Is that your wife's wedding dress, Lance?" asked Manawa.

Lance shrugged. "She doesn't seem to wear it any more. Shame to let it go to waste."

I laughed. It was the first laugh I'd had since the whole sorry Jordan affair had reared its ugly head. It felt good - a small reprieve from the pang in my chest that had been growing a little more each day since. If I'd had any previous experience with it, I suspected I might recognise it as heartache.

Manawa's eyes flicked up to my face then back to the

rum and coke she was pouring. "Good to hear some colour in your voice, Sadie. It must've been a hell of an ailment to knock you out for three days."

She was no fool. I knew she meant "ailment" in the broadest sense of the word.

"Was it to do with Callum?"

"Partly."

She grunted. "I've wondered why he's looked so sour the last few days. He only just took that terrifying leap of faith into the chasm of love and I take it you've given him a hard landing?"

Chasm of love? I very much doubted that. "What's your policy on employing someone with a criminal conviction?"

"Why? Are you thinking of getting one? I hear they're the new tattoos."

When I didn't answer, she said, "Poor bugger. You'll have shaken the foundations of his universe."

"Yes." As dramatic as Manawa's comment sounded, right now if felt like an apt description. I tipped the IPA tap towards me and began to fill a glass. "It's not for anything serious. If I'm lucky, I'll get diversion, but if I don't, you have to think about whether you still want me working here."

"What's it for?"

"Burglary."

Manawa raised her brows. "Burglary? You?"

"I *had* been thinking of getting a tattoo of Justin Bieber on my back, but I'm scared of needles."

Manawa's brows remained raised.

I sighed. "It's a long and embarrassing story. I'd rather tell you only if I need to."

"Are you reformed?"

"One hundred percent."

"Then we're all good."

I looked up from filling the second glass and met her eye. Her face bore its usual stern expression, but I had no doubt she was sincere. "Thank you."

I put the transaction for the two beers through the EFTPOS machine and asked, "Where's Mitchell?"

Manawa jerked her head in the direction of the store room. "Padding his bra? Removing the curlers from his hair? I've no idea. He's watched YouTube videos all day about how to soften the masculine lines of the face with make-up. I don't know what he's using. The only make-up I own is a dried-up tube of under eye concealer."

The storeroom door opened and Flick stepped out, closing it behind her.

Manawa looked her up and down and said, "What are you doing in my storeroom?" She pushed past her and made a grab for the door knob. "My husband better not have been in there with you. The only person that gets to be in the storeroom -" She pushed open the door and stopped dead in her tracks, staring into the room's interior. An absent-minded "with" fell out of her mouth, before she stepped inside and slammed the door closed behind her.

Flick raised her arm and tapped at her watch. "Thunderbirds are go. I'm predicting what with having to negotiate stockings and a dress that I had to lube his arse up to get into, a time of three minutes, seventeen seconds. Not their longest, but legit above average. And he'll have to work harder on account of the lack of kissing."

"Lack of kissing?"

"Took me one hundred and eighteen minutes to make him look less lumberjack and more fire bunny." She mimed a fire blazing from her skull. "He better not be messing up my artistry."

At three minutes and twenty-five seconds, the storeroom swung wide and a beautiful red-headed woman in a purple sequinned halter-neck dress stepped out to the sound of cat calls. She had a fine nose, sweeping cheekbones, full lips and arched eyebrows. Mitchell was unrecognisable.

"Ladies," he called to the pub floor in a falsetto. "Are we ready to get this auspicious evening underway?"

A chorus of camp affirmations answered him and he sashayed around the bar to join them.

The storeroom door whined open and Manawa crawled out on her hands and knees. She stopped at my feet and raised a hand. "Sadie, help me up."

I pulled her to her feet. She staggered back against the service bench and placed a hand to her cheek. Her mouth flapped open twice before any words came out. "I had no idea how sexy a man could look in lipstick and a gorgeous dress."

A hairy-shouldered man in a matted blonde wig and crushed velvet tube dress cleared his throat.

Manawa turned and eyed him, her face expressionless. "I stand corrected," she said tonelessly.

As Flick engaged the man in a conversation about the merits of depilatory cream or waxing, a Go-Go Girl with a blue French bob teetered through the double doors in four-inch heeled boots. She shouted, "He's here," and my heart leapt like someone had laid defibrillator paddles on my chest and turned them to full power.

The men arranged themselves into their idea of feminine poses. Those on bar stools crossed their legs and laid hands on knees, while others flicked their hair and placed hands on cocked hips.

"That -" Manawa pointed out at the pub floor. "- Is a

faithful representation. God, it's hard being sexy all of the time."

The pub doors cracked open. Fingers curled around the edges of the wood. The doors pushed forward.

A laughing Callum stepped over the sticky floorboards and I put my fingers in my ears as whistles and whoops filled the air in a deafening wave.

"I make it 6.20 pm," Manawa shouted and turned to write the result in the matrix. The room surged forward towards the scoreboard, jostling to make sense of the final numbers.

Callum's eyes swivelled from the stampede of stilettoed men to me and the grin dropped from his face.

The throbbing in my chest unfurled and surged into my limbs. I couldn't move. I was cast in an impotent stasis.

His lips shifted into the ghost of a smile and he turned to the door.

The break in eye contact gave the ache a reprieve and it receded, freeing my body from its paralysis. I ran to the end of the bar. "Callum, wait."

He stopped and turned.

I ground to a halt three steps away from him, breathing hard, like I'd run a hundred metres, not fifteen. "I, um, wanted to say how much I appreciated you being present today. It was incredibly kind of you."

A nod. "It's only Gerry who needs to thank me. I did it for him."

I sucked in five more slowing breaths before managing an "I see". The ache dropped to my stomach. "I'd better get back to work."

Callum ran a hand through his hair. "I didn't." He put his hands in his pockets and looked at his shoes. "I didn't just do it for him." After a beat, he raised his eyes and met mine.

I was caught by the blue, a blue so pale as to be irides-cent. The ache turned warm and molten, and hummed with restless energy.

Someone shouted, "Callum, get over here for a drink, man," but he didn't look away.

We clearly had some shit we needed to resolve. And we needed to do it right now. "Are you free to talk?" spilled out of my mouth in a rush.

He nodded. "I'm off the clock. Swung by here on my way home."

I looked at Manawa.

She raised her eyebrows, then lifted her chin as if to say get out of here, and I turned and strode out through the double doors, hoping Callum would follow.

Once outside and into the quiet of the early evening, the urgency evaporated with my confidence. I wasn't sure what to do next.

I looked around the car park, searching for a place that might afford us privacy and comfort.

"Would you..." Callum faltered. "I've got the squad car. Should we sit in there?"

I nodded.

He led me to the farthest corner of the car park and held the door open while I climbed in. Then he walked to his side, removed his stab-proof vest and threw it onto the back seat. It took him five seconds between closing the back door and opening the driver's to climb in, which was, it was fair to say, rather discouraging.

He settled into the seat, placed his feet on the pedals, then pulled his legs back, his knees framing the steering wheel. Gripping the wheel, he stilled and stared at his hands.

My heart rate ratcheted up in tempo with each second he remained silent.

I opened my mouth to prise open the conversation we needed to have when Callum asked, "How are things at home?"

I blew out a puff of air. "Delicate. Bloody awkward. They're booked in at the motel. They decided to stay the night to avoid driving the long distance in the dark, so that's given things a little more time."

"Good. That's good."

"Mum spent the afternoon with us while Dad and Uncle Peter did, I don't know, whatever they needed to do, but they're all having dinner together, so that's a good start."

Callum nodded and twisted his hands over the wheel. "I'm glad." He still hadn't looked at me since he'd climbed into the car.

I reached out a hand and laid it across the top of his left one, stilling it.

He stiffened.

Prising his fingers open, I pulled his hand onto the centre console and wrapped it between my own. A hand sandwich.

Callum looked down at it for several seconds, then up at me.

"I'm really sorry you're hurting, Callum. That my thoughtless actions put you in a position where you were forced to make a really shitty choice."

"You left me with no choice, Sadie," Callum said, quietly.

And yet, his words, his look in the pub told me that maybe, probably, after a few days' space, things were beginning to look a little different. "At the time, yes. It would have been a hell of a thing to wrap your head around."

He gazed down at our hands again, opened his mouth, and closed it again.

"You know everything now. There's nothing else hidden. The motivations for all my actions are laid out for you to pick through, and what I want to know is do you still think I'm someone who would make it impossible for you to -" I broke off, steeling myself to say the words neither of us had mentioned to each other before. "- Be in a relationship with?"

Callum turned his hand over and gripped the one I'd placed on top. "I'm not sure. I'm still working through my anger at your stupidity. It hasn't been easy to reconcile the person I've come to know with the person who did that."

"I don't recognise that person, either. I'm pretty sure she's not me. At least what she did isn't part of the shape of Sadie Quinn."

"You sure she isn't? When you're pushed into a corner, you're not going to lose control?"

"No. I don't think I'll need to. I have people in that corner with me now."

Callum looked out the windscreen and said nothing.

My chest tightened with each of my heartbeats. I wanted to keep pushing, to argue the worthiness of Sadie Quinn, but I also knew I needed to tread lightly. One false move and this delicate dance would be over.

After enough time for me to have planned my humiliating but graceful retreat, Callum spoke. "It's a big thing to ask me to trust you, Sadie." He turned to face me. "Something like that has the power to undermine my standing here, let alone put me in an impossible position professionally. I mean, we're not talking about a little office indiscretion here. My job is upholding *the law*. It doesn't get much more serious than that."

"I know. Even if I was thinking straight at the time, I couldn't have anticipated...you." *Finding you.* My fingers itched to touch his face, to cup his cheek, slide my knuckles down his cinnamon skin. "You know I could never knowingly put you in that position." I slipped my fingers through his and whispered, "I really want...us. I think we can be a *good* us."

Callum's thumb moved over the back of my hand and he whispered back, "When I overlook the bombshell you dropped, I think we can, too."

My heart lifted and expanded so it filled the whole of my chest. "Can you overlook it? On a more permanent basis, I mean?"

"I'm -" He paused, his eyes flicking between mine. "-Beginning to think I might be able to. As long as it stays between you, me and Gerry."

"And Manawa."

Callum raised an eyebrow.

"She's my boss. I had to tell her and give her the option to fire me."

"What did she say?"

"She said as long as I was reformed, she was happy."

Callum nodded slowly and a smile tugged at one side of his mouth. "Why do I feel like she's just put me to shame?"

"It's Manawa. She could put the most virtuous of us to shame." I took a deep breath and willed myself to say the right thing, even if it diverted the course of our conversation towards a full stop. "But you have to do what feels right by you, not her," I said, hoping that at the very least, Callum was still open to an ellipsis.

"Yes."

It wasn't much of a clue, and his lack of willingness to expand pushed me to speak without engaging my brain. "I'll get diversion, and we can laugh about this with our grand-children." I winced. It was probably a bit early to be intro-ducing the concept of procreation. "Who...may or may not...share our genetics." Oh God.

Callum's lips twitched. "You *might* get diversion."

I decided to go for broke, seeing the only way was up from the verbal hole I'd dug for myself. "If I get diversion, can I be your girlfriend?"

"If you get diversion, I promise I'll consider you along with all my other offers."

"Oh, you've got others, have you?"

"Hello, man in uniform." He gestured to his clothes. "I'm overwhelmed by ch-".

I leaned over and stopped his words with a kiss. I inhaled his cinnamon skin and closed my eyes against the tingle along my scalp as he kissed me back.

He raised a hand to the back of my head and pulled me closer. "I really loved your T-shirt," he said against my lips.

"Thanks. I'm working on bringing my head in line with it."

"Good." He pulled away and rested his forehead against mine. "You've made it a little hard for me to feel lately, but *that* I am definitely proud of you for." Then he brought his mouth to mine for another kiss. "Beautiful Sadie Quinn."

EPILOGUE
FIVE MONTHS LATER – ST ANDREWS MALL, AUCKLAND

CALLUM'S HAND was warm in mine.

I peered down at our entwined fingers, brushing my thumb over the fine golden hairs on the back of his hand.

He brought his lips to my temple, his warm breath skating across my skin and a familiar pressure pushed against my breastbone. An expanding ball of warmth and light. It had been building ever since the Auckland police had sought what they called an "alternative resolution", part of a new drive to settle minor law infringements out of court. My alternative resolution couldn't have been more surprising. Jordan had sat across from me in the mediation room and been the first to apologise. Step nine of twelve, he said, on his road to addiction recovery.

When I emerged from our meeting to a waiting Callum, the defensive perimeter he'd carefully placed between me and his heart crumbled away. We were free to let each other in completely.

Three weeks and a trip to court later, Poppy secured the hallowed Diversion Prize without a single blurted recrimination. It had allowed us to pursue our next project with no distractions.

I smiled at Callum, then looked past him to scan the shoppers.

We sat at a table with Mum, Uncle Peter's wife and my sister, several tables away from where Poppy, Dad and Uncle Peter sat.

The three men fidgeted, twisting napkins and rotating cups in saucers. Their heads swivelled as they watched the crowd in the mall pass.

One by one, their gaze locked on an approaching figure.

He stopped at their table and with a scraping of chairs, they pushed themselves to their feet.

The man held himself erect, his spine straight despite his age. He was taller than Poppy, but shorter than his sons.

Poppy's chest rose and fell rapidly. His lips formed the word "Gerry" and he extended a hand.

The man took it, and a smile lit up his face. Pulling Poppy towards him, he wrapped his arms around him and clapped him on the back.

"Owen," he said.

Eddie's son.

THANKS FOR TAKING THE TIME TO READ MY BOOK

I hope you enjoyed it. Please consider taking the time to leave a review. As an independent author, reviews help support my work so that I can produce more great novels for you to read. If you're not sure where to post a review, try the Goodreads website or your favourite online bookstore.

ACKNOWLEDGMENTS

This book has borne various iterations and Sadie has travelled several different paths until the story settled into its current form. It needed a lot of shaking down until it felt right. And it feels really right. Thank you, Sadie, for finally emerging as the incredible woman you are. I loved writing your story.

Thanks to my very colourful wether, Woolly Wonka, for being the inspiration for Obi-Wan. You are a clown and a goof and you bring me endless joy.

To my childhood and dear friend, Olivia Gibson, thank you for your policing advice. I might have added some creative license here and there. Please forgive me.

Thanks to my editor, Ray Collins, for your enthusiasm for this project. And to Kura Carpenter for your feedback on an opening that didn't serve the story well. I am eternally grateful for your honesty.

Bailey McGinn, you have surpassed yourself yet again with another fabulous cover. I think this one's the best yet.

To my mum, who's always my alpha reader and utterly convinced that anything I write is perfect. Thanks for your bias. I do have to ignore it, but it makes me feel wonderful.

ABOUT THE AUTHOR

Merren Tait writes quirky and irreverent romantic comedy about empowered women, and her books have earned a reputation for living up to the laugh-out-loud promise of the genre. *The Year of the Fox*, her first novel, has been optioned for television.

Merren has lived a series of bookish lives. Her first incarnation was as a book-hungry child, then as a mildly pretentious English literature student. Her third life saw her teaching English to somewhat-willing high school students, and her fourth, sharing her love of books as a librarian. Now she has been reincarnated as a fiction creator.

She is of Scottish, Ngāti Apa ki te Rā Tō, English, Irish and German extraction and attributes her cross-cultural comedic flair to the enthusiastic interbreeding of her ancestors.

Merren lives in a small house on a large piece of land

near Raglan, New Zealand, where she dreams up fabulous names for her chickens, like Princess Layer.